MENSCH

a novel

J MILO

Mensch
Copyright © 2021 by J. Milo

For more about this author, please visit jmiloauthor.com

This is a work of fiction. Names, characters, businesses, places, events, locales, and incidents are either the products of the author's imagination or used in a fictitious manner. Any resemblance to actual persons, living or dead, or actual events is purely coincidental.

For permission requests, write to: jmiloauthor@gmail.com

Editing by The Pro Book Editor
Interior and Cover Design by IAPS.rocks

eBook ISBN: 979-8-218-09731-8
paperback ISBN: 979-8-218-09732-5

1. Main category—YOUNG ADULT FICTION / Coming of Age
2. Other category—FICTION / Action & Adventure

First Edition

TABLE OF CONTENTS

Mensch:
a person of integrity and honor
—Merriam-Webster

CHAPTER 1

San Diego, 1969

Adversity toughens manhood, and the
characteristic of the good or the great man
is not that he has been exempt from the evils
of life, but that he has surmounted them.

—Patrick Henry

IT FELT FUNNY, BEING OUTSIDE without my cover. It had been four years since I felt the cool breeze run through my high and tight. *This is going to take a while,* I thought as I walked across the parade grounds of Balboa Hospital to the chow hall for my last breakfast of powdered eggs, SOS, and crappy coffee. There were some things I wouldn't miss about the navy. This episode of my life was coming to a close, and the bright day whispered promises of new opportunities waiting just beyond the gate.

Bob Dylan's "Lay Lady Lay" on Armed Forces Radio seeped through the speakers as I shuffled along the chow line and headed for a seat. Johnny was sitting at one of the tables, massaging the stump that used to be his arm. His jet-black hair shone brightly under the mess hall lights. He looked up with a grin as I slid my tray onto the table.

"Hey, short-timer. How's it going?" he asked through a mouthful of lumpy Cream of Wheat. "Are you ready to enter the real world?"

I sipped my mug full of tepid java, wondering the same thing. "As ready as I'll ever be. It's going to be an adjustment, that's for sure." Looking into my cup, I saw that the oil slick on top of the coffee had an iridescent glow. "How's the arm?"

He grinned—Johnny always grinned—and gurgled, "Feels pretty good today, hardly any of that phantom pain. A few more weeks of therapy and I get my prosthesis. Then I'm outta here. Mom wrote and said that the whole town of Nowata is planning a big homecoming and they have a cashier's job lined up for me at the feed store. Then it's off to Stillwater in the fall on the GI Bill. Can you imagine this Okie redskin with all those cowboys? I can't wait to shake it up. How's that leg of yours? Can't hardly notice your limp."

I reached down and massaged the six-inch scar running diagonally across my thigh, smiling. "Getting better, but I won't be running any marathons for a while."

He reached across with his good arm and handed me a ring of keys.

My smile disappeared. "Are you sure you want to give her up? She's your pride and joy."

"You paid me top dollar, and besides, I can't quite handle a stick shift any more. There's a new GTO with automatic transmission calling my name. Besides, I owe you, Luke."

"You don't owe me shit, Marine," I growled. This was a conversation I didn't want to have.

But Johnny persisted. "Me and seven other guys sure as shit owe you, Corpsman. You dragged our asses out of that clusterfuck. You deserve a lot more than a '65 Mustang and that Silver Star. Those assholes should give you the Medal of Honor. Hell, they should give you the keys to the White House. Kick that sorry asshole out."

I cringed. "They need to give the medals to those guys who didn't make it. Better yet, get us the hell out of that Godforsaken country. It's not our fight, and our boys are just fodder for the generals' and politicians' egos."

As we were talking, a huge shadow fell over the table. Baby Huey slipped in beside Johnny and said, "Hey, Doc. Hey, Johnny. What are you two shitbirds up to?"

His real name was Howard, but due to his size—six feet, six inches tall in his stocking feet, with a girth of 225 pounds—and gentle disposition, the moniker was a natural. The burns along one side of his ebony face and neck took away from his otherwise natural good looks.

Johnny punched him in the arm. "Hey. Doc's mustering out today. We were just talking about the state of the world and our place in it." His lopsided smile returned. "Nixon announced that he's pulling out twenty-five thousand troops. That's a start!"

Huey let out his deep baritone laugh. "What about the other four hundred and fifty thousand? He's just playing politics. As long as we're over there, shit like My Lai is going to happen. And those hippy-skippy assholes sitting outside the base with those ridiculous signs can paint all of us with those atrocities. I'm not a pacifist, but that war is just wrong!"

"Well, I guess it ain't our concern anymore. It's someone else's problem now." I got up and shook Huey's huge hand. "So long, big guy. Stop by if you're ever up my way."

He pulled me into a bear hug that nearly crushed my ribs. "I still can't believe you carried me all the way to the LZ. Johnny's right, they need to give you more than a crappy piece of metal for what you did. Stay safe, Doc."

I just shook my head and retrieved my hand from his big mitt. "You would have done the same for me." I grabbed Johnny's shoulder. "Johnny, you better keep in touch, or I'll hunt you down and rip off your other arm."

"You too, Luke." Johnny wasn't grinning for a change. He hung his head, refusing to meet my eyes. "I'm gonna miss you."

———•———

After emptying my tray, I left the mess hall and walked past two buildings, then entered the admin building.

"What are you going to do, now that you're a free man?" Lieutenant Grogin asked as he handed me my discharge papers. "You know that reenlistment offer still stands. Ten big ones in your pocket and we'll fly you to 'Nam to sign the papers so it'll be tax free. The navy needs men like you. You could chart your own course if you chose to stay."

"Thanks, sir, but my baby sister's graduating with her bachelor's degree next week, and I'm gonna be there. Then, I'm off to school on the GI Bill for my own college career. Who knows after that? The navy's been pretty good to me, and I might consider reenlisting, but I want to get my degree and experience something else, maybe helping others with something other than a tourniquet and a morphine syringe."

"Well, Captain Perdue has been summoned to the Pentagon, otherwise he'd be here to see you off. I've heard him on the horn discussing you. Best of luck, Sailor."

I gave him a smile and walked out into the sunshine, heading for the barracks.

⸺•⸺

The hike down the street to the barracks took only a few minutes.

There, I picked up my seabag, then threw it into the trunk of the Mustang, climbed in and headed out. It was another cloudless San Diego day as I drove under the towering palms and eucalyptus trees and out through the gates of Balboa Naval Hospital. The glow of the sun trickled through the foliage, throwing nymphlike shadows that danced across the hood of the convertible. Near the gate a small group of long-haired protestors clustered. They yelled, waved their signs at the car, and gave halfhearted peace signs. Some of the peace signs were with one finger. They seemed so young. I wondered at the difference between their world and mine, and if the wounds that this war had created could ever be healed. With a quick wave back, I shifted into third and drove down the hill.

Tuning the car radio to K-Earth 101, I navigated the narrow streets, jumped onto El Camino Real, and headed north. I could have taken the new interstate and saved a lot of time, but I was drawn to the old two-lane by something deep inside. There was no rush; Riley's graduation wasn't for another week. In the words of my old friend, Andy, I had nothing to do and all day to do it.

As I navigated the narrow streets of San Diego, the roadside signs alternated between US 1 and 101 without any logic, but the brass mission bells that hung on shepherds' hooks led the way. I cranked up the radio as The Kingsmen sang one of my favorites, "Louie, Louie." I couldn't figure out what they were singing, but I was pretty sure it was erotic.

Two hours later, the sweet smell of caramel corn invaded the open cockpit of the Mustang as I passed through Santa Monica and spied the giant Ferris wheel suspended in the mist over the ocean. A few miles later I cruised into Malibu and my stomach was making threatening noises. I spotted a hole-in-the-wall beachside café and pulled onto the gravel among the half-dozen or so vehicles. Soft music strummed through the outside loudspeakers, and the blackboard out front advertised a blackened mahimahi sandwich special that sounded good.

After finding a table and ordering, I sipped my iced tea and watched the surfers trying to find a wave. The water was churning, not much action though. Harbor seals poked their heads above the surf and taunted the interlopers. The sandwich was every bit as good as I had hoped. Tangy tartar sauce teased my tongue, and the tension in my shoulders and neck started to ease as I stared across the blue waters. Something about large bodies of water calmed my inner being.

The afternoon sun warmed my head and shoulders on the winding course up the Pacific Coast Highway. Coming over a hill and around a curve, I was surprised by a flash of light and smoke billowing from an area along the coast. A dark projectile climbed out of the smoke, headed out to sea, and banked left, running parallel to the coast while navy cruisers tried their best to shoot it down.

Must be the boys at Point Mugu playing war games, I thought. Just then, a dartlike projectile shot from one of the ships and the target missile burst into flames. "Nice shooting, sailor!"

The Mustang's motor purred, and the car dropped into the western edge of the Oxnard Plain. The memories began to crystallize, and my mind drifted back to that summer.

And what a summer! The summer of the great adventure…

CHAPTER 2

Trouble in Paradise, 1957

There is nothing permanent except change.

—Heraclitus

O H BOY! TWELVE YEARS OLD, and school was out for the summer—it couldn't get much better than that. I'd just finished my paper route and didn't have a care in the world. The sun was shining, and as I pedaled my bike through the treelined avenues of Redfield, I was going through all my vacation plans. The Boy Scout jamboree was coming up in three weeks, and I still had a few activities left before I earned my next merit badge for First Aid. Maybe Riles would let me practice putting a splint on her arm.

The air was heavy with the smell of citrus and cut grass as I rounded the corner of our street and almost ran into Mr. Dominguez's milk truck.

"Better watch where you're going, Luke. Not everyone keeps their eyes out for wild boys on bikes like I do," the ever-happy, rotund man said. Then he laughed. "Don't want to have to peel you off of my grill."

"Sorry, sir. I wasn't paying attention," I hollered as I slid to a halt in front of our house. "How's Cindy?"

Mr. Dominguez had already rounded the corner, so I didn't get an answer. Cindy was Mr. Dominguez's daughter. She was a year ahead of me in school and beginning to fill out in all the right places. I had a huge crush on her, along with every boy in my class. Much to my consternation, my feelings went unnoticed. The lovely lass didn't know what she was missing.

Walking into the house, I could hear music coming from the television in the living room. Bill Haley and the Comets were rocking around the clock on *American Bandstand* while my little sister, Riley, sat glued in front of the set. The cast of kids in the studio were swaying to the rhythmic beat of the song.

"You're gonna get cancer sitting that close to the TV, Riles. You're being bombarded with radiation," I said on my way to the kitchen.

She stuck her tongue out at me. "That's an old wives' tale. Mr. Tucker said so in our science class. He said that the radiation from television cathode-ray tubes is insufficient to cause any harm." She looked back at the TV. "Bring me a glass of juice when you come back, please."

Riley was nine years old and already the genius of the family. While I was a good student, she took school way too seriously and never failed to get straight As. I didn't even try to argue matters of science with her. She knew things I didn't even know that I didn't know. Tall for her age, and lanky, she had blue eyes and curly black hair cut in a pixie, as well as freckles covering her nose. She looked like our mother must have looked at her age.

I, on the other hand, was just plain average. Average height, average weight, and straight brown hair that I inherited from our dad. Just an average guy.

Riley and I were three years apart, but we were best friends. Both of us were somewhat bookish and shy, so we didn't have other close friends. Our life was simple. Dad was a hardworking man who earned enough for us to be in that mythical American middle class, even if we were on the lowest rung. He had served in the army in Europe. He never spoke of the war, but I had once stumbled upon an old shoe box in the garage that held artifacts from his service, including a Purple Heart with a bronze oak leaf cluster. I think that meant he had been wounded twice.

Mom and Dad had been childhood sweethearts and married as soon as Dad received his discharge in 1945. They'd built a loving home for us here in the valley. Then, Mom died suddenly when I was eight and Riley was five. Her death had driven the three of us closer to each other.

I could sense trouble as soon as I walked into the kitchen. Dad was home in the middle of the day and having a quiet conversation with my mom's half-sister, Aunt Helen, at the table. They didn't seem to notice my presence, so I grabbed a couple of glasses and poured some juice into each. As I slipped back into the living room, I heard Dad say, "It will only be for a short while."

Back in the living room, the undulating rhythm of Chuck Berry's "Maybelline" thrummed from the television while Riley tried in vain to match the gyrations of the pretty teens on the tube.

I put one of the glasses on the coffee table for her. "Keep it up, Riles. Your invitation from Dick Clark is in the mail," I quipped while walking back to my room.

She ignored me while desperately jerking her hips about a half-second behind the beat.

I closed my door to the noise from the TV, put the juice down, sat on my bed, and pulled my knapsack from underneath. This pack had been my dad's while he fought across Europe. It contained all of my earthly treasures and epitomized my adherence to the Boy Scout motto to Be Prepared.

I wasn't sure what it was that I needed to be prepared for, so the contents were a jumbled assortment of unrelated items that my imagination had invented uses for, including an old tarp, a ball of string, and two sticks of beef jerky. The remaining treasure included Dad's old mess kit, a dented canteen full of water, my lucky rock that I was sure was flint in case I needed to start a fire, and of course my prize possession—my official Boy Scout knife. Wrapped in genuine simulated bone, this knife was the ultimate survival tool. Besides two blades, it included a corkscrew, a can opener/screwdriver, tiny scissors, and an awl that had a sawblade on one side. I couldn't wait to try it out at the jamboree.

I took care to inventory the pack's contents as I placed each item in its proper place. I was looking forward to camping.

Later that evening, I was watching the news on television, and Riley was in her room reading. I wasn't really into the news, but all three stations broadcast at the same hour each day. Dad came in and sat on the couch next to me.

It had been four years since Mom had died, and I could still see the pain etched into his face. Riley and I missed her like crazy, but I could tell that our pain was nothing in comparison to the emptiness and loneliness that my dad felt. His pain never got in the way of the love and affection that he shared with us, though. It was like he was filling in for Mom as well as being a great father. In my mind, he was doing an amazing job.

The anchorman was talking about some place called Vietnam and said an American had been killed there. I asked Dad where Vietnam was.

Dad frowned and sighed, "It's in Southeast Asia. Our boys don't need to be involved in that place. Eisenhower needs to keep us out of other peoples' troubles. He knows better."

"How come you were home in the middle of the day? What was Aunt Helen doing here? I thought she went to Hollywood to become a star."

"She came back to town a while back. I asked her to come over as a favor, and I need to talk to you about that." His shoulders slumped a little before he went on. "They let me go at the shop two weeks ago. Business is really slow, and they had to let all of the mechanics go except Fred. And they only kept him on because he's the owner's brother-in-law. I've been looking for work all around, but there's not anything available. The government is calling it a mild recession, but it doesn't feel that mild to me. Anyway, I've got to find work and there's none around here, so I asked Helen to take care of you and your sister while I look. We don't have enough money for next month's rent and expenses."

A knot formed in my stomach, and I jumped up stuttering, "Where are you going? Why can't we just go with you? Aunt Helen is nice but kind of scary. Remember that one time she accidentally left me and Riley at the baseball game because she went off with that popcorn man for a drink? You always said that she was too wild and unreliable."

"I know, but she's your mother's half-sister and our only relative. She's agreed to take care of you while I'm looking for work. I've heard that there's plenty of work up north. I can't take you with me because I'll be on the road and won't have time to look after you and your sister. You guys can stay at Helen's apartment. It'll only be for a short time, and then we'll settle wherever I find a job. I need you to look after Riley while I'm gone. Can you do that for me?"

His shoulders folded in and his hands were shaking. I could see tears forming in his eyes and there was no way that I was going to add to his angst, so I nodded and gave him a hug while I brushed a tear from the corner of my eye. "I won't let anything happen to Riles. I'll take care of her."

Boy, I sure didn't know what I was getting into!

●———————————●

The conversation with Riley didn't quite go as smoothly. She pitched a complete hissy fit and hid in her room. Dad spent a lot of time talking to her, his voice too quiet for me to hear. I could hear her crying softly after bedtime, though. I don't think any of us slept well that night.

The next morning was overcast and dreary, just like our moods. We packed our clothes, and Dad drove us in our old Chevy to Aunt Helen's apartment on the other side of town. On the way, we passed a group of hobos gathered outside the Salvation Army Mission. I thought I was being clever when I pointed at them and mimicked some of the older kids. "Look at those scroungy bums. They're pretty useless. Why don't they get a job?"

Dad's jaw was set as he pulled the car to the curb. "Come with me." I was a little nervous in the midst of these strange men, so I hung back as we walked over to the group. Dad said hello and shook one of their hands. "Don, I want you to meet my son Lucas. Luke, Don served with me in Europe. He was one hell of a marksman. He picked off a machine gunner who had us pinned down from three hundred yards. Saved us a lot of casualties."

Don looked down and mumbled something. My dad squeezed his arm, then handed him a five-dollar bill and a pack of cigarettes as he walked away.

Back in the car, Dad turned a stern face to me, "Those fellows that you call 'bums' are God's children just like you and me. Life has thrown them a curveball, that's all. Of course, there are some bad apples just like everywhere, but they deserve our respect and help. You never know when you might need the same."

"You see, while we were in Europe, we all experienced more horror than any person should ever have to endure. And that horror overwhelmed some of us. For Don, the tipping point was when he saw the atrocities committed by the Nazis at Buchenwald. What we found there made us all sick."

We continued across town to an area of rundown buildings with weeds for lawns. All of the businesses had bars across their windows. It seemed like every other shop was a liquor store or a pawnshop. We pulled up in front of a dilapidated two-story apartment in desperate need of paint.

The building was practically falling apart, and the hallway smelled of cigarettes and liquor—and maybe urine. Aunt Helen welcomed us with hugely theatrical hugs. Her hair was a strange yellow color with black roots, and her eyes twitched nervously. She weaved as she led us to the spare bedroom.

"You're going to have to share this room, and there's only one bed. Luke, we'll make up a bed on the floor for you, and you can pretend that you're at one of those cam-pout things that you love. I hope that's okay?"

"No problem, Aunt Helen. I like sleeping on the floor. I guess I won't be going to the jamboree, so I'll just have my own right here. I can probably use a couple of blankets to make a tent. Don't worry, I won't have a campfire."

She grimaced. I figured she didn't know that I was kidding.

Dad brought our clothes up in two cardboard boxes, and Riley set about putting hers into the lone three-drawer dresser. I put my box and knapsack in the corner of the closet and went about folding a blanket that would serve as my mattress.

When I got to the kitchen, Dad was handing Helen a handful of cash. "This should keep you afloat for a while. I'll send more if I get any work along the way."

Then he got down on one knee to be at my level and handed me two dollars, "Luke, take care of Riley and your aunt. I'll write and let you know how things are going, and with any kind of luck, I'll send for you soon." He looked me in the eye. "In the meantime, you're the man of the house." My chest tightened, and I felt a strange weight on my heart. All I wanted at that moment was to live up to his expectations.

We walked out to the street, and Dad pulled me into a big hug. "I love you son. I'm going to miss you and your sister like crazy. Say your prayers every night and be sure to include me. Take care of Riley." His shoulders slumped as he got into the car. He started it and waved as he pulled into the street.

As the old Chevy turned the corner, I wiped the tears off of my cheeks. I sat on the curb and pulled off my shoes, then folded the dollar bills and placed one in each. I didn't know why, but I had a feeling that I would need that money for something other than candy and comic books.

I got up and was walking back when Helen come out the door of the apartment complex. Her smile was gone, and she lit a cigarette. "Now, let's get a few things straight…"

CHAPTER 3

Across Town, 1957

*Affliction comes to us, not to make us sad
but sober, not to make us sorry but wise.*

—H. G. Wells

IT'S AMAZING HOW A FEW miles can change your life. Living with Helen was not exactly enjoyable. Her rules included staying in our room unless it was time to eat. She didn't exactly exude maternal empathy. We could go outside, but the neighborhood was in bad shape, and groups of greasers not much older than me were always hanging out on the street corners.

Each corner had its own ethnicity: Hispanic, Black, White, you name it. It didn't seem to matter which group—they all hated me and anyone else who ventured into their territory. The few times that I ventured out, I was challenged by mean-looking guys who seemed to think that roughing up a smaller kid somehow made them tough. Maybe they were acting this way because they'd never had anyone to show them a better way to act.

Once, when I was walking to the store to get something for Riley and me to eat, a group of Mexican kids came up and started taunting me. I tried to ignore them, but they just got into my face and then began shoving me. The leader of this gang grabbed my hair and punched me in the stomach. He swore at me in what I assumed was Spanish, then called me a dumbass gringo. As I was bent over, they tripped me and began laughing as I fell to the ground. While I was on the ground, each of them came up and kicked me, again and again. Eventually, they tired of the "game" and moved on down the block.

I was a slow learner, but after getting knocked down and kicked by a group of Chicanos, I decided the streets were not for me or Riley.

It turned out that Helen had a boyfriend, or should I say boyfriends. She was pretty enough, but in a coarse, used-up sort of way, and her friends were just as coarse. These were nasty-looking men who didn't seem to have much in the way of employment since they were there at all hours, smoking and drinking beer.

To a man, they were mean-spirited souls. They would swat at me as I passed through the living room and laugh if I cried out. The looks they gave Riley made me uncomfortable, and I made her stay in the room whenever one of them was in the apartment. Cigarette smoke choked the air, and liquor bottles crowded the kitchen counters. If we'd been able to get out of that dismal place even for a short while, our sadness could have been alleviated. I would even have welcomed spending time at school over the boredom of staring at those four walls.

It sure was turning out to be a lousy summer vacation.

We were on our own for meals, forced to forage through a diminished supply of TV dinners and cans of soup. I tried to press the issue of nutrition with my aunt, but she would either cuss at me or throw a few dollars my way and tell me to buy something good, which meant avoiding the toughs while making my way to the store three blocks away.

We got a letter from Dad two weeks after he left. It was postmarked Portland, Oregon. He told us how much he missed us, saying that the trip north was uneventful, and while he'd found some part-time work, there weren't any permanent, full-time positions to be had. He was headed for Seattle, where rumor had it that jobs were plentiful at an aircraft company. He asked us to say our prayers for him and said that he would send for us as soon as he could. His note indicated that he'd included some money for us and Helen, but the envelope had already been opened, the funds appropriated by either Helen or her latest man.

One night, a few days after the letter, a man came to the apartment and started yelling at Helen. He said he wanted the money that she owed "them." It evolved into a terrible fight. Riley and I cowered in our room while the two of them screamed and cussed at each other. It got physical and we could hear furniture being tipped over and dishes breaking. The sound of a slap echoed through the apartment and Helen began wailing. I wasn't sure what to do when I heard Helen cry out that she would get them the money as soon as she scored. The door to the apartment slammed shut, and there was only the sound of Helen's whimpering coming through the thin walls.

The next morning, Helen came into our room and told us to pack our stuff because we were moving. She looked nervous, and her face and arms were covered with bruises. When I started to ask where we were going, she interrupted and told me to shut up and pack.

After we had finished, we piled into her old DeSoto and headed out of town. How the heck was Dad going to find us now?

CHAPTER 4

Jack Ranch Café, 1957

I know some lonely Houses off the Road
A Robber'd like the look of –
Wooden barred,
And Windows hanging low…

—Emily Dickinson

THE OLD CAR WOUND THROUGH orange groves, the air sweet with their nectar. We lost the radio signal as we ascended a high pass and dropped into a hot, dry valley. Two hours later, we pulled up to a rundown, single-story house that hadn't seen paint in a long time. The house was set back from the road and sitting on a half-acre lot. Behind the house was a nice-looking vegetable garden that included rows of corn, tomatoes, and a number of low-growing plants.

When we pulled onto the gravel driveway, an older, sunbaked man came out and stood on the porch. His face was deeply lined, and he was lean with thinning hair. His clothes consisted of a soiled long-sleeve shirt and faded coveralls. I could tell that the lines in his face weren't laugh lines.

Helen got out of the car. "Come meet your Uncle Walt."

I didn't know we had an uncle, and I asked her who he was.

"He's not exactly a blood relative, he's just a close friend. You'll be staying with him for a while so I can get to LA for some interviews. Get your stuff out of the car."

I was getting a little tired of being left at strange houses. "What do you mean? You told Dad that you would take care of us, and now you're going to take off? That's not right!"

I hadn't realized that the old man had walked up behind me, so the fist to the side of my head was a complete surprise and knocked me to my knees. "Shut up, kid. You don't get an opinion. Keep your yap shut unless I ask you to open it. Pick up your stuff, and you two get in the house. You're staying in the back bedroom."

Now, I'd been in my share of scrapes and been beat up by bigger boys, but for my entire twelve years, neither my dad nor any other adult had ever laid a hand on me. This stung, but I wasn't going to let this grizzled old bastard have the satisfaction of seeing me cry. It didn't stop Riley, though. She began to bawl and started hitting the old guy in his leg. He pushed her away, and I grabbed her arm. "Come on, Riley. Let's go." I knew better than to take on someone twice my size, but that didn't mean our "discussion" was over.

For the first time, I felt hate for a fellow human being. It wasn't a good feeling, but I knew that I would pay him back eventually.

Helen didn't bother to stick around to say goodbye, leaving in an oily cloud of smoke before we had even reached the porch. Walt was waiting for us with his gnarled hands on his hips when we came up the hall and into the living room. "This arrangement ain't my idea, but since I'm stuck with you, we'll make the best of it. You, boy, will earn your keep by tending my garden, and you, young lady, will keep up the house cleaning."

Looking around the dusty room, it didn't seem to me like anyone had been performing that particular task in a long time. The place was filthy and covered in a thick layer of grime. The windows were almost opaque with muck. Mold gathered in the corners and appeared to be growing.

Walt growled, "We eat breakfast at seven and dinner at six. Ain't no lunch. After you finish your chores, you're on your own. Just don't get into trouble."

We left Riley to her assignment and went outside. Walt took me around back to some stairs leading to a root cellar. "There's a rake down there. Get it and start weeding the garden. I'll be back before dinner." He called the last words over his shoulder, already walking away.

The sky was cloudless and the temperature was up, probably into the eighties. The root cellar was cool enough to bring out goosebumps on my arms. I found a single bulb light hanging from a cord in the middle of the room and pulled the chain. The eight-by-twelve room had been carved out of the dirt. Black Widow spiders scrambled from the light. Crude shelves lined the hardpacked adobe. Hundreds of mason jars filled the shelves, each with a small paper label. I read some of the labels: corn, tomatoes, beans. I knew where to go if I got hungry.

I found the rake, turned out the light, and headed for the garden. Next to the garden were an apple and an apricot tree. The apples were still small, and the apricots were full grown but had a green hue to them. Maybe another two weeks, I thought.

The garden was about ten by twenty feet with neat rows. Each row had one or two different vegetables assigned to it. There were tomatoes, onions, radishes, and squash. Behind the low-lying plants, beans crawled up small trellises, and behind those stood the corn. Nothing had ripened yet in the early summer, but when it did, there would be quite a haul. Walt obviously knew his gardening.

I needed to find a way to let Dad know what was happening and where we were. I set about pulling weeds.

Walt lived in Cholame.

Now, Cholame was a miserable little speck that lay on Highway 41 near the junction with Highway 46. It consisted of…well, nothing. Its only claim to fame was the site of James Dean's fatal automobile accident. That, and a handful of earthquakes each year. Otherwise, there were only thousands of acres of cattle ranches and the Jack Ranch Café, which catered to the truckers and tourists who passed through. No wonder Walt felt comfortable letting us wander free.

The only saving grace to living with Walt was the slight improvement of the meals over Helen's. The food was plain, but hearty, and it didn't come out a box. Walt would prepare dinner using the vegetables from the cellar and meat from a large freezer located in the kitchen. He mentioned once that his ex-wife had canned all of the vegetables in the cellar. I bit my tongue so I wouldn't make a smart-ass comment about knowing why she was an "ex."

After dinner, Walt would settle in front of the TV with a large jelly jar of whiskey while Riley and I cleaned up and then went outside to find something to occupy ourselves. We wandered everywhere—which meant nowhere in Cholame. The horses and cows from the ranches could keep us occupied for a while. One rancher grew stands of wheat in a field, and we would pick the ears and roll them between our palms until the chaff fell away. The kernels made a gum-like treat for us to chew on. By the time we got back, Walt would be passed out in front of the TV and we would slip off to our room.

The Jack Ranch Café was the only sign of life in that miserable corner of the world. After finishing our chores, we would hang around outside and watch the people as they came and went. The truckers were there to grab a quick bite, but the tourists wandered around and commented about the shame of losing a great talent at such a young age. Some of the women would actually tear up. Making such a fuss about someone who hadn't done anything but act in a few movies seemed silly to me.

Walt would typically fix breakfast, tell us what he wanted done, and then leave for the day. I was never sure where he went, but he always reeked of liquor when he returned.

One day, he returned early and in a foul mood. I was daydreaming while I weeded, and he walked up behind me and kicked me in my backside. "You dumb son of a bitch. You pulled up one of the onions, damnit!" He ripped off his belt and began whipping me with it. "Get in the cellar, now."

I scrambled out of range of the belt and ran to the entrance of the cellar

"Get in there, and don't come out until I tell you!" I ducked down and slid into the darkness. Walt slammed the door behind me, and I heard the latch drop.

It was dark and cool down there. I reached for the chain on the light and pulled, but nothing happened. Feeling around, I discovered that the bulb had been removed. I could hear Walt stomping around upstairs, and every once in a while, he would let out a stream of cuss words. After what seemed like an eternity, I was getting antsy. I wasn't sure when he would let me out, and I sure wasn't staying put until he came back. Luckily, I had my scout knife with me. I opened the saw blade and began prying the latch up.

Then I heard Riley crying. I began to panic, my hands started shaking and I almost dropped the knife.

I finally got the latch up and pushed the door open. Apparently, I had been there longer than I thought because it was starting to get dark. Scrambling up the stairs, I ran across the yard to the back door. Then I heard Riley screaming, "No, Uncle Walt. Please stop."

The house was in shadows when I entered, but I heard the sounds of a struggle coming from the back bedroom. Riley was screaming.

"Be still, you little bitch! I'm not going to hurt you." Walt growled.

I crept into the room and saw Riley in a prone position with her pants pulled down. Walt was on top and struggling to pull her underwear off. Riley was crying, "No, no, no!"

An anger that I had never felt erupted in me. The knife was still clenched in my hand, the blade still out. I ran over to the bed and swung at Walt with a fury. The knife struck him in his buttocks, and he let out a roar.

He fell on the floor, but almost immediately, he got up and came at me. "You little son of a bitch, I'll kill you."

I scrambled out of his way, but he grabbed my arm. As I twisted, his fist hit me hard in my stomach. I doubled over and couldn't breathe. Another fist glanced off my head, and I went down. He brought his boot up and was getting ready to kick me when I heard Riley scream as she jumped on his back and wrapped her arms around his neck in a stranglehold.

As they flopped around the room, I caught my breath and slowly got up. Walt had managed to pull Riley off his back, throwing her against the wall. She scrambled away, and he went after her once more. I couldn't catch my breath and my head was spinning. I wasn't sure how to stop this monster.

Then I spied the bedside lamp that had fallen on the floor in the ruckus. It was about two feet long and had a heavy metal base. I grabbed it, and just as Walt had grabbed Riley and was bent over, trying to wrestle her into submission, I swung at his head as hard as I could.

The sickening sound of the impact with the back of his skull filled the small room, and Walt crumpled to the floor. Riley's soft sobs and my labored breathing were the only sounds.

I was trembling and just wanted to lie down and rest, but I knew I had to move. Approaching Walt, I saw a large gash in his scalp and shuddered. "Shit, I think I killed him. We have to get out of here."

Riley's was shaking and her sobs became heavier as I struggled to remain standing. "That was terrible. I was scared to death. Shouldn't we find someone to help?"

I picked up my knife and wiped it on the drapes. "All the people around here are friends with Walt. How do you think they'll treat us? Besides, I'm done trusting adults. Get your shoes on and grab some clothes—we're getting out of here."

I threw some pants, T-shirts and socks in Dad's knapsack and went to the kitchen. There wasn't much, but I found two cans of soup and a box of crackers and threw them in with my clothes. In one drawer, I found a flashlight and some matches and tossed them in as well. I was just closing the drawer when I spied a long, sharp knife used for filleting fish. After wrapping it in a dishtowel, I put it in the bottom of the pack. Then I ran down to the cellar and grabbed some canned apricots and beans.

When I got back to the bedroom, Riley had stacked some pants, shirts, and underwear on the bed. She was still pale and trembling. "Where are we going?"

I hugged her and until she settled a bit then stuffed her clothes into the pack. "We have to find Dad. He's the only one who cares about us. He'll know how to get us out of this mess."

Her eyes brightened at the mention of him.

"Are you ready?" I asked. "Let's go!" I thought about checking on Walt, but the thought made me want to throw up. I was pretty sure he was dead.

His TV was still playing as we went outside and started toward the highway.

CHAPTER 5

Truckin', 1957

*How did I escape? With difficulty. How did
I plan this moment? With pleasure.*

—Alexandre Dumas

A LUCENT HALF-MOON WAS HANGING OVER the horizon as we headed down the dusty road toward the highway. I held Riley's hand, and some cattle lowed softly as we passed by. I wasn't real sure about what we were doing, but I knew we couldn't stay here. We had to find Dad.

Riley was shaking and whimpering. I put my arms around her and gave her a tight squeeze. She became calmer, and we started out again. As we walked, I squeezed her hand and told her that I was going to take care of her.

Bright lights shone through the windows of the café as we approached. A couple was just leaving, and I pulled Riley into the shadows with me. The woman was prattling on about James Dean as they got into their car and drove off.

The twangy notes of a country ballad filled the night air. A bit later, a blue pickup pulled in. Two men in long-sleeve work shirts and baseball caps got out and headed for the door.

"I hope we catch something besides rockfish and ling-cod this time," one of them said.

The other guy grunted as he pulled up his jeans that had slid down to display the upper reaches of his crack, "The fish report on the radio said that bonito are running out of Oxnard, so we should have a good catch this time. The boat doesn't leave until three, so we can take our time here and have some burgers and a couple of beers with time to spare."

Now, I wasn't sure where Oxnard was, but I did know that you caught rockfish and lingcod in the ocean, and I knew enough geography that if we followed the coastline, we would eventually end up in Seattle. We ducked down and scooted over to the truck. Lying in the back were a couple of poles, two large duffle bags, and a pile of burlap sacks jammed up against the cab. I boosted Riley up and climbed into the bed. We arranged the sacks, making a relatively soft surface, and then pulled a couple of them over our heads. "Try to get some rest, Riles," "It's going to be a long night."

Trucks rumbled down the highway and cars came and went. An hour and a half later, the two men staggered out of the café, each with a six-pack under his arm. "Damn, they make a mean burger!" the shorter of the two said. "And the beer is ice-cold. Did you see the way that wait-ress was giving me the eye? Maybe we should stay here."

"Naw, we got some fish to catch. Besides, she wasn't giving you the eye. She's got more class than that. She was giving *me* the eye. Maybe she'll be here when we come back. I gotta take a piss before we head out." They weaved over to the side of the building, and I could hear liquid spraying against the clapboard.

I was questioning my decision and wondering if we should get out rather than risk having a "James Dean" with these two, but before I made up my mind, they jumped in the truck and we headed down the road. Riley had fallen into a disturbed sleep, and the motion of the truck made her wake up. She jerked and started to rise, but I held her down, "Stay down or they'll see us." She lay back down, and I put my arm around her shoulders. Giving me a half smile, she faded off again.

The night was cloudless, and the stars were like tiny gems in the sky. I lay back on the sacks and wondered what the hell I was doing. Maybe we should have just stayed and face the music. I mean, we were just kids. I was pretty sure that not all adults were like Helen and Walt. They would understand. Right?

But I wasn't in the mood to trust any strangers. My head hurt, and I was scared. The only thing that I knew was that our dad would protect us. We just had to find him.

The truck motored down the two-lane highway, and I stared at the stars through my tears, Finally, I nodded off.

•————————•

I woke to a feeling of vertigo as the truck spun wildly in an arc and then smacked against a rock fence with a loud, sickening crunch. Riley cried out, and we bounced around the bed, slamming against the cab. Luckily, the pile of gunny sacks pretty much cushioned the impact, but it was enough to knock the wind out of me.

When the truck settled, I slid over to Riley and asked if she was okay. "I'm alright, but that was really scary.

What's going on?" Just then, we heard a low moan coming from the cab. I pulled Riley out of the bed and sat her beside the rock wall.

"Stay here. I'm going to check out the truck."

I scrambled to the front and peeked in. The driver was slumped against the steering wheel and appeared to be unconscious. The window was down, and I reached in and shook him a couple times. "Are you alright, mister?"

He didn't answer, but his chest looked like he was breathing. I heard another moan from the passenger side of the cab. I couldn't see in the dark, so I ran around the hood and looked in. The other man was leaning back, blood spurting from a large gash in his arm. His eyes were glassy, and he was shaking.

The sight of the blood brought bile up into my throat, and I bent over and retched. I was scared to death. I was shaking as I struggled to recall my first-aid training from the Boy Scouts. I knew that I had to stop that bleeding or the guy would die. I opened the door to the truck, and the guy fell out onto the ground. I pulled my T-shirt off and pushed it against the wound. The blood squirted around my fingers, and I thought I was going to faint for a minute. The bile rose up, and I retched to the side.

The flow of blood seemed to be slowing, though.

Riley was sobbing, and I yelled at her to grab the flashlight from the pack and to try to flag down some help.

It seemed like I held that blood-soaked rag on that guy's arm forever. I don't know why, but I kept talking to him and telling him he would be alright. I was shaking and in a daze myself when I heard someone walk up behind me, "It's okay, son. I'll take over from here. You did good."

I looked up, barely registering the person who had arrived.

They continued, "Now, you need to go over to the ambulance and get checked out. They'll clean that blood off of you, too."

I guess I got up too quickly, because my head started spinning, my knees crumpled, and I sank to the ground.

"Just take it slow, son. You've had a helluva shock. Stick your head between your knees for a minute until you get your sea legs."

I did as he said, and a little while later, I was able to get up and walk to the ambulance, where the other EMT checked me out and cleaned me up.

Riley and I huddled together and after a half hour or so, a highway patrolman came over with my pack and talked to us. "Looks like they're going to be alright. The EMT says you saved that guy's life by controlling the bleeding. Where'd you learn to do that?"

I slipped on a clean T-shirt from the pack. "I kinda just reacted. I've been studying for my Boy Scout first-aid merit badge, and it said that one of the first things to do was stop the bleeding."

"Well, I'd say you earned your badge and then some. Good job, young man. They're going to transport your dad to the hospital in Oxnard, and we'll follow in the patrol car. You two need to get checked out before we take you home."

Riley started to say, "He's not—"

I kicked her and shook my head. "Thank you, sir. We haven't ever ridden in a police car. Let me get my pack."

Luckily, he didn't seem to notice the back and forth.

As we drove, the cop sipped a thermos of coffee and talked to us about the wreck. "My name is Deputy

Swenson. Your dad has a concussion, and his buddy lost a lot of blood, but the EMTs say he'll make it thanks to you. Seems like your dad had a snootfull. He either wandered off the road, or an animal wandered in front and your dad jerked the wheel and lost control. You kids are lucky to be alive."

We arrived at the ER ahead of the ambulance, and Deputy Swenson escorted us into the lobby. The bright lights made us squint as we plopped down on plastic chairs.

The cop dropped coins into a vending machine and handed us each an RC Cola. "You guys wait here, and a nurse will come check you out in a little while. Give me your phone number, and we'll get someone to come pick you up."

I was at a loss and began to stutter and mumble. I figured our goose was cooked, but then Riley spoke up and gave him our old phone number. As he walked away, I smiled and gave her a little shake, "Quick thinking Riles. No one will answer the phone, and that should buy us a little time. How do you feel? Do you need the nurse to check you out?"

"No! I'm okay," she started walking in the opposite direction of the cop. "Let's just get out of here and find Dad."

I grabbed the pack, and we slipped down the hallway to the side door of the hospital.

CHAPTER 6

On the Run, 1957

Virtue consists in fleeing vice.

—Horace

T HERE WAS A FINE MIST in the air, and it carried a slightly salty taste. We slipped out the door and onto a loading dock and were well on our way across.

We scrambled off the dock and started running down the dark alley just as the back door to the hospital opened and the cop barged out. "Hey, where are you kids going? Get back here! He jumped down and started running after us. Damn it, what's with you two?"

We skittered around a corner and dashed across the street. Up ahead was an empty lot, and we ran for it. The cop was really quick for a big guy, though, and he was almost upon us. Just then, Riley tripped and fell flat on her face into the dirt. I reached down and pulled her up, and we sprinted toward a fence at the back of the lot. The cop reached for me, but I was able to avoid his grasp, and he let out a few choice swear words. About ten yards from us, I spotted a hole in the fence, and I yelled at Riley to go through it. She crawled through on her hands and knees, and I pushed the backpack through behind her.

Before I could make it all the way, the deputy grabbed my foot and pulled me back. I started swinging at him with both fists, trying to squirm away, but I really wasn't doing much in the way of getting free. He was just too big and strong. He pinned both of my arms and told me to settle down.

The cop pulled me to my feet, "What the hell's wrong with you, kid?" "No one's going to harm you."

"Let me go! Let me go! You're hurting me!" I cried, twisting to no avail. He just held me at arm's length. "You're not going anywhere. Just tell me what's going on."

His grip tightened, and it was really starting to hurt my wrists. As I struggled, I noticed a shadow coming up behind the cop. It was Riley—she had crawled back through the hole in the fence and snuck into position, kneeling down onto all fours just behind his legs.

When she was in position, I pushed at the man with all I had. Stumbling back a step, he caught his legs on Riley's back and tumbled over her. With a punched exhale, he released his grip on me. "Son of a bitch!" he shouted as he hit the ground.

I ran to Riley and pulled her up. Together, we slipped through the fence and darted between the dark buildings. Riley was giggling the whole time. "Always worked when we were wrestling with Dad."

We fled down the darkened streets. Whenever a car passed, we faded into the shadows.

We had been going for long enough that I was out of breath when I saw a police car inching down the street in the opposite direction. We dove into an alley and behind a dumpster. The car's spotlight flashed over us, and the car continued down the street. I was pretty sure I recognized the driver as Deputy Swenson. Riley started to get up, "That cop was pretty nice. I hope we didn't hurt him when he fell. Maybe he can help us."

I held her down, "Yeah, he seemed nice enough, but he probably doesn't know about Walt yet. He won't be as nice when he finds out that I killed someone. I don't think we should take a chance and trust him."

When the taillights disappeared around a corner two blocks away, we crawled out and began to move down the street. "We need to figure out where we are and how to get to Seattle," I said. "Dad's the only grownup that I trust.

We kept to the shadows and made our way along the foggy streets of Oxnard. Every time we saw car lights, we would disappear into a doorway or down a dark alley. A while later, we saw two other cop cars slowly cruising the streets, only these were city police cruisers. "The highway patrol guy must have put the word out on us. The more people looking for us, the better chance they have of finding us. We've got to find a good hiding place."

Just then a sinfully luxurious aroma reached our noses. My stomach growled, and Riley said, "I'm starving. Can we eat something?"

"That's a good idea," I whispered. "Let's find out where that smell is coming from. Maybe we can get some."

•———————•

As we exited the alleyway, I spied a light from a business a few doors down spilling across the otherwise dark street. We snuck along to the shop. A painting of a strange-looking donut with a face and the words "Spud Nuts" were stenciled across the front window.

The door was unlocked, so we slipped inside. A little bell tinkled above the doorway. There were six tables with chairs along the window and a counter and stools in front of the kitchen. Sitting at the end of the counter was a large coffee urn and an assortment of coffee mugs. A voice from the back yelled, "The donuts won't be ready for another twenty minutes. The coffee is hot. Grab a cup, have a seat, and I'll be right out."

Soon, a man wearing a sweaty T-shirt and an apron tied around a huge belly came through the batwing doors leading to the kitchen. Each massive arm had a tattoo on it. One said, "Navy" and the other said, "Mom."

"Well, well what have we here? What are you two urchins doing out at four thirty in the morning?"

I ignored his question and smiled. "Mister, we're hungry and wanted to get some donuts from you, but we lost our money. Is there anything we can help you with to earn a meal? I'm a really good worker, and my sister can sweep your shop."

The two dollars Dad had given me were still tucked into my shoes, but I wanted to save it as long as I could.

The man's face softened. "Hmmm, let me think. You know, I might have just the thing. Jay was helping me, but he got a better job up in Ventura. Come with me."

He led us into the kitchen to a large stainless-steel sink filled with bowls and utensils. "You kids wash these up, and we'll get you some of the finest donuts in the land."

I pulled a step stool over to the sink for Riley to stand on, then filled half of the sink with soapy hot water and the other with just water. Helping Dad with the dishes had been routine for us since Mom had passed away. While I washed, Riley rinsed and placed each item on the drainboard. With both of us working like that as a team, we were finished quickly.

The baker was loading large trays of sweet morsels into the display case. "Have a seat at the counter and I'll get some hot chocolate for you." He filled two coffee cups with tan liquid and brought them over, then placed a plate stacked with glazed donuts in front of us.

The hot cocoa warmed our stomachs, and the man wasn't lying—those were the best donuts that I had ever tasted. The fact that we hadn't had anything to eat for hours might have had something to do with it, but they were delicious. Between bites, Riley said, "These are really good, mister. How do you make them so light and delicious?"

He sat across the counter from us and lit a cigarette. "You can call me Cookie, little miss. That's the question everyone asks. I can't tell you all of the secret ingredients, or everyone would copy me and I'd be out of business. But I can tell you we use potato flour instead of wheat. That gives them the special flavor. I had some of these in England during the war. I was a cook in the navy, so I bought this franchise as soon as I got my discharge. This shop makes me a pretty good living." His eyebrows arched up. "Now that you know my name, how about letting me know yours?"

Before Riley could answer, I stood up to shake his hand. "I'm Joe, and this is Cathy. We just moved here. Our mom is in bed with a cold, so we came looking for food. Thank you for the delicious food. We'll finish cleaning up and then leave you alone." I carried our plates back to the kitchen as Riley tagged along.

We had just finished drying the dishes when I heard the bell above the front door ring out. Cookie called out,

"Good mornin', Sam. How's one of Oxnard's finest doing this morning? Grab a cup and I'll get the order for the precinct ready."

I looked through the gap in the kitchen door and saw a police officer sitting down at one end of the counter. Cookie had his head tilted toward him and was saying something, pointing toward the kitchen.

I ducked back into the kitchen, "It's another cop, and I think Cookie is telling him about us." I grabbed the pack and headed toward the back door, with Riley right behind.

I pushed on the door, but it wouldn't budge. After a couple more tries, I realized it was stuck. I was starting to panic as I looked around. Then I saw a door leading to a small restroom. Pulling Riley into the room, I latched it. Above the sink was a half-opened casement window. I clasped my hands together, interlocking the fingers, and Riley stepped into the cradle. I boosted her, and she pushed the window up and scrambled through. I had just pushed my pack over the sill when Cookie rattled the door. "Hey, kids, come on out. I've got someone for you to meet." I pulled myself up and through the window, dropping onto the ground in another alley.

"Let's get out of here," I called to Riley, and we began jogging away from the donut shop and onto another street. Dawn was breaking and it seemed like the fog had thickened as we loped down the street, turned the corner and ran past an all-night café, where one lone patron sat hunched over a newspaper and a cup of coffee at the counter.

We darted across the street without looking. A car skidded to a stop in front of us, horn blaring, and the driver yelled, "What's the matter with you crazy kids? Get out of the road."

Up ahead, a bridge crossed a small ravine. Railroad tracks ran under the bridge and disappeared into a copse of eucalyptus trees. We half ran, half slid down the bank and charged into the trees. As soon as we were within the shadows of the trees, I turned and studied the road. It didn't look like anyone was following us, so we slowed down and made our way into the thicket. Crawling under bushes and over downed trees, we moved away from the road.

After a few minutes, we came upon a downed tree about three feet in diameter. The trunk had fallen across a slight depression, forming a recess underneath. Brush had accumulated across the back of this depression, creating a natural alcove. I was feeling pretty puny by now, and Riley was really dragging. Clearly, we needed to rest.

"This looks like a good hiding place to me. We should be okay to rest here," I said, and she nodded. "You sit by that tree and I'll fix this place up."

Using my knife, I cut some saplings and leaned them against the opening of the hollow. It took a few minutes, but I was able to form a framework that was solid enough for me to pile brush onto. When I was finished, our hiding place was camouflaged enough that someone happening by wouldn't even know it was there. As a final touch, I pulled branches and brush away from the back of the den until I had a small tunnel leading ten feet out the back that was just big enough for me to crawl through. I turned to ask Riles what she thought of my handiwork, but she was sound asleep. Her mouth hung open, and some spittle dripped down her chin.

While she sat there gently snoring, I gathered up eucalyptus leaves and piled up a four-inch bed inside the hideaway. I figured the eucalyptus oil would keep most insects from invading our space, but for extra protection, I pulled the tarp from my pack and laid it across the top of the leaves. I led Riley to the bed and let her lie down gently, then covered her with my sweatshirt.

Once she was settled, I scouted around the area to make sure we were safe before joining her in the den. I made a pillow from the pack and laid down. I barely even remembered closing my eyes.

When I jerked awake, it took me a few minutes to figure out where I was. The sunlight came at a soft angle through the trees. I figured it was midmorning. Riley lay sprawled on the other side of the enclosure, mumbling in her sleep.

I lay back and thought about our situation. We were alone in a strange place with no one to care for us. I had a vague idea of where we wanted to go, but no idea how to get there. I wondered if maybe I had moved us from a bad situation to a worse one. Maybe I wasn't being fair to Riley. She hadn't done anything wrong, and now she was in some danger. I was starting to think that I should just give up and turn us in, hoping that someone would understand why I had murdered Walt.

But that would mean putting our trust in adults I didn't even know. And adults really hadn't proven to be too trustworthy lately. Even if they believed me, what would they do? Dad wasn't around, and we had no other relatives. That meant foster care and probably being separated from Riley—unacceptable. I had promised Dad that I would take care of her, and that was what I wanted to do. Then again, maybe I wasn't doing the right thing by dragging her along on my odyssey. Maybe I was putting her in danger. We weren't even sure where Dad was. My thoughts kept swirling around and falling over themselves.

Riley woke a little while later and said she was hungry. I opened one of the jars of apricots, and we spooned them out with my knife. The fruit was good, but it wasn't nearly enough to fill us. I dug out the beef jerky and handed her a piece.

As she chewed on the dried meat and sipped water from the canteen, Riley asked, "Now what?"

"I've been thinking about that," I said. "I promised Dad that I would take care of you.

But that was before everything fell apart. They're looking for me because of what I did to Walt, but that isn't your fault. I'm heading toward Seattle, but if you want to turn yourself in, I'll understand. They will take care of you, and you'd be well fed and safe."

Tears streamed from her eyes, but I could tell they weren't from sadness. She was angry.

Rising, she slugged me in the arm. "You're not going anywhere without me, Luke! You're my brother, and I feel safe with you. Please take me with you." She threw herself at me and sobbed, "If you're going, then I'm going with you."

To be honest, I was relieved. I wouldn't have known what to do if she and I were separated.

I softly patted her shoulders. "Okay, then we're a team. We'll stay here tonight and then figure out our next move. In the meantime, I need to scout around and check things out just to be sure we're secure here. Hopefully, I can find us some more food, and I need to fill the canteen. I'm going to be moving around quickly and don't want to worry about you getting caught, so you need to stay here." Riley looked like she was about to say something, but I continued before she could. "No one will find you, but if you need to, you can sneak through this tunnel and run up to the road. Go to the café that we passed, and I'll find you there." She wasn't happy about my leaving, but she bit her lip and nodded. The sun was rising and slowly burning away the fog that blanketed the woods.

The remnants of the fog created an eerie glow as I moved through the brush to the street. Traffic along the street had picked up. I figured I wouldn't stand out since there were pedestrians walking along the sidewalk.

I crossed the street and headed down the block. Turning a corner, I spied a church in the middle of the block, and when I headed over to it, I found a spigot along the side wall. Someone was playing "How Great Thou Art" on the church's organ.

I pulled the canteen from the pack and had just started filling it when I noticed groups of people leaving the church and entering an outbuilding. Once the canteen was full, I walked over to see what was going on. The gathering seemed to be composed of multiple families, with children of all sizes running about. Peeking into the building, I saw a half-dozen tables covered with white cloths. Each table was packed with a variety of casserole dishes and serving platters piled high with an assortment of scrumptious-looking goodies like fried chicken, hot dogs, sandwiches, and corn on the cob. One table was dedicated to desserts and was sagging under the weight of cakes, pies, and an assortment of cookies. People were moving among the tables with paper plates and plastic silverware.

The aroma emanating from that hall made my mouth water. I wasn't sure what the occasion was for this potluck, but I was pretty sure that God wanted me to partake in his bounty. After all, Jesus said, "Feed my sheep," and I figured Riley and I were about as helpless as any sheep. We had been raised Catholic, but I didn't think eating Protestant food was any more than a venal sin. So, I ditched the pack along the side of the building and slipped into line. The organ in the church squeezed out a refrain from "Amazing Grace" as I squeezed in between two families, hoping that each would think I was with the other one.

The organist had switched to "Onward Christian Soldier" as I slipped out of the hall, my plate piled high with food and cookies stuffed into my pockets. I picked up the pack and headed for the woods.

A cop car was nearing at just that time, so I turned into the lobby of an apartment complex until they passed by. Once the coast was clear, I crossed the road and started down the bank near the overpass.

Entering the woods, I smelled smoke. After looking around for a moment, I spied a campfire in the shadow of the bridge. Curiosity got the best of me, and I angled over to check it out. Men and women were huddled around the campfire, and there were tents and lean-tos scattered about. A large black pot hung from a tripod over the fire, and I recognized this as a hobo encampment. Someone was playing "Ode to Joy" on a harmonica. I wondered what these poor souls had to be joyful for.

As I turned to leave, a gravelly voice startled me from behind, and I almost dropped the food that I was carrying. A massive man with a jagged scar across his cheek and broad shoulders said, "Those Baptists sure know how to put on a potluck, don't they? It's enough to make a believer out of you."

I backed away from him and was turning to run. He let out a belly laugh, "Y'all are welcome to join us. Be a lot safer than that spot where your sister's at. Hooligans come through those woods all the time, partying and looking for trouble." He smiled at me and held up two huge hands. "I'm Cletus. Ain't nobody here going to hurt you or your sister. After you finish your meal, come on back and you can flop with us. It'll be a lot safer."

I remembered what my dad had said about most hobos being down on their luck and harmless. Plus, this guy seemed kindly and sincere—for some reason, I trusted him. He wasn't telling me what to do. He was just treating me like an adult. I stopped backing up and stood up straight. The man was still twice as tall as me. "I'm Luke. How did you know we were here?"

"We make it a point to know what's going on around our camps. It's important for our survival. How about it? You going to join us? There's always room for more in the hobo jungle."

I told him that we might come over later, but I needed to talk it over with Riley. Then I rushed into the woods.

CHAPTER 7

Hobo Jungle, 1957

I'm not a vagrant… I'm a hobo. Big difference.

—Lee Child

I SCRAMBLED INTO THE THICKET AND down to our hideout, where I ducked inside. Riley's face lit up when I crawled in.

"I was really getting scared. I kept hearing sounds, and some people walked by just a few feet away. I thought they were going to find me."

I laid the paper plate down between us. "It's okay now. I brought some food, and I think I may have found someone who can help us. Let's eat, and I'll tell you all about it."

It turned out Cletus was right—those Baptists really knew how to cook. Riley devoured two chicken legs while I scarfed up a slice of ham and cornbread. We both enjoyed corn on the cob and shared a can of crème soda. The cookies were absolutely scrumptious. I had oatmeal-raisin, and Riley ate two chocolate chip cookies. She was pretty much addicted to all things chocolate.

I lay back with a very happy tummy. Riley was licking chicken grease off her fingers, and I told her about my adventures at the church and then running into Cletus. "If that man is right, then we can't stay here. If trouble starts, we have no way of defending ourselves. I just don't know if we should trust him." I shook my head. "Then again, we can't go back out on the streets. The cops will get us for sure."

Riley pulled on my arm to hug me, "Dad always says you need to trust your feelings. You said that this Cletus guy seemed alright. If he wanted to hurt us, wouldn't he have done something to me while you were away? And he could have grabbed you, too. We need help, and he's the only one offering."

I nodded and let out a sigh. We really didn't have a choice. "Okay, let's get our stuff together and see if we can find Cletus, our new best friend."

As it turned out, Cletus ended up being not only our friend but our mentor in the ways of the road.

●————————————●

I hid Riley behind a tree outside the encampment and walked in. About a dozen men were scattered about. Some of them were sleeping, while a half-dozen were huddled around the campfire. They were a motley-looking crew of all sizes and shapes.

Everyone ignored me as I walked up and asked for Cletus. I raised my voice and tried again, but the men seemed lost in their own thoughts, either staring off into space or down at the coals of the fire.

This wasn't getting me anywhere, and I was getting flustered. I stood there for a while. I didn't know what to do, so I began to walk off when one of the men croaked, "Ain't here." I looked at him for more, and he finally said, "Be back in a while. You wait." He was bald, and one of his eyes stared off in another direction when he looked at me. "Bring your sister. She's safe here."

I wasn't sure what to do. I couldn't leave Riley out in the woods, but I didn't want to unnecessarily expose her to another situation like Walt or some unknown danger here in the midst of these strange men. I was about ready to grab Riley and take our chances on the street when Cletus emerged from a clump of bushes and let out something between a laugh and a snort. "So you made it. Glad you decided to join us. Welcome! Go grab your sister, and we'll get you settled."

I went and retrieved my pack and led Riley by her hand into the camp.

"There's a spot over by my tent," Cletus continued. "Go ahead and put your pack down there and help me make a lean-to with this piece of plastic."

After we had erected the lean-to, I gathered a bunch of eucalyptus leaves underneath and laid the tarp from my pack over them.

Cletus handed me an old wool army blanket. "Here, this will keep that ole Oxnard fog off you two. Once you get settled come over to the campfire and I'll introduce you kids around."

We arranged the blanket, and I gave Riley's hand a squeeze as we walked to the campfire. Cletus stood up and raised his voice. "Listen up, everyone. We have some visitors to our little community." Then his tone turned more menacing. "Treat them with respect, or you'll answer to me. Now, why don't you younguns tell us your names and a little about yourselves so we can get to know each other."

I tried to stand tall. "My name is Lucas. I'm twelve, and this is my sister, Riley—she's nine. We are on our way to Seattle to find our dad. He's up there looking for work."

"It's a pleasure meeting you, Mr. Lucas and Miss Riley. As you know, my name is Cletus. You can call me Clete."

He gestured at the man with the wandering eye. "This here's Stitch. Stitch got his name because he was a tailor in Dayton, and he's a mighty fine one. If you need anything sewn up or mended, he's your man. Seems he came home early one day and found his wife in bed with his brother. When he discovered them, they weren't even embarrassed, just laughed at him. He packed up some clothes and left. Been on the road since, but before he went, he made sure his brother wouldn't be giving him any nieces or nephews. Made quite a mess, ain't that so Stitch?"

Stitch just grunted in response and turned toward the fire.

A skinny man sitting across from us pulled out a harmonica and started softly playing "Battle Hymn of the Republic." Clete pointed at him. "Now that 'bo playing the mouth organ is Eddie. He was a member of the First Marine Division, defending democracy against the onslaught of communism in Korea. He lost most of his toes serving our country. Tell them about it, Eddie."

Eddie looked down and began speaking in a low voice. "We landed at Wonsan in North Korea. Then that genius MacArthur sent us into a trap. We had them on the run by Thanksgiving, but Mao sent his troops down from China and a hundred and twenty thousand of them ambushed us at the Chosin Reservoir. Man, it was cold, down to minus thirty and more. Our guns froze up, and none of the vehicles would run because the batteries were frozen. We had to fight our way down seventy-eight miles along the Hungnam road, the only way out. The cold, plus the harassing gunfire, slowed us down till it seemed like we were crawling down that road."

He stared off into space, seeming to lose his train of thought for a second. "Thank God, old General Smith sent Chesty Puller to bail us out. We finally made it out, and they stuffed us into ships and we waved goodbye to North Korea on Christmas Eve. Anyway, I made it, but frostbite took most of my toes. Lost a lot of friends in that country, and I guess it messed up my head, 'cause I've been living on the road ever since my discharge."

"Your head ain't messed up, Eddie," Clete growled. "It's all those politicians who keep sending young boys to do a fool's errand who are downright evil. We're just cannon fodder to them. You lost your toes and don't even qualify for a Purple Heart. Damn desk jockeys writing the rules!" He stood and shouted, "Theirs is not to reason why, theirs is but to do and die." Then he stomped off.

"Ole Clete gets emotional about that kinda stuff," Eddie said. "He lost a bunch of his buddies at Omaha Beach. He was wounded pretty bad himself, but the thing that put him on the road was the Dear John he got while he was in the hospital. The guy still pines, but he's real blowed-in-the-glass, and it's time he found someone new and moved on. He's too smart to waste his life on the road. Did you know he was a Rhodes scholar before the war?"

Eddie pointed to a black man sitting off by himself, reading a book. "That 'bo over there is Tom from Mississippi." Tom looked up, smiled, and nodded. "He keeps to himself, but he's really smart. He was the first from his family of sharecroppers to graduate from high school and was on his way to college. But the white trash from his hometown didn't cotton to an uppity negro maybe being better than them. The night before he was supposed to leave for school, they broke into his home, beat up his folks, and started to string him up. Had his neck stretched out tight when neighbors ran them off and cut him down. He never did get to college. He figured no matter what he did, some redneck would be around the corner, waiting to knock him down."

Next, Eddie gestured to an emaciated man who was passed out under a large oak. "Red's over under that tree. Stay away from him. He's gentle enough most of the time, but if he doesn't get his fix of horse, he gets real nasty. He was in a really bad car accident a few years ago, and they gave him morphine for the pain. He got to liking it a little too much. Lost his job, and his wife left him. Graduated to smack here on the streets."

The shadows were getting long, and the fog was rolling in when Cletus wandered back to the campfire and stood near the cooking pot. "Getting pretty late. You kids will need some spending money if you're going all the way to Seattle. I heard Sun Bright Farms was hiring pickers. We'll have to get up early and get over there if we want a job. There's a washstand on the other side of that blue tent if you want to clean up before settling in. We'll go over some of the rules for the camp in the morning."

Riley and I cleaned our faces and hands, then wandered over to our shelter. Cletus was standing outside of his tent. "You kids get your rest. Picking strawberries is hard work, but you'll be able to pick up enough cash to move you up the road a ways. Good night, now." We said good night as well and slipped into the lean-to. Riley lay on one side and I sat on the other. "Cletus is nice," she whispered. "I feel a lot safer here with him here. What's a rogue's scholar?"

I laid down on the tarp. "I think he said roads scholar. I'm not sure, but it must have something to do with knowing all there is about being on the road." I sighed. "They all seem nice. It will be good to earn some money for our trip. I just hope that Clete can point us in the right direction for Seattle. Good night, Riles."

Eddie was playing "Beautiful Dreamer" on his harmonica as we drifted off to sleep.

———————

The sound of people moving about woke me. Riley was already up and sitting against the side of the lean-to. "Hey, how long have you been awake?" I croaked through a throat that was still half asleep.

"I woke up about an hour ago, and I've just been listening to those men moving around. I can smell food. Do you think they'll share with us? I'm starving." That was one thing about Riley, her stomach always comes first.

Just then, Cletus's voice boomed out. "Hey, kids, better get a move on. Those strawberries won't pick themselves. Come on out and get some porridge while it's hot. You're going to need your energy if you want to earn some money."

We scrambled over to the cooking pot, where Eddie was standing with two chipped mugs full of steaming oatmeal. He handed one to each of us with a smile while he looked off in the distance.

I guess it was because of all the fresh air, but that was some of the best oatmeal that I had ever tasted. It had a slight taste of cinnamon, with a sprinkling of raisins throughout. Clete was kneeling down and stoking the fire.

"We're going to catch a ride with Miguel. He's one of the migrant workers who follow the crops wherever they lead. He says the field where we'll be picking isn't very big and we'll be done by early afternoon. Have you two ever picked strawberries before?" We shook our heads, and he stood up and continued, "Well there's always a first time. When you're picking, look for a berry that's completely red, firm, and dry. Don't pick any that are still yellow or look rotten"

We walked over to a road that ran parallel to the train tracks. "Miguel says that Star Bright is paying seventy-five cents per flat," he continued. "That's good money around here. Most adults can earn two or three dollars per hour, but it's hard, backbreaking work. You bend, stoop, or squat for hours at a time. Since you're inexperienced, you kids might pick up four or five dollars." He pointed. The cough of an engine sounded behind us. "There's Miguel's truck. Let's go."

We climbed into the back of a weathered pickup, sat on the bed among a half-dozen Hispanic men and women, and took off down the road.

A while later, we turned down a dirt path to a large field covered with low-lying plants sprinkled with bright red fruit. When the truck stopped, everyone hopped out, grabbed a wooden flat and a dozen baskets, and headed into the field. We followed along as each picker went to the head of a row, knelt down, and started picking.

•————————•

It turned out that "backbreaking work" was a gross understatement. Riley and I worked a row together. Though she tried valiantly, the effort was just too great for a nine-year-old city kid. She ended up keeping me company instead, offering encouragement and eating every other strawberry that she found.

The effort was just about too much for a twelve-year-old as well. It was all I could do to continue picking all the way to the end of our row. Besides an aching back, my fingers were soon raw, and I could barely kneel down because my knees were so sore. I ended up with a lot of respect for those men and women who faced this agony every day.

On the positive side, we picked seven flats and earned five dollars and twenty-five cents. While we rode back to camp, Riley smiled at me through red-tinged lips. "That was hard, but we did really great. Five dollars should help us on our trip."

I nodded wearily and handed her three of the bills. "Here, put these in your shoe where they'll be safe. I'll hide the others. When we get back, I'll talk to Clete about us getting on the road."

————————

When we returned to camp, Riley and I washed up and then walked up the street to a little neighborhood store. I pulled out two dollars and bought a bag of rice and a can of coffee to take back to the camp for the hobos. We splurged and spent the extra quarter on treats. Riley had an Orange Crush, and I had my favorite, a Grape Nehi. I'd had a lot of water from the water buffalo in the strawberry field, but that soda sure felt good sliding down my parched throat. We had a nickel left over even after that, so we bought a handful of penny candy.

Eddie was softly playing "Home on the Range" on his harmonica when we returned. Clete was sitting by the fire.

He looked up and smiled, "You kids did good today. How are you feeling?"

We handed him the rice and coffee and slumped down beside him. "We're really tired," Riley moaned. "I didn't realize how hard that would be. How does anyone do that all the time?"

Clete massaged his back and nodded. "It is hard work. But it's honest work, and those people are honorable people. They may be poor, but it's folks like them who keep this country fed. There are others like them who work hard all across America. They are the backbone of this country.

"Now that you two are official members of our little enclave, I need to explain how things work around here. You've met some of the folks here, and you can see that they're pretty much like anyone else in society. There's good and bad. They just want to get along each day in relative safety. The difference between these hobos and so called 'society' is that for whatever reason, they've chosen to live on the road. They've shunned the normal structure most others need. Most of them are solitary souls who want to be left alone and who will leave you alone.

He got up, stretched his back, and waved his arm around the camp.

"And hobos aren't tramps or bums either. A tramp only works when they're forced to, and a bum won't work at all. Hobos work wherever we go, just like those Mexican migrants we worked alongside today. We are traveling workers—we may be homeless, but we value and embrace our independence. We decide our own life and won't let another person run or rule us.

"But even the most independent of us understands that there are basic rules that must be followed in order to assure our survival. So, there are hobo rules that have evolved to ensure our little subset of society functions effectively. These rules vary from camp to camp, but they each have a common thread based on respect for our fellow humans."

"Hobos respect local laws and always try to find work wherever we can. We find work by doing jobs that no one else wants. We try to stay clean and set a good example so that locals will leave us alone. We respect nature more than most because we live in it."

I was waiting for more of the rules, but his expression shifted. "Now, I'm getting a little hungry. How about we finish this discussion over some stew? Remember what I said about us hobos staying clean. Time to wash up."

We walked over to the wash pan sitting on a fifty-five gallon drum and washed our hands. When we got back to the fire, Clete handed us each a steaming mug and spoon. "Grab some bread over there. It's good for sopping up the gravy. This luscious stew is courtesy of Mrs. McIntyre. She's resting over in that tent. She made this mulligan stew by combining the food some of the boys got from panhandling this morning."

I glanced toward the tent, but the flap was closed, so I couldn't see anyone. We wandered over to a downed log and sat down.

"Now, getting back to your lessons about hobo life. Where were we? Oh yeah, if you angelinas are going to be traveling around, you'll need to learn a few hobo signs. These signs are a method of communication between hobos. You'll need to be alert to them because they describe important local information about a town or area."

This sounded interesting, and important. I leaned in as he continued.

"If you stay on the road long enough, you'll learn them all, but you need to know these basic signs to stay out of trouble." He grabbed a stick and drew an X in the dirt. "A big X means everything is okay, and if the X has a circle around it, then it's a good place for a handout." He continued drawing as he talked. "If the X has what appears to be water waves above it, then the water is safe to drink. A sketch of a cat means a kind lady lives at the house, while a rectangle with and elongated base means a gentleman lives there. There are others that you'll pick up as you go along."

He laid his hands on his knees with a loud slap. "Okay, that's enough lessons for now. There's another hobo rule that applies now that everyone has eaten. When you're in a community jungle like the one we're in right now, it's important that everyone pitches in and helps. How about the three of us pitching in and cleaning up?"

Riley jumped up. "I'll wash. You can dry, Luke. You can put things away Mr. Clete" She gathered up all of the dishes and utensils and headed over to the wash tub.

•———————•

Eddie was playing "Down in the Valley" on his harmonica as we lounged around the fire. Clete stuffed an old stogie between his teeth, looked over at us, and smiled.

"We need to figure out what to do with you two. Part of the hobo code requires that we protect and take care of children. You're welcome here as long as you like, but if you're runaways, we should consider getting you back with your folks."

I stood up and started pacing back and forth. "We're not runaways, Mr. Clete, We're looking for our dad. He lost his job and left us with some people while looking for work. Some of those people were bad, so we took off. Last we heard, he's in Seattle, and that's where we're heading."

Before I knew it, I'd told him the whole story. "I didn't mean to kill Walt," I finished, "but he was going to hurt Riley, so I had to stop him." Tears formed in my eyes. "We can't go to the police, because of what I did. It's a big mess. We have to find Dad."

Riley grabbed my hand and squeezed.

Cletus nodded. "That's quite a kettle of fish. I think the police should understand your motives if you explained the whole story to them, but given my experiences with the law, maybe not. Even if they did, they would probably throw you into some home while they sorted everything out. And you might be separated. Not good. Then again, Seattle's a long way from here.

"Here's what I think. This town's getting too familiar for me, and I've been thinking about moving on. What do you think about me tagging along for a while? I can continue with your hobo education, and maybe I'll see some new country."

Before I had a chance to reply, Riley jumped up and hugged him around his big neck. "Thank you so much, Mr. Clete. You're the best! We could really use the help." I felt a huge release of the tension that had enveloped me.

The shadows were getting long, and the light was fading. "Okay then, that's settled," he said. "Why don't we hit the sack, and tomorrow we can come up with a plan to get you and your daddy back together."

We said our goodnights and headed to our lean-to, where Eddie played "Taps" and Tom softly sang,

"Day is done, gone the sun,
From the lake, from the hills, from the sky,
All is well, safely rest, God is nigh."

He had a nice, deep voice. Riley and I held hands and said our prayers before fading off to sleep.

———————

We woke to the sound of someone pounding on the side of the lean-to. "Wake up in there. The bulls are clearing out the camp. Get your stuff together and get out of here," Eddie was saying. "Get into town, and don't come back here. The bulls are ornery, and they don't care who they hurt. Clete says to meet him at the Baptist Church at first light. Now git, before they catch you."

Riley and I jumped up and stuffed our meager belongings into the pack, then slipped out of our nook. I heard men shouting as we crept toward the woods, yells and cries coming from the camp. A large man swung a black baton at one of the hobos, and it hit his head with a sickening crunch.

I grabbed Riley, and we started running into the darkness.

CHAPTER 8

Riding the Rails, 1957

*Even if you're on the right track, you'll
get run over if you just sit there.*

—Will Rogers

T HE NIGHT WAS PITCH BLACK. Fog filled the air,
dampening the sounds of the fight in the camp. My
heart was pounding as I pulled Riley along. After a block,
we slowed and began walking. We were becoming adept
at moving from shadow to shadow. We wandered up one
street and down another until we found ourselves in a residential district. The lights were out in most of the houses,
but a few streetlamps provided enough light to mark our
way.

I spied a garden hose lying across a front lawn and
stopped to fill our canteen. As I approached the house
to turn on the spigot, a dog barked and jumped out from
behind a bush, wagging his tail. After my pulse settled
down, I reached my hand out to her. She sidled up and
began licking my fingers. "Good girl," I whispered as I
petted her and then put the cap back onto the canteen. She
sniffed me, licked my hand again, and then wandered back
to the house.

"I think we need to get out of this neighborhood. If someone sees two kids wandering around in the middle of the night they're going to get suspicious and call the cops." Just then a car came ambling around the corner and pulled up to a house three doors down. Riley and I dove behind an old trailer parked in the driveway. The car's passenger window was open, and a newspaper flew out and landed on the path leading to the house. The car moved on down the street, stopping at houses along the way to disgorge another delivery.

Once it had turned the corner, Riley and I got up and began walking. "I'm all turned around and not sure where we are," I said. "Let's get to a main street and then maybe we can find the church. We don't want to be late and miss Clete."

That is if Clete survived the raid at the camp. I kept that thought to myself so Riley wouldn't start to worry.

"Okay, Luke, but I'm hungry. Can we get something to eat?"

I grinned to myself, *That's my sis.*

<hr>

We backtracked to a main thoroughfare and headed in what I hoped was the right direction. Traffic had picked up, so we had to go slow and stay in the shadows. When we reached a fairly main intersection, we spied a Speedee Mart in the middle of the block. I sat down, untied a sneaker, and retracted one of the dollar bills, putting it in my jeans pocket. We moved up the street to the doorway next to the store, and I creeped around and peeked in the window. A large clock on the wall said it was five. Two customers were at the counter.

I went back to Riley. "There are two people in there. As soon as they leave, we can go in and get some food. We need to get in and out in a hurry, so you need to think about what you want. Let's go."

We scrambled into the store and went straight to the refrigerated section, where I grabbed a pint of chocolate milk. Up another aisle, we found the pastries. Riley grabbed some chocolate-covered miniature donuts, and I scooped up a package of Hostess Twinkies. We finished off our haul with two bananas and a handful of beef jerky—a real gastronomical delight, all of the food groups.

The store's sound system was playing Harry Belafonte's "Banana Boat" song and the clerk was singing along as he checked us out. I thought about asking directions but didn't want to raise the cashier's suspicions.

When we got back outside, the sky above the mountains to the east was glowing with the morning light. I heard a train a few blocks away and started in that direction. Glancing down the road at another cross street, I saw the Spud Nuts sign. "I know where we are now. The church is just a couple of blocks away."

Upon reaching the church, we sat on one of the benches in the back and ate our meal. It was almost full daylight when a lamp came on in the front room of the parsonage. After a few minutes, the door opened and a figure dressed in black came out and started up the pathway to the church. As he came closer, I could see a wispy-haired, middle-aged man deep in thought.

He started when he saw us. "Why, hello children. You're certainly up early this morning. Have you come to pray?"

"No, sir. I mean, yes, sir. Um, we're waiting for our uncle," I stammered. "I mean, we pray, but we're not Baptist, so I'm not sure we should."

The preacher let out a guffaw. "Out of the mouths of babes. I know many Baptists who would run me out of town on a rail if they heard me say this, but the Lord doesn't care about our denomination. He loves all of us, and he cares about our souls, not our memberships."

He steepled his fingers before his lips. "I have a thought. While you wait for your uncle, would you join me in thanking God for another glorious day and asking Him to guide our paths for the day? It's something that I like to do as I set out each morning."

We nodded our heads, and he continued, "Dear Lord, thank you for all the blessings that you have bestowed on us. Please have mercy on our sinful souls. As we move through our day, we pray that we maintain the virtues of patience, understanding, and compassion. Bestow on us the gifts of fortitude, slowness to anger, kindness, and wisdom. We ask this in the name of our Lord, Jesus Christ, Amen."

We responded with our amens, and just then Clete came around the corner. "Good morning, Padre. That was a nice prayer. Since the children and I will be traveling today, can you give us a blessing for our trip?"

"Of course. There's nothing like Psalms for a good blessing—let's go with Psalm 121:8. 'The Lord will watch over your coming and going both now and forevermore.' Now, I'm afraid I'm up against an appointment. Mrs. Guilfoyle needs to tell me about her neighbor's sins. Should prove to be an interesting morning. Be safe, and my prayers are with you as you travel."

The preacher walked away. Clete turned to us, and I could see a bruise forming on his cheek. "That was a pretty good dustup back at the camp. Eddie said you made it out, but I was still worried. I'm sure glad you're okay. Those bulls are a mean lot. Now we need to get moving. There's a northbound train leaving in about an hour, and we're going to be on it."

I'd seen it plenty of times in the movies, and I got excited and chirped, "Are we going to hop the train as it goes by? That sounds like a blast!"

"I don't think so," Clete growled. "That's a fool's game. Hopping trains is extremely dangerous, and anyone who does it without getting hurt is lucky. I figure I used up all my luck on Omaha Beach. Besides, I'm too damn old to be running after trains. No, we're going to sneak into the yard and climb into a boxcar after the bulls make their checks. Let's head out—those trains don't wait for anyone.

Clete led us through some trees and out a gate at the back of the church's lot. From there, we followed my previous route to the overpass covering the hobo camp. As we dropped down to the tracks, I could see that the camp had been thoroughly trashed. Tents and clothing were strewn about, and the campfire had been doused. The cookpot was dented and buried halfway in the ashes. Eddie was sitting on a tree stump, a gash in his cheek. Dried tears streaked his face as he looked down upon the bent harmonica in his hand. The image made me want to cry.

"Why did they do this?" I wondered out loud. "We weren't hurting anyone! It's just plain mean!"

Clete shook his head. "The Railroad will tell you that they're protecting their property. They say they want to ensure everyone's safety and that our camp is a threat. But the violence says otherwise. The bulls don't have to beat and abuse people to get them to move. It's more about power. The men they hire to enforce their property rights are bullies by nature. And like all bullies, they're cowards, traveling in groups and preying on those weaker than them. It's unfortunate, but the bulls are a hobo's biggest danger."

He reached out for the man. "Let's go, Eddie. Guess we won't be havin' any music on our trip." Together, they picked up their knapsacks and canteens and slid into the brush, with Riley and me following.

We started up the draw by the railroad tracks. Across the way and halfway up the block, I saw an F.W. Woolworth's department store and had a thought. I yelled at Clete, "I need to go to the store real quickly. Do we have time? Riles, you stay here with Clete and Eddie. I'll be right back." I started running up the street before he could answer.

"You better hurry up, boy! We got about ten minutes." His voice faded behind me in the distance.

I was back in eight with a brown Woolworth's bag in my hand. Clete scowled at me, and we started toward the rail yard.

* * *

We huddled behind an old shed at the edge of the yard. Railroad ties were stacked near the shed and the smell of creosote was palpable. Clete pointed. "We're gonna be riding open-air style in that train on the fourth track over," he whispered. "You see, the bulls are checking all of the cars because it's ready to take off. Once they're finished with their checks, we'll sneak over to that open boxcar and get settled. I normally don't like doing this in the daylight, but the fog's rolling in, so that should give us some cover. We'll go the long way around to keep trains between us and the bulls. Just follow my lead and stay alert." He gestured to a spigot protruding from the shed. "Make sure your canteen's full. We don't know when we'll get another chance to fill up."

I watched the bulls walking along the tracks, sticking their heads into all of the cars and even checking the undercarriage. When they reached the end of the train, they turned around and repeated the process on their return trip to the roundhouse. When they were finally out of sight, Clete waved us forward and we scrambled, hunched over, to the boxcar. He boosted each of us up and through the double side door.

"Slide over to the corner out of sight until we get underway," he whispered.

Clete and Eddie clambered up and sat beside us. The floor of the boxcar was covered in a layer of gray dust, and debris lay strewn about. It reeked of whatever contents had been carried in it before—a mixture of ammonia and rotten fruit. The doors opposite the one where we entered were fully open. A short time later, the car jerked, twice, and we began to roll through the rail yard. As we started toward the edge of town, it picked up speed and blew a mournful tone from its horn.

Clete indicated that we could move around and make ourselves comfortable, but the car was jerking and bouncing so much it was difficult to stand, so we kinda slithered over to the doorway and sat watching the industrial buildings move past in a blur.

Eddie was sitting next to Riley. I reached over and handed him the Woolworth's bag. "This is for you, Eddie."

The man took the bag with a puzzled look on his face. "What is this? Ain't no one ever give me anything before. You should be saving your money." He opened it and peered in. His chin quivered, and he looked over at me with a smile. "Well ain't you something else. Damn, boy!" Then he pulled out a shiny new Hohner harmonica.

Riley held my hand. "Will you play us a song, Mr. Eddie?" Eddie blew the dust out of the harmonica and started playing "12 Bars Boogie Woogie."

Clete put his beefy arm around my shoulders and murmured, "You're a good man, Lucas." I looked up at him, and I couldn't swear it, but it looked like the big man might have been a little misty. Me, meanwhile—I felt a little warm all over…and maybe a little misty. But it was probably all the soot from the train.

———•———

The train poked along, pulling into sidings to let other trains traveling south to pass, then all at once the view from both sides opened up to competing vistas. On one side, the coastal mountains provided a backdrop to the verdant fields of the Oxnard Plain. On the other, we were treated to whitecaps exploding across the blue Pacific. Cumulus clouds skittered across the horizon. Sunbathers were soaking up the rays on the beach, and off in the distance we could see the Channel Islands.

A little while later, a little white sign on a post announced the town of Ventura, and the train began to slow.

Clete leaned over. "This train isn't supposed to stop in Ventura, but if it does, the bulls will probably pull an inspection. We need to be ready to take off if we see them coming." We gathered our stuff together while he peeked out one door and Eddie did the same at the other.

Prepared as we were to take off running, it turned out that we didn't need to. The train slowly creaked and groaned past Ventura's few tall buildings and back out into open country. As we rolled out of town, the mountain range seemed to come right down onto us, and the tracks cut along a wall of granite. Looking at that great stone edifice wasn't very entertaining, so we all sat on the ocean side and watched a pod of dolphins playing fifty yards off the surf line.

Eddie was in the corner playing "Turkey in the Straw," and Riley had curled up for a nap.

Clete started talking. "You know, when I came ashore at Omaha Beach and saw the carnage there, I thought that was the worst thing that would ever happen to me. Half of my unit was killed before we ever got off of that damned Higgins boat. And that thought was reinforced as we fought our way through the hedgerows and across Europe. The atrocities we witnessed were horrific, and I couldn't understand man's inhumanity. But at least I understood the driving power of greed and the lust for power some people possess. Throw in a little insanity, and it's explainable…not justified, but explainable.

I took my gaze from the sparkling ocean to watch the darkening emotion on Clete's face.

"The thing that pushed me over the edge was the pain of betrayal. It's one thing if someone who's not close to you lets you down, because there was never a deep commitment. But when someone that you love, trust, and depend upon turns their back on you, the pain is almost unbearable. Your whole foundation is shaken, and you lose your trust in anyone. You build a protective shell around yourself.

His sadness was palpable, and I put my hand on his arm and squeezed. He took my hand in his and a smile returned to his big face.

"Being around you kids the last few days has cracked that shell. I feel a stirring, and I think I'm ready to begin life again. Who knows, maybe I'll meet someone and settle down." Clearing his throat, he growled, "Anyway, I just wanted to say thanks." He rolled over and went to sleep.

I sat in the doorway, daydreaming and staring off at the waves crashing in the surf. A few minutes later, something caught my eye. There, on a rocky point jutting out to sea, three boys sat on long, pointed boards. A swell rose behind them, and they started paddling toward shore like heck. And then the darndest thing happened. The swell seemed to catch one of the boards and began to propel it faster and faster toward shore, and the boy stood up on the board. He and the board sailed toward the rocks, and then he kicked his heel. His board turned, and he slowly sank into the ocean and began paddling back out.

Eddie had scooted up beside me. "They call it surfing. Started in Hawaii, I think. We'll be coming into Santa Barbara soon. It's a passenger stop only, so we probably will roll on through. Keep an eye out, just in case."

Santa Barbara appeared to be a pleasant town, a nice little garden of Eden nestled up against the green foothills. White stucco houses with red tile roofs dotted the landscape, but the grime of the buildings and the groups of homeless wandering the street made me wonder if this picture-perfect setting might just be a façade.

"Goleta is the next town. It's more industrial, and the train will probably stop there. There's usually not a lot of bulls around, but you better wake your sister just in case. I'll get Clete up."

The mountains pulled away as we left Santa Barbara and entered a flat plain interrupted by low-rise, light-industry buildings. On a point jutting into the ocean in the distance, we could see Spanish architecture buildings under construction. The train slowed and came to a creaking halt. We kept watch out of both doors, but no one materialized except a couple of hobos, who nodded their greeting and continued down the tracks. Our boxcar bumped around as other cars were added and subtracted to the train, and after about forty-five minutes, we slowly began to creep away.

As soon as we left town, the train began to skirt the rocky coast. The rolling hills covered in golden grass to our right were dotted with herds of black cattle. Meanwhile, the ocean opposite was aquamarine and tranquil, and we watched seals and sea otters swimming and lazing in the afternoon sun. I pulled the beef jerky from the pack and offered some to Clete and Eddie. They both declined, but Riley took two and settled at the oceanside door.

Clete pulled a half-smoked stogie from his pocket and lit it, staring out to sea. "Isn't this gorgeous? The sun's shining, the weather's balmy, and the ocean is picture-perfect. It's days like this that make the hobo life idyllic. Not a care in the world, and about as much freedom as a person could have." He sighed. "But these days are few and far between. The rest are hard."

The miles rolled on, and the clacking rhythm of the wheels on the tracks lulled us to sleep. I was pretty far gone, dreaming of Cindy and those little bumps in her sweater, when an explosion pulled me out of my reverie.

The train was still skirting the ocean, and on the other side, earthmoving equipment was clearing an area from the thick scrub brush. Off in the distance, tall, odd-shaped buildings rose like inverted Ls.

A while later, we passed a lonely siding and covered platform in the middle of nowhere. The small white sign identified this spot as Surf. A road led due east through farmers' fields toward a small town.

Eddie was watching gulls and terns ride the currents in the wind. "That little town is Lompoc. I spent some time there working the fields. Not much to it except a couple of strip joints catering to the military at Camp Cooke. There's a pretty Spanish mission and a federal penitentiary. You know, Luke, I've been thinking that you should learn to blow this mouth organ yourself. You want me to teach you?"

I nodded enthusiastically. "That would be great. I always wanted to take music lessons, but we never could afford them."

Eddie was very patient as he walked me through the basics of how to hold the harmonica and then how to relax my mouth and breathe with it. Soon, I was playing single notes without too many flubs. After a while, I mastered "Happy Birthday." Later, I was blowing "Amazing Grace" well enough that Riley recognized it when she woke up, and she even applauded. It was a simple piece and I wasn't able to bend the notes yet, but it felt pretty good to be able to play it. I was jammin'.

The train kept clack-clacking away, and we passed through Guadalupe and entered an area covered by sand. Some of the dunes rose thirty feet in the air, punctuated with clumps of creosote. Out of the corner of my eye, I spotted what appeared to be a giant sphinx jutting out of the sand. I started to point it out to Riley, but we turned a corner and it was out of sight. I shook my head, thinking for a moment that I'd imagined it

Clete slid up beside me and chuckled. "Cecil B. DeMille filmed *The Ten Commandments* here back in 1923. They built up a whole set to simulate the Egyptian countryside and then buried the set when they were finished filming. Some of the old props appear after a strong windstorm pushes the sand away.

"The train will be pulling into Pismo Beach soon, where the rails turn east. We'll get off there. There'll be bulls, so we need to scramble as soon as the train stops. There's a hobo camp down the road, and Pismo is always a good place to pick up some work. You and Riley should get ready."

CHAPTER 9

Clam Chowder, 1957

*Clam chowder is one of those subjects, like politics
or religion, that can never be discussed lightly.*

—Louis Pullig De Guoy

A S WE LEFT THE SAND dunes behind us and came over a small hill, I noticed a grove of eucalyptus and cypress trees that seemed to be alive with thousands of Monarch butterflies. Their gold and black wings fluttered, making the trees shimmer. To me, it looked like some kind of magic.

It was late afternoon when we rounded a bend and crossed a dry creek bed. An arched sign straddled the main street, proudly announcing "Clam Capital of the World." Next to the sign sat a giant concrete clam. The train lurched and squealed as it slowed to a stop on a siding near the center of town. Clete pointed at three rough-looking men crossing the tracks toward us. He and Eddie helped us down on the opposite side of the car, and we took off running in the direction of the beach.

The bulls didn't have much interest in catching us. They fell back and stopped as soon as they reached the edge of the yard. We jogged down the street and ducked into an alley that led us to the dry creek bed. After dropping down the bank, we headed upstream to a stand of eucalyptus trees. There was a small clearing in the middle of the trees, and a half-dozen tents were spread around a fire pit. The place was deserted save for one woman standing at the fire, stirring a large pot. She was skinny as a rail and had a pipe jutting from her teeth, many of which appeared missing.

Clete approached her. "We're passing through. Mind if we share your fire and spread out our bed rolls?"

She grunted. "He'p yourself. Got any tobacco? I'm plum out." Clete handed her an old, half-smoked cigar, and she proceeded to shred it and tamp a wad of tobacco into her pipe. She pulled out a match, struck it on a rock, and then held it to her pipe. Blowing smoke out of the side of her mouth, she said, "Pretty safe around here. The townsfolk leave us alone, and there's plenty of day work if you're inclined.

We thanked her and walked to the edge of the clearing. Clete began clearing an area for his tent while Riley and I began scrounging material from the detritus lying about to make a lean-to. We found an old rectangle of plywood and propped it up against a tree.

Watching us struggle to keep the plywood upright, the woman wandered over and handed Riley a large old tarp. "Here, this will work better. Stretch your rope tight between those two trees and drape the tarp over it. You can hold the corners down with some large rocks." We did as she said, and then I spread some eucalyptus leaves on the ground and covered them with our small tarp and blanket. "It gets cold and wet at night here in Pismo, and you're going to need another blanket. Go grab one out of the community pile."

She pointed at a pile of blankets and old articles of clothing neatly folded and stacked on a tree stump. Riley and I sorted through the stack and found two army-green wool blankets. When we had finished, she puffed on her pipe, nodded, and walked away.

Clete was finished with his spot, and I noticed that Eddie hadn't set up his tent and was sitting on a rock softly playing "Home on the Range" on his harmonica.

Riley walked over to him. "What's wrong, Mr. Eddie? Aren't you feeling well?"

Eddie took his harmonica from his lips and smiled. "No, honey, I'm alright. I'm heading out tonight on the nine-o-five for Reno. I noticed Sam Tooley's moniker on the water tank coming into town. I've been trying to catch up to him for a while. He and I were members of the 'Frozen Chosin' together."

I walked over. He put an arm around each of us, pulled us into a hug, murmuring, "I sure have enjoyed your company. I'll miss you and that big galoot over there. Take care of him. I'm positive that we'll cross paths again. Lucas, would you like this fine harmonica back?"

"No, sir! I bought that for you," I managed to say as I hugged Eddie around his neck. "Thanks for the lessons. I'll pick up one along the way."

Eddie smiled and stood. He shook my hand and did a formal bow to Riley, tipped his cap to Clete, and walked away blowing "Auld Lang Syne." Watching him go, I felt a hole open up in my heart. Riley took my hand in hers, and we stayed like that until Eddie turned the corner.

We finished fixing up our camp. By then, the shadows were long and there wasn't enough time to do anything else, so we decided to explore the town while it was still light out. Before we left, the old woman approached us and asked us to keep an eye out for any sources of tobacco.

Pismo was a typical beach town. The buildings were dingy, and all the streets seemed to have a slight slant toward the ocean. Catering to the tourists, every block seemed to contain at least one bar and three restaurants. Hotels crowded the ocean, their balconies hanging dangling off the backside. We wandered by one large and extremely loud cowboy bar, where Patsy Cline's melodious voice carried through the batwing doors. Men with big hats and bigger belt buckles were staggering in and out.

We turned left onto a steep street that angled toward the beach. At the end, we turned left again and found a pier jutting out about two hundred yards into the ocean. The lights along the pier had just come on in the dusk, accentuating its form and making for a beautiful scene. Walking out onto it, we passed men and women with their fishing poles held out over the water. I peered into a couple of buckets and spied some perch and rockfish. In the shadow of the pier, a couple of guys were in the water, doing that surfing thing. We watched in amazement as they caught the waves and performed an acrobatic balancing act while they hurtled toward the shore.

On the way back toward camp, we walked along the seawall and past a bait shop. I smiled at an elderly Asian man behind the counter, and he waved us inside. He was slight of build, with salt-and-pepper hair and a wispy mustache. "Do you two want to earn a little money?" He smiled. "I've got a whole bunch of chores, and I'm getting a little old to keep up. I can pay you each seventy-five cents per hour." We both nodded, and he handed us each a lollipop from a jar on the counter. "Okay then, be here tomorrow bright and early and we'll get you started. Should keep you busy for three days."

I noticed a couple of cold cigars in an ashtray, one half-smoked and the other with about a third remaining, and asked if I could have them. The old man arched his eyebrows suspiciously and told me I was way too young to be smoking.

I was prepared for that. "Oh no, sir. I don't want to smoke them. I need them for a summer assignment that I'm doing about the dangers of smoking."

He squinted at me, chuckled, and handed them to me. "In that case, it's okay. Just don't try to get me to quit. It's my last remaining vice."

We were pretty elated with our newfound employment and headed back to camp. There, the old woman was sitting at the fire with Clete. I gave one of the cigars to her and handed the other to him. The woman thanked me and shredded hers, stuffing the loose tobacco into her pipe. Clete lit his stogie with a match while the woman fussed with her setup, lighting and tamping the tobacco until it was lit. We all sat around the fire, lost in our thoughts, those two puffing away, Riley and I licking our suckers.

After a few minutes, I told Clete about our wanderings and the job we were going to start in the morning.

"I know who you're talking about," the woman jumped in. "That's Tim. He's a good man. He'll treat you fairly." She got up and poured some soup from a kettle on the fire into two mugs and handed them to Riley and me. "Don't forget to bring back some tobacco."

Clete spoke up. "Sounds like you'll be busy for a few days. I found a job, too, chipping paint from an old trawler at the dry dock in Shell Beach. Pays pretty well, so how about we meet up tomorrow evening after work and I'll treat you to dinner? I've got just the treat for us. Now, I don't know about you, but I'm bushed. I'll see you in the morning. Don't forget to wash those dishes." We wandered over to the wash bucket and rinsed our cups out, said our goodnights to the old woman, and headed off to our makeshift tent.

———————•———————

Clete was already gone by the time we got up the next morning. The fog was so thick everything was dripping wet. I made a note to myself to thank the old woman for recommending the extra blankets.

When we got to the bait shop, we had to wait for Tim to check out some customers. When he was finished, he smiled and said, "Good morning, young people. We didn't get to introduce ourselves last night. I'm Tim Kawai." I didn't think anyone would be looking for us this far from Cholame, so we introduced ourselves with our real names.

"I'm glad you're here," he said as he turned and opened a door behind the counter. Come on to the back and I'll get you started."

We skirted the counter and entered the back room. The walls were lined with shelves from floor to ceiling, crowded with detritus of all shapes and sizes. A pile of about a hundred empty cardboard boxes occupied one corner. In another, a shrine of some sort stood on a small wooden table. A workbench and stool dominated the center of the room, covered with various types of fishing tackle.

"As you can see, I'm not very organized. I can't seem to find anything. I need you two to clean and straighten up this room and organize the inventory. You can start by breaking down those boxes and taking them to the dumpster down the alley. That should keep you busy for a while.

I'll be at the counter helping customers if you need any-thing. Just come out front when you're finished with the boxes." Just then, a little bell over the front door chimed, and Tim headed out to greet his customer. Not long after, the smoke from a cigar wafted into the back room.

It took almost two hours to clear out all the boxes. Riley and I would separate the bottom flaps and collapse them to lay them flat. Whenever we made a large enough pile, I would carry them out the back door and down the alley to a dumpster that was already half-full of trash.

When we finished with those, I stepped over to the shrine in the corner for a closer look. It appeared to be a finely crafted miniature model of a building with a con-cave roof and red doors. A chrysanthemum was painted on the front in intricate detail. There was a rope hanging across the top, a pair of vases, candles, and some white dishes. As I was checking it out, Tim came up behind me. "I see you found my *Kamidana*. It is Shinto and means 'god shelf' in English. I'm a third-generation American and was raised a Lutheran, but after I returned from the internment camp, I wanted something to tie me to the ancestors."

He glanced around the room and grinned. "It looks like you two did a fine job with those boxes. Let's just sit here and have some tea for a while before you begin your next task."

He went to the front and came back with a tea service tray that held a porcelain pot and tiny cups decorated with fine paintings. Pouring the green tea, he continued, "I am a red-blooded American. Grew up with baseball and apple pie. I don't speak Japanese, and I've never been to Japan. After Pearl Harbor, though, everyone was in a panic. Just like Irish Americans and Italian Americans, we Japanese

Americans tended to cluster together. But we look different and speak a language with 'funny' intonations, so we were suspect. In the panic of those days, there was no way for the authorities to sort out who was loyal or who was not. So, they pulled us out of our homes and sent us to live in compounds surrounded by barbed wire and guards.

"I was lucky in that I had no remaining family, but many suffered under the sparse conditions. While the program created hardships, conditions in the camps weren't horrendous—we had a roof over our heads and plenty of food. Segregating us Japanese made sense, but the program, like most government programs, was not well planned and rife with abuse. And we got through it relatively unscathed. My only regret was that I was too old to serve in the military and fight for my country like many of those who went to the camps."

He smiled. "Enough about me. Please be kind enough to tell me a little about yourselves. I am an old man, so excuse me for prying, but I perceive that you have a story to tell."

I had already fabricated a story. This man seemed nice enough, and I wanted to share our story, but I was still cautious about the possibility of him turning us over to the authorities. I had just started to tell my fable when Riley blurted out, "Oh Mr. Tim, we're looking for our dad. We think he's in Seattle."

I panicked, ready to bolt. She sobbed and continued on with all the gory details, including telling him that I was a murderer. That detail caused Tim to sit back and look at me with fresh eyes.

"Well now," he said when she was done, "that's a lot of excitement for someone as young as you two. I'm amazed that you've made it this far—that's quite an accomplishment. I understand your reluctance in going to the authorities. My experience with government types has demonstrated that they will follow some protocol that is not necessarily the right course of action. So, your secret is safe with me. That doesn't solve the problem of finding your dad, though. Since you'll be with me for a couple of days, let me think about how to move you forward." He slapped his hands on his knees. "Now, I think it's time to get back to work. Do you think you might be able to organize the chaos that I've created in this storeroom?"

And with that, we went back to work. We pulled jars of salmon eggs, tackle, and lures off of the shelves and began to group similar items together, then place them into bins. I would clean the shelf while Riley printed a descriptive label—her penmanship was much neater than mine.

After about three hours, we'd made good progress and had almost finished one wall of shelves. Riley had been making noises for a while about how hungry she was, so we walked into the smoke-filled front room and asked Tim if we could take a break. He said he spent his lunches playing canasta with friends and was just ready to close up.

He walked us out and locked the door, then handed Riley a dollar. "Take your brother down that alley to Rosa's in the next block. Tell her Tim sent you, and she'll fill you up with the finest Mexican food on the central coast. I'll be back in an hour."

Rosa's was a little hole-in-the-wall with four tables and an aroma that made my mouth water. "Guadalajara" was playing on the juke box when we entered. Rosa herself had dark hair pulled back in a bun and was one of those people who seem like they must always be cheery. She stood about four feet, six inches tall and was as wide as she was tall. After we told her that Tim had sent us, she sat us at a table by the window and proceeded to lavish scrumptious dishes onto our table, beginning with a basket of tortilla chips and a bowl of spicy salsa. I had a Chile Verde burrito and a carnitas taco with rice and beans, while Riley chowed down on a cheese enchilada and two chicken tacos. Rosa followed up these culinary delights with flan for Riley and tres leches cake for me.

Our tummies were happy, and when we thanked her and tried to pay, she pushed my hand away. "Tim is a special person. He helps everyone in the neighborhood, and if he's a friend of yours, then you're a friend of mine. Friends don't pay at Rosa's. Tell Tim I'll see him Thursday night for the merchant's meeting."

We had time to kill, so we sat on the seawall and watched as the surfers performed their stunts in the waves next to the pier. I pointed at them. "One of these days, I'd like to take a try at surfing. It looks like a blast."

Then I noticed a pawn shop on the corner, so I wandered in. An old harmonica lay under one of the glass shelves. I pointed to it and asked the proprietor how much. He said he wanted seventy-five cents. Digging into my jeans, I could only come up with sixty cents. I didn't want to take off my shoes and spend any of our paper money, so I headed for the door. Luckily, the guy took pity on me and let me have it for the change in my hand. There sure were a lot of nice people in this town.

When we got back, we tried to return Tim's dollar, but he refused. He said that it was a thank you for brightening up his day. We went back to work, and by five o'clock we'd completed another wall of shelves.

Tim walked in and admired our work. His almond-shaped eyes lit up as he beamed. "Just look at this. If I didn't know better, I'd say I walked into the wrong place. I swear I didn't even know that wall was blue. And look how organized those shelves are. That's going to make my life a lot easier." He lit a cigar and blew out the smoke. "I've got to get moving, or I'll miss my turn at the weekly bocce ball tournament in the park. And later there's a string quartet playing under the stars. Please say you're coming back tomorrow."

We assured him that we would be, then walked off while he locked the door and headed in the other direction.

On our way to the camp, I pulled a dollar from my shoe and bought a sack of pinquito beans and a bag of flour. Clete hadn't returned by the time we got back to camp, so we handed the beans and flour to the old woman. She grinned around her pipe and told us to call her Nora.

We decided to pitch in and straighten up the camp. She sat on a decaying log, watching us fill the water jugs and gather downed branches for the fire. When we were finished, I walked over to her and gave her two of the cigar butts that Tim had given me. She smiled and shredded one, stuffing the tobacco into her pipe. Grabbing a twig from the fire, she turned the burning end toward herself and lit the pipe.

The three of us were sitting around the fire daydreaming when Clete walked into the camp carrying a pile of clothes. His face was clean shaven, and his hair was slicked back, and the outfit he was wearing was crisp and clean.

He put the pile of clothes into his tent, then came over to the fire and sat down.

"The boatyard let me wash my clothes in their deep sink, and I hung them out to dry this morning while I worked. I showered using an old hose to get some of the grime off and scraped my face in the mirror in the restroom." He smirked. "I feel like a new man. Now, I'm starved, how about you guys?"

"Me, too!" shouted Riley. "I could eat a horse." No big surprise there—the girl was a bottomless pit. I was ready to eat too, though. Rosa's food was wearing off after a busy afternoon. Part of being a growing boy, I guess. I reached over and handed Clete the rest of Tim's partially smoked cigars.

He nodded his appreciation and examined them before picking the longest and lighting it. "I told you we were going someplace special, so why don't you get cleaned up and we'll head out."

After we'd scrubbed ourselves and put on some clean clothes from the pack, we headed off along the street. Around three blocks down, Clete pointed across to a one-story building with a blue roof. A neon sign announcing Fish Bowl in multicolored letters sat on a pole out front. We scooted across the street and when we entered, we heard a shriek and a loud "hello" in a funny accent. Sitting on a perch was a large Mynah Bird, its head canted sideways as it watched us. A voice from the kitchen shouted for us to sit anywhere. The weather was mild, so we found a table out front with red-checkered cloth.

After we sat down, a large rotund man wearing a greasy apron and chef's hat came around the corner. "Son of a bitch," he shouted as he rushed over and grabbed Clete in a huge bear hug. "Clete, you old dog! Where the hell have you been? It's been at least four years." He held him at arm's length and shook his head. "Merle is off buying supplies, but he's going to freak out when he sees you."

Clete extricated himself from the man's grip and beamed, "Hi, Al. How are you? I didn't realize that it's been that long."

They plunged into a conversation about old times, so Riley and I went back into the restaurant and examined the bird. It squawked a lot, but its vocabulary seemed to be limited to "hello" and "goodbye," which it yelled at us when we walked back out to the table.

As we approached the table, the chef was saying, "I'm pretty sure you weren't gone long enough to have two children of this age?" He squinted at Clete. "Besides, they're not ugly enough to be related to you. How about introducing me?"

"Lucas and Riley, say hi to Al. He and his buddy Merle and I go back all the way to England, where they pretty much constantly tried to poison me. Al, I would like you to meet my new friends. This young man is Lucas, and the lovely lass is Riley. We ran into each other down in Oxnard. They are on a quest to find their father, and I came along for part of the ride." He proceeded to tell an abbreviated version of our story to Al.

The new man gave us a worried look. "What a tale. I hope that you're successful, but you're in good hands with this guy. I don't have children myself, but my observation is that they are continually hungry. How about it—do you feel like having our specialty?" I glanced at Clete, and he smiled and nodded, so we did too. "I'll be right back with three platters."

Al brought iced tea for Clete and two RC Colas for us. Glen Miller's "In the Mood" came through speakers hung under the eaves. While we waited for our meal, Clete told us about Merle and Al. "They were cooks for our outfit in England and followed us into France after D-Day. They did the best they could with the supplies they were given, but army food is army food. While we were stationed in England, the two of them wandered about the region picking up recipes and culinary techniques. But British food is pretty different. They have things like bubbles and squeaks, steak and kidney and black pudding. I don't mean to slam the Brits, but their diet just wasn't what we red-blooded Americans wanted. Merle and Al, however, found one meal that resonated with us, and that was fish and chips.

"So, they scoured the countryside and found a really good recipe. When they returned to the States after the war, they took their backpay, headed for the West Coast, and opened this restaurant in 1947. They refined the recipe over the years, and now they have customers coming in from all over."

The tables inside began to fill up, and a waitress materialized from the back room to attend to them. A while later, Al brought out three dishes piled high with batter-encrusted Haddock wrapped in newspapers, piles of french-fried potatoes, and a scoop of coleslaw on each. He placed containers of tartar sauce in front of us and pulled a bottle of malt vinegar from the pocket of his apron. "The Brits eat their fish and chips with vinegar, but some Americans can't handle the strong taste, so there's catsup on the table if you would prefer."

In spite of our large lunch, we both dove into one of the best meals I had ever tasted. The batter was crisp with a satisfying mix of spice, yet the fish within was light and airy. The french fries were just the way I liked them, crispy on the outside while the potato within had a meltin-your-mouth texture. I sprinkled a little vinegar on part of my fish and found the taste much to my liking. Riley didn't care for it, so she slathered her fish and fries with catsup and gobbled up every morsel. Neither of us was a fan of the coleslaw, but we had been raised with the requirement to eat our vegetables, so we swallowed it down. Fortunately, there was only a small scoop.

People came and went for takeout orders as we ate. Looking up, I saw Clete watching a pretty woman walking in. She was dressed in hospital scrubs, and her blonde hair was pulled into a ponytail. They smiled at each other as she walked by. It made me feel good to see him opening up a little and maybe getting past the pain in his heart.

We finished our meal and were wiping the grease off our fingers when the woman walked out, balancing two sacks of food in her arms. As she walked up the sidewalk and slipped her wallet into her purse, a handkerchief fell out and fluttered to the ground. Clete jumped up and picked up the cloth, then ran after the lady. We watched from the table as he caught up to her at the corner. He handed her the handkerchief and began to carry on a conversation, both of them smiling. After a minute, they said their goodbye, and she ventured out into the crosswalk.

While Clete looked after her with a goofy expression, a car came speeding up the street—from my vantage point, it appeared to be on a collision course with the woman. The driver must have noticed her and hit the brakes, but not soon enough. Clete took one look and dashed into the street. I didn't realize a man that big could sprint like that. He ran between the car and her, pushing her to the side just as the car was about to strike.

It barely missed her, but Clete wasn't so lucky. The front bumper made contact with his hip and threw him in the air, where he did a cartwheel and landed in the pavement. Fortunately, the car came to a halt just inches before the front wheel would have rolled over him.

Pandemonium broke out. The woman screamed, the driver of the car jumped out and was crying over and over about how sorry he was. Riley and I screamed and ran across the street toward Clete, tears streaming from our eyes. Onlookers gathered around, and one man tried to stop Riley and me from getting to him. There was no force on earth that could keep us from our friend—I dodged around him, Riley slipped between his legs, and we fell to the pavement next to Clete.

The lady had jumped up from where she'd fallen and rushed to his side. She yelled at the crowd to back away and for someone to call an ambulance. Then she got to her knees and began to check him over. His head was bleeding from a large gash across his forehead, and his right leg was turned in a direction it wasn't supposed to. His eyes were open but unfocused. The lady still had the handkerchief clutched in her hand and began to apply pressure to the wound in his head.

I was crying softly, but Riley was wailing and rocking back and forth. The lady smiled at her. "Don't worry, I'm a nurse and I think he'll be okay. I don't know for sure, but he doesn't appear to have internal injuries."

She asked our names, then spoke to us in a calm and soothing voice. "My name is Marilou. Why don't you sit by me and help me take care of your dad?" She put her free arm around my sister and held her close. Sirens wailed in the distance. She stroked Clete's cheek and whispered, "The ambulance is almost here. We'll take him to the hospital in Arroyo Grande, and I promise they'll take excellent care of him. I work at that hospital, and he will be my number one patient. He saved my life, and I'll make sure they treat him right. I'm not leaving his side until he's in the clear."

The ambulance pulled up and the EMTs jumped out grabbed a stretcher and knelt down by Clete. One of the emergency workers attached a blood pressure cup to his arm while the other found a vein and inserted an IV. He looked over at us. "Hey, Marilou. Nice to see you. This guy's lucky that you were around."

"I'm the lucky one, Ted. I wouldn't be here if it weren't for him. He saved my life! He's my hero." Tears fell from her eyes.

Ted and his partner dressed Clete's head wound and completed their inspection of the rest of him. "His vital signs are steady. No signs of injuries to his spinal column. Looks like a compound fracture of his femur, possible concussion, and that cut on his head is going to require some stitches. Can't tell, but I don't see any signs of internal injuries." Clete moaned as they attached a neck brace and straightened his leg to get him onto the stretcher.

Marilou held his hand while they wheeled him to the ambulance, and we crowded around it. They lifted him into the back, and Marilou climbed in after. We began to climb into the small space as well, but Ted held out his arm to stop us. "I'm sorry kids, but I'm not allowed to let you ride with us. Go home, and your mother can bring you along to the hospital."

Riley began wailing again. "We don't have a mother! Clete is our best friend, and he's taking care of us. Please don't leave us here. Please take us with you, Miss Marilou. Please!"

Marilou looked out the back of the ambulance. "I can't leave your friend. Try to find a ride to the hospital. If you don't make it, I'll send someone for you as soon as we get Clete stabilized." The EMT closed the door to the back of the ambulance and climbed into the driver's seat, and they left us standing there with tears streaming down our faces.

●———————————●

We sat sobbing on the curb with our arms around each other. People milled about and then began to slowly disperse. The show was over. The cops were checking the scene, measuring skid marks and examining the damage to the car.

One of them, a stout woman with short, dark brown hair, started walking over. "That was a terrible thing for you two to see. It seems your dad is very brave, but also very lucky. I just heard from the hospital that he doesn't have internal injuries. Do you want us to drive you home?"

Riley blurted out, "He's not our dad! He's our friend, and he was taking care of us." Then she realized what she'd said and clamped her mouth shut.

"Hmmm. That's interesting. Where are your parents?"

I grabbed Riley's hand and pulled her up. We started backing away while she continued toward us.

Then Al walked up and said, "That's okay, Officer. Thank you for your concern. I own that restaurant over there, and these two and Clete had just finished eating when the accident happened. I'll make sure they get home safely."

The cop arched her brow and looked at us with what may have been concern or suspicion. "Well, you two are witnesses to the accident. Let me get your names and addresses, and I'll follow up later to get your statements after you calm down."

Al didn't miss a beat. "That's why Clete was watching them. They're in the process of moving to San Luis Obispo, and we haven't learned the new address. Would it be alright if they call when they get settled? These kids are really not in any shape to answer questions right now."

The officer's eyebrows scrunched into a frown while she absorbed this information. I was holding my breath and getting ready to bolt. Then she nodded. "I can see that they're pretty shaken up. Let me get your information, sir, and then you're free to leave."

Al rushed us into the Fish Bowl and sat us at a table, then went behind the counter and handed us each a soda. He grabbed a clean towel and tried to wipe the tear stains from our faces.

"You two just sit here and relax. Clete did that same kinda stuff throughout the fight in France until he got wounded. I don't know how many lives he saved, but I was one of them. He never seemed to worry about his own safety. As soon as Merle gets back with the van, we'll head over to the hospital and find out how he's doing. He just left LA so he should be here in a couple of hours."

I jumped up, knocking my chair over. "We can't wait a couple of hours. We need to be with Clete, now! How far is the hospital?" I picked up my chair, grabbing Riley's hand without waiting for a reply. "Thank you, Mister Al. We'll get a ride to the hospital, and when we get back, we'll come and let you know how he is. C'mon, Riley."

We took off running toward the park.

There, we found Tim sitting on a blanket next to a stunning Asian lady, listening to the string quartet. Her eyes grew wide with surprise when Riley ran to Tim and threw her arms around his neck and began blubbering.

I explained what had happened and asked if Tim could possibly take us to the hospital. By then, the woman had pulled Riley onto her lap and was hugging her closely.

"Lee," Tim said, "these are my new friends that I told you about. They transformed my shop into a highly organized operation. Do you mind if we cut the concert short so I can help them get to the hospital?"

"Oh, of course I don't mind. These two are precious. And if they made your shop more efficient, then you can spend more time with me. Besides, this music isn't that good. Let's go."

We left the park and headed to a side street, where Tim's car was parked. I was worried about the possibility of the police finding us at the hospital, but my concern for Clete was too strong to hold me back. The melodious sounds of Dvorak's *American* followed us out of the park. It was a little classical for me, but to my untrained ear, the quartet sounded pretty good.

●———————●

As it turned out, Lee was also a nurse at Arroyo Grande Hospital. She put her arm around Riley and said she knew Marilou and that she would take good care of Clete. She was trying to put us at ease, but unfortunately, we were just too worked up.

Within twenty minutes, we'd pulled into the hospital parking lot. Lee took us in a side entrance and asked us to wait while she checked with the receptionist. Soon, she wandered back and told us, "Your friend is in surgery on the third floor. Let's go up and find out more details. They don't normally let children up there, but I know the head nurse, so we'll be okay as long as we stay out of the way."

We entered a service elevator with doors on both ends and rode silently to the third floor. Following the signs to the OR, we turned the corner and spied Marilou pacing in the hallway. Riley ran up, and Marilou knelt down and folded my sister into her arms.

"He's doing well. They just finished repairing his leg—it was broken in three places. His head took twenty-three stitches, and he has a pretty good concussion, but no other internal injuries, thank God!"

She greeted Lee and Tim and led us to a bench along the wall. "They'll take him to his room shortly, and we can visit him there. He's going to be pretty drugged up, but I'm sure he'll be happy to see you. You won't be able to stay long, but don't worry, I'm going to be personally taking care of him through the night. Can you tell us how to get in touch with his wife or family?"

When I said he didn't have a wife, a small smile formed on her lips. We had just begun to tell the story when the OR's double doors slammed open and they wheeled a gray-faced Clete out on a gurney. We all jumped up and followed down the corridor, but we had to wait outside the room while the orderlies and Marilou got him into bed and hooked up all the monitoring equipment.

When we finally entered the room, I was taken aback by Clete's appearance. His skin was sallow, and he had a bandage around his head. His right leg was elevated by a system of pulleys. In spite of all this, he was able to give us a crooked grin when he saw us. Marilou sat next to him with his big hand in hers.

Clete's eyes were drooping, his voice slurred. "Hello, my friends. Sorry I messed up our dinner. No dessert to-night, I guess."

Riley held on to his other arm and hiccuped. "Mr. Clete, we were so worried about you. Are you going to be alright?"

"Oh sweetie, I'll be good as new in no time." He smiled at Marilou. "I appear to be in good hands." His voice faded and his head lolled to the side.

"He's fading fast," Marilou said. "They pumped him with a bunch of pain killers—I'm surprised he's even still awake. Maybe we should let him rest and visit again tomorrow?"

•————————•

We stopped by the Fish Bowl to let Al know what was going on, and then Tim and Lee dropped us off on the street near the hobo camp. Tim wanted us to come home with him, but we said we would stay in the camp and make sure Clete's gear was safe. We told him that we would come work at the bait shop in the morning until the hospital visiting hours began.

Lee hugged both of us as they left, and then we began collecting Clete's gear.

•————————•

We woke early the next morning and found our way to the bait shop, where we began sorting through the remainder of the inventory in the back room. We did the best we could, but our hearts weren't really into it.

Tim closed the shop at ten to give us a ride to the hospital. Along the way, we spotted a Hispanic woman standing on the corner, selling cut flowers. "I believe Miss Manners says that one should always bring a little something to brighten the room when visiting someone in the hospital," he said.

He pulled over and bought three bouquets.

Lee met us at the hospital entrance and shuttled us past the reception desk and up the elevator. When we walked into the room, Marilou was holding a straw to Clete's lips. Clete smiled and lifted his hand in a wave. Black and blue bruises covered his arms and jaw, and both elbows were wrapped in bandages. His pallor had pretty much returned to normal, though. He was a mess, but he sure was a sight for sore eyes. He patted the bed next to him, and we both climbed up. "I guess I messed up our travel plans. I'm sorry, kids, but it's going to be a while before I hit the road again."

Marilou spoke up. "The gentleman who hit Clete is completely despondent about the accident. He has guaranteed to pay Clete's hospital bills and rehabilitation expenses, but he'll need someplace to live while he's mending."

She continued, "I have an extra room, so Clete can live with me while he recuperates. It's the least I can do. Clete told me about your situation—I'm pretty sure we can squeeze you two in, too, if you don't mind a couch and the carpet? Then, when Clete is back on his feet, he can help you find your father."

"Thank you, ma'am, but we can't wait that long. We miss our dad terribly, and we know he'll be worried sick about us." Clete gave her a "told you so" look, and I continued, "We'll be fine as soon as we get to Seattle. Clete has taught us a lot about traveling."

Just then, Al walked in with another bouquet, followed by a beanpole of a man with hound dog eyes and a wispy tassel of hair on his head. Clete smiled and said, "Hello, Merle. HI, Al. Welcome to our gathering."

"We were just discussing the plight of these two young people. They are intent on continuing their travels without my assistance, but we have concerns because they're so young. I've witnessed how resourceful Luke and Riley can be, still it's a big and dangerous world out there."

Al frowned. "Well, we need to figure this out soon. That lady police officer came by the shop this morning to check up on the kids. She was upset because the 'parents' hadn't contacted her last night. We put her off with excuses and promises to remind them to call, but I think she's getting suspicious. She said she was coming to see you this morning to gather your statement about the accident and would question you about the children. I'm afraid that when she finds out that the children are homeless, she'll take them to some foster facility."

Riley started sniffling, and I spoke up, maybe a little more loudly than necessary. "All of you have done enough! If the police find out, you'll get into trouble. We'll be leaving right away, and we'll be okay. We just want to be with our dad."

Tim put his hand on my shoulder, giving it a squeeze. "It's alright, young friend. I think between all of us in this room, we should be able to figure out how to get you safely on your way. While we were talking, I was thinking. You can't take public transportation without an accompanying adult, but we have a friend who drives a delivery truck with stops up the coast all the way to Monterrey. He's coming through town tomorrow, and you could ride along with him that far, anyway."

Clete smiled. "That's a good start, and Monterey is a friendly town. I can give you some contacts who are good people, and they can help with the next leg of your journey. Let's write down a plan and draw out a rough map for your trip."

CHAPTER 10

Pismo Beach, 1969

Every soul that touches yours—
Be it the slightest contact—
Get there from some good…

—George Eliot

IT SEEMED APROPOS THAT ROGER Miller was singing "King of the Road" as I navigated through the shade of the Eucalyptus trees, their branches shimmering in the broken sunlight. The gold and black undulations of the butterflies still mesmerized after all these years. Off to the right, near the creek, the hobo camp had been replaced by scores of ticky-tacky houses. The sight made me sad.

I drove down the familiar street past a shuttered Fish Bowl. Merle had passed away two years ago from a massive heart attack, and Al had moved to a retirement community in Scottsdale. The memory of that succulent fish made me smile. I wondered if the Myna bird was with Al.

The bar on the corner still stood, though now it was called Harry's. I spied cowboy boots and big hats.

I drove up the hill and crossed the freeway, then backtracked to Arroyo Grande. On the same corner as twelve years earlier stood another Hispanic lady, with a baby on her hip, selling cut flowers. I stopped and bought her entire inventory, then proceeded to the town's cemetery.

After reviewing the directory, I slowly made my way to a section that was shaded by a beautiful oak tree. There, side by side, stood two headstones, each adorned with both a cross and a chrysanthemum, one for Tim and one for Lee. They had married shortly after Riley and I left, and five years later, a horrific traffic accident had taken them from us.

I knelt down and cleared away the weeds and debris. Mist clouded my eyes as I laid two bouquets beneath the headstones of these gentle people who had helped us so much.

After a short prayer, I wandered to another section of the cemetery and found Merle's headstone. I cleaned his grave and laid another bouquet down. We hadn't gotten to know the man very well, but he had given selflessly to our odyssey.

I headed up the highway. K-Earth 101 was almost out of range, but up on this hill, Aretha Franklin came through loud and clear with "I say a Little Prayer for You."

———•———

Cal Poly campus lay nestled in the foothills near San Luis Obispo. I stopped at the Registrar's office for directions to the philosophy building. As I drove down the narrow university streets, my almost-new Mustang drew envious stares from students scurrying between classes and lounging on the expansive lawns. A few of the young men had shoulder-length hair and tried to give me the stink eye. I figured it was my military cut that made me stand out. But most of the kids seemed complacent, just enjoying their sheltered life. I wondered how I would fit into "academic" life.

Since Cal Poly was an engineering school, the philosophy department was relegated to some of the older buildings. Checking the map, I found my way to a broad, one-story clapboard building that looked out of place on the modern campus and headed inside.

After listening to my request, the receptionist smiled and dialed a number on a black telephone. Eyeing me up and down, she spoke into the handset. "Professor Harding, there's a young man here who says he's looking for an old 'bo who used to ride the rails with him…"

A loud whoop echoed down the hall, and a door slammed open. Heavy footsteps raced toward me, and I found myself enveloped in a suffocating bear hug.

Clete lifted me off my feet and growled, "Damn, boy, you're a sight for sore eyes! I've been on pins and needles all morning." He let me go and held me at arm's length. He was a big man and outweighed me, but I stood two inches taller. "Come to my little office. Can I get you some coffee or water?" He led me down the hall, and I noticed a slight hitch in his gait.

Clete's office was small. A gray metal desk sat in one corner, and a matching table surrounded by four chairs occupied the other. Most of the walls were covered by shelves straining under the weight of hundreds of books, but the wall behind his desk held his degrees and two pictures, one of Marilou and one of Riley and me that someone had snapped on the day of our departure so many years ago.

Clete noticed me checking out the pictures and put his arm around my shoulders, "The people in those pictures are the most important people in my life. The two of you and Marilou helped me to understand that there was meaning to my life. The bravery of you and Riley inspired me to get off the road. And Marilou's love has kept me grounded all these years. I am truly a blessed man."

He led me to the table and poured coffee into two porcelain mugs, handing me one. "Marilou is sad that she's missed you. Now that she's the head of nursing at the hospital, she's required to attend meetings all over the state."

I sipped the coffee and set the cup down, "Will you be able to make it to Riley's graduation? She's counting on it, and she'll be devastated if you don't come."

Clete smiled and nodded his big head. "We wouldn't miss it for the world. We'll be leaving this weekend. Marilou has all of next week off, and my classes wind up this Friday. Are you sure there's room for us at your place? We can always stay at a hotel."

I frowned and shook my head. "There's no way that we're going to let you do that. Besides, we have plenty of room. Now get me up to date about you and Marilou. It's been a long time."

We talked into the early afternoon. It had taken two months of intense therapy for Clete's leg to heal after we left Pismo Beach. During that time, he and Marilou had fallen in love. I could see a light come into his eyes every time he mentioned her name. They married in 1959, and I could tell the spark was still there.

Before the war, Clete was well on his way to an advanced degree, and as soon as his leg allowed him, he resumed his academic pursuits. He received his doctor of philosophy in less than a year and snagged a teaching position at Cal Poly as soon as he graduated. Four years later, he was the department head. He became animated when he described a course that he was offering in the fall studying itinerant workers the America—including a section on hobo life.

With a little prodding by him, I described my stint in the navy. I tried to keep it light, but Clete could tell that I was holding back. He knew better than to push me, though, and he let me gloss over some of the details. It just wasn't something I wanted to talk about.

Later, we walked under a bright blue sky over to the cafeteria for a late lunch as I told him about my future plans. "I can't wait to get to college. I've been accepted at Seattle University, University of Washington, and Gonzaga. I decided on Gonzaga. It's more expensive, and it'll be a real stretch, but I'll get by on the GI Bill and working part-time. Now that Riley is graduating and getting a job, I won't need to send money home anymore."

A funny look came over Clete's face, then disappeared quickly. I wondered what that was all about but kept it to myself. It was none of my business—he was full of mysteries.

"That sounds like a good plan," he said. "Are you leaning toward any degree?"

"As a corpsman in the navy, I got to help people. I would like to continue with that. I would love to become a doctor, but that's pretty much a pipe dream. I was thinking about some sort of therapy work, but I'll be happy to get my nursing degree. Maybe Marilou can give me some pointers."

We talked into the early evening, comfortable with each other as only old friends can be. Clete told me that Eddie had caught up with his friend in Reno. On a whim, he had bet some money on a long shot in the Belmont

Stakes and his horse had come through, instantly making him a man of means. He and his buddy used the money to buy a section of land in North Dakota and were making money hand over fist growing sugar beets. It turned out they were more than just friends—they were living together and a very happy couple.

After we walked back to Clete's office, I got ready to leave. Clete handed me a package. "Eddie's sorry he can't make Riley's graduation and sends his best. He sent this for you and said to give you a big hug."

We held on to each other, the big man crushing me in his massive arms, and then I headed down the hallway. I gave the last bouquet to Clete's receptionist before walking outside and down the path in the fading light. When I got to the car, I opened the package and found a new Hohner Crossover harmonica and a handwritten note.

Dear Luke,

I've often thought about you and your sister and wanted you to know how much your presence in my life means to me. Your kindness and bravery set an example for me (and Clete if he'd admit it). Please accept this little gift. I still have the harmonica that you gave me so many years ago and play it often. Playing has helped me get past my demons and I hope it does the same for you.

Yours truly,

Eddie

P. S. Give my love to Riley and tell her how proud I am of her.

I had continued with the harmonica and could even play pretty well, but I hadn't taken it out much in the last few years—'Nam got in the way.

CCR's "Fortunate Son" drifted over the lawn from one of the dorms. I ran my hand across my eyes, put the car in gear, and drove away headed toward Highway 1. Thoughts of those days traveling along the Big Sur coast filled my mind.

CHAPTER 11

The Oranges of Hieronymus Bosch, 1957

*When California was wild it was the
floweriest part of the continent.*

—John Muir

T HE FOG HAD ROLLED IN and covered Pismo Beach with a blanket of gray. A panel truck pulled up in the alley behind the bait shop at eight, and a middle-aged man and woman got out of the cab. The man had a full head of hair and pork-chop sideburns. The lady was of medium height, with curly red hair and a smile that formed twin dimples on her cheeks.

Tim introduced us to Chuck and Sally. Sally gurgled, "I love the ride up the Pacific Coast Highway through Big Sur. For me it's almost a religious experience. I ride along with Chuck whenever I can get a few days off from work."

Chuck chimed in, "Having company on the haul up the coast is a blessing, and today I'm thrice blessed. Go ahead and throw your pack in the back. We arranged some boxes for you to sit on behind the seats. We need to get underway to make our schedule."

We hugged Tim, and over our objections he pushed twenty-five dollars into my hand. "This is the money that I owe you, and the rest is from all of us. You two have been a bright spot in our lives the last few days. Please stay in touch and let us know when you're back with your dad." He handed me a paper bag. "I packed some sandwiches and apples for you."

We piled into the truck behind the seats and Chuck headed toward the highway.

I wasn't sure that we were headed in the right direction as we seemed to be heading inland, but after twenty minutes we passed through San Luis Obispo and exited Highway 101 turning northwest on Highway 1. The fog grudgingly dissipated, and off to the right I saw a large compound surrounded by two fences topped with barbed wire.

Chuck saw my gaze in his mirror, "That's the California Men's Colony, also known as 'The Country Club.' The prison is low-to-medium security. It's called that because of all the facilities and programs included with a rent-free vacation for the inmates. They have their own hospital and library, and the inmates can attend adult classes."

A short while later, a bay came into view as we topped a hill. Seemingly in the middle of the bay stood a huge granite hill jutting from the water, dominating the vista. This rugged-looking rock was surrounded by sailboats and fishing vessels bobbing on the sparkling water. A sign along the highway announced that we were entering Morro Bay.

The road turned north and began paralleling the coast. Gulls and terns were floating on thermals above the blue water. In the distance, I could see massive commercial ships headed in both directions. We turned left toward the ocean in a scrubby beach town, and Chuck pulled up to a market housed in a weather-beaten building encapsulated in cedar shingles.

He shut down the engine and turned in his seat. "This is our first stop. I need to unload some boxes. You should get out and stretch your legs. It won't take me long, so stay close."

I grabbed one of the boxes and followed Chuck into a wood-floored mercantile. An Asian man said hello and told him where to set the boxes.

While they completed paperwork together, I wandered around the store. Oriental singsong music was softly playing in the background, and a strange but not unpleasant scent filled the air. The bins in the back of the store contained all sorts of strange produce. There was long green grass that smelled of lemon. I recognized ginseng and ginger. The meat section dominated one wall. Cuts of beef and pork lay in the refrigerated cases below. Above me fresh, plucked chickens were hanging by their feet, next to a whole pig hanging upside down that appeared to have been mummified. As we left, the Asian man smiled and handed me two morsels of rice candy wrapped in paper.

We continued north and soon entered the small town of Harmony. Sally smiled and told us the story of the town. "This area used to be surrounded by dairy ranches established by Swiss immigrants. The ranchers formed a co-op and built a creamery here in town. They say that the ranches used to feud, and during the early part of the century, the range wars peaked with a murder." She giggled. "Who knew dairy farmers were part of the wild west? The creamery made the best butter, and we used to buy some to distribute, but they closed a couple of years ago when high grazing prices drove the ranchers out of business.

Now the town has pretty much dried up except for a few artisan shops and a restaurant."

We pulled up next to a restaurant located in a large U-shaped building, and I helped Chuck deliver a few boxes. Climbing back into the truck, we pulled out of town and turned north on the highway.

Just minutes passed, and I spied a sign that sent an involuntary shiver through my body and made me take a deep swallow. I caught my breath and asked Chuck, "Where's that road go?"

"That's Highway 46. It goes over the hills to Paso Robles. It crosses through some pretty ugly country, and after intersecting with Highway 41 at Cholame, you can get all the way to Fresno. You kids are probably familiar with Cholame—you know the place where that big movie star died in a car wreck a few years ago? We have to use 46 whenever this highway gets blocked by landslides in Big Sur. I hope we don't have to, though, because it adds an extra day just to go around and back down."

I glanced at Riley, and she stared back with wide eyes.

We held our breath as we passed the intersection, and a short while later we veered onto a street bisecting the town of Cambria, where we made another delivery at a grocery store. Instead of having to double back to the highway, we were able to follow the street on a loop through the artsy town and connect with the Pacific Coast Highway to the north.

Our next stop was unscheduled. We pulled up to a line of cars being directed by a highway patrolman around a large mass lying across our lane of the road. "Uh-oh," Chuck muttered, "looks like one of the young bulls is sunning himself on the road again. We strained to look out the truck's windows at a huge seal. A patrolman was trying to coax the animal off the road, but the seal wasn't having anything to do with it. He raised his head, displaying a massive, elephantine snout, and roared his displeasure at the cop.

Looking across the road to the beach, I could see dozens of these creatures lying in the sand and soaking up the sun. The large bulls would raise their heads and roar at each other. The females quietly nursed their young.

We finally inched our way past the elephant seal.

On we went up the road. The ocean was a gentle blue, and the seabirds effortlessly rode the currents. At the small town of San Simeon, we left the highway and began an ascent up a low hill to the east. After traveling about five miles, we crested the hill and were rewarded with a magnificent view.

Before us lay a compound that could only have been described as a castle. The Southern-Spanish-Renaissance-styled structures complemented the surrounding countryside. Each building was in itself like a palace. The main structure could have contained the whole town of Cholame and had room to spare.

Chuck pulled around to the service entry. "There's just support staff living here now. Old man Hearst left it to state of California, and they're trying to figure out what to do with it. It's going to take a while for the staff to unload their deliveries. Why don't the two of you take a look around, but don't get lost."

It would have been easy to get lost in that wonderland. The buildings themselves must have covered five acres. Palm trees dotted the landscape, and every building seemed to have at least one large fountain and dozens of statues to complement its design. We wandered around and peeked into a few windows, spying rooms full of artwork and exquisite furniture. Each arched doorway stood at least ten feet high and was surrounded by ornate columns and stonework.

A cook was working in a huge kitchen, and when we peeked in, she smiled at us and waved us over. "What are you two munchkins up to?" she asked in a heavily accented voice. She had a round face and blonde hair pulled up into a bun. We told her we were helping deliver supplies.

"I've just made some strudel," she said as we started to leave. "Would you care to try some?"

My sister, with that bottomless pit, smiled and nodded enthusiastically. "Gut, I like to share my creations. My name is Anna. Let me fix some plates for you." She gave us plates covered with thin sheets of pastry wrapped around an apple filling, then brought over two glasses of milk, reached for a mug of coffee, and sat down at the counter with us.

While we savored that mouthwatering concoction, she told us about William Hearst's castle. She entertained us by describing the continual construction that had taken years, followed by grand parties attended by many famous guests, including Charles Lindbergh, Winston Churchill, Clark Gable, Cary Grant, and the Marx brothers.

We finished our treat, and after thanking her we decided to head back before Chuck had to look for us. We must have taken a wrong turn, because we came upon a huge swimming pool surrounded with beautiful sculptures. The vista of the ocean behind the pool was breathtaking.

We finally found our way to the truck just as Chuck and Sally were closing the back doors. We piled in for the ride through the golden hills toward a gleaming blue ocean.

●————————●

After we had descended the hill and turned right, we passed another elephant seal rookery, the beach and rocks teeming with mounds of blubber. The ocean was alive with multiple shades of blue, and we spotted dolphins performing their sinuous dance in the surf. I could taste the salt in the crystal clear air. In the distance, I could see a vertical structure surrounded by native plants that were ablaze with color.

Sally pointed. "That's the Piedras Blancas Lighthouse. It's not very tall anymore, since they had to tear down the top floors that were damaged during an earthquake."

Winding along the coast for a few miles, we turned into the parking space for a newly constructed two-story building advertising itself as "Ragged Point Inn and Resort." Chuck told us to stretch our legs while he carried two boxes into the service entrance.

Ten minutes later, we were traveling north again, and the road began to wind its way along cliffs overlooking the sea. Whenever we reached a canyon formed by a swift running creek, the road would turn inland until it could find a suitable place for a bridge to cross the expanse.

We passed through a community called Gorda, and after that I dozed for a while.

The truck's suspension wasn't great, and the seemingly endless curves and hairpin turns began to make me nauseous, waking me up. I looked over at Riley—her face was slightly green, and she was squirming. She was suffering, too.

I was just about to ask Chuck to pull over when we rounded a curve and came to a halt behind a line of cars. Up ahead was a highway patrol vehicle with its amber and blue lights flashing, and beyond that stood a large pile of two-foot boulders and rubble. Chuck cussed under his breath. "I was afraid of this. Looks like that late-season rain caused a landslide. I'm going to go check it out."

Riley and I jumped out and followed. The patrolman was ensconced in a tan uniform with a smokey bear hat and had mirror-like sunglasses covering his eyes. He was helping cars perform three-point turns to head back down the road. He turned toward us, "Sorry folks but the road is closed until DOT can get up hear with equipment to clear the mess. They're on their way, but it will be at least three or four days before they can clear, regrade, and repave."

I walked up to the slide with my sister to check it out. The debris had covered three quarters of the road, and there was about a yard between the rocks and the edge of the cliff, which fell two hundred feet down to the ocean. The trooper waved his arms, "You kids be careful! That ground may be unstable."

We backed away to the truck, where Chuck and Sally were huddled. "Sorry kids, but we're going to head back. It's getting late, and it would take too long to go up the 101 and back down. We'll just wait until we get word that the road is open and try again. We can drop you off at Tim's on our way."

I glanced at Riley, and we communicated silently. "Thank you, Mr. Chuck," I said, "but we really need to keep going. I think we can find our way around the slide and then head up the road." I grabbed my pack and started toward the fallen rocks.

Chuck started to say something but cut himself off. Shaking his head, he finally sputtered, "I know you kids are missing your dad, but it's dangerous out here. Come back with us and we'll get you on your way soon."

We waved. "Thanks, but we've got to keep moving."

I saw Chuck head over to the cop, saying something under his breath. The cop glanced our way, and I grabbed Riley's hand. We sprinted along the edge of the cliff and to the other side. The cop yelled, but it was too late. We had escaped again.

Our freedom was almost short-lived. There was another highway patrolman on the other side turning the southbound traffic around. Fortunately, his back was turned to us as he spoke with a traveler. We rushed over some rubble and dove into the heavy brush just as his radio squawked something about kids running away. We watched him through the camouflage of the leaves while he looked around, shrugged, and went back to directing traffic.

●———————●

After crawling along for a while, we left the brush and began walking up the road. A few cars passed us, but I was wary of asking for a ride. We rounded a few curves, and I noticed a dirt road leading along a creek and up a canyon. There were fresh tire tracks dug into the dirt. We were still feeling the nauseating effects of the winding road, so we decided to see we could find a place to camp around there.

We had only gone a few hundred feet when we heard a car coming up the road. Its engine roared as it slid around the corner in a cloud of dust and pulled up beside us. A balding man with wispy white hair clinging to the sides of his head and sad eyes hiding behind round glasses leaned out the driver's window. "Hello, young ones! You're a long way from home. I'm headed to the old convict camp—can I offer you a lift?"

We must have looked apprehensive. "Don't worry, I and my friends are quite harmless. Some may be a little hedonistic, but they won't bother you."

I looked at Riley, and she shrugged her shoulders and gave me a little nod. "Thank you, sir. We're on our way to find our dad and wanted to camp up here for the night. But, we don't want to bother anyone."

"Trust me, young man, you won't bother anyone. And you won't have to camp, because there are many buildings up here where you can find shelter. My name is Henry, and I rent a shack at the camp. Hop in and I'll give you a lift."

We piled into the old Chevy coupe and introduced ourselves. While we rode up the hill, Henry told us about the labor camp. "It was originally built to house the convicts who were part of the construction crew building Highway 1 through Big Sur in the 1930s. After the highway was complete, many of the buildings were left standing. I rent my shack for five dollars per month—heck of a deal! Now tell me a little about yourselves and how you ended up out here in the middle of nowhere."

We had just pulled into the camp compound when we finished our story. We left out the part about killing Walt this time.

His expression migrated from disbelief to amazement and then to one of admiration. He clapped his hands and grinned, "You are certainly the bravest couple of juveniles I believe I've ever run across. I understand the pull of family—I recently returned from New York, where I had to bury my mother. I brought my sister to California, and she's now living comfortably in a home where they're taking care of her. You two are pretty tough to make it this far. We should be able to hook you up with someone to give you a lift at least part of the way north." He pointed to a wooden structure in the middle of the compound. "You can stay in that shack. Mine is next door, so I can keep an eye out for you. Go ahead and make yourselves comfortable, or at least as comfortable as you can be without all the crass conveniences of modern life. When you've settled in, come over to the campfire. Today marks summer solstice, and there will be a whole lot of celebrating tonight."

The interior of the shack was relatively clean, and there were two cots lining the walls. We pulled the blanket from the pack and made up one of the beds for Riley. "What's a solstice?" she asked.

I wasn't real sure, and I told her so. I wandered around the shack to see how secure we would be. The front door could be secured with a fairly sturdy latch. The wood frames of the windows were swollen, and I was unable to open either of them. The back door of the shack didn't have a lock, so I rigged up a rope to hold it shut. I formed the knot so I could easily release it in case we had to exit quickly. Satisfied that we would be safe, I wandered outside with Riley close behind.

The camp consisted of a dozen old clapboard buildings along a bluff overlooking the ocean. There were six cars of varying vintage parked haphazardly around the compound. People were milling about a huge bonfire. I could see Henry, puffing on a pipe, in deep conversation with a middle-aged woman. Before heading to the bonfire, we walked around the compound.

The view down to the ocean was breathtaking. Gulls gliding on currents rose to our level and above. In the distance, we could see whales breaching the surface and releasing their breath into the air. Huge redwood trees surrounded the camp. Some rose over two hundred feet and were six feet thick at the base. As we walked about, a shadow fell over us, blocking the sun for a moment. Looking up, we saw a gigantic vulture with a wingspan wider than a car is long. We weren't sure if the vulture was going to swoop down and grab us, so we scrambled under the porch of one of the shacks.

Someone chuckled from the doorway behind us. "Don't worry, those condors will only get you if you're dead. And you two look pretty alive to me." A pretty woman in her twenties stepped out. She was wispy, with bobbed, dark brown hair. Her breath held a hint of liquor as she reached for our hands. "I'm Eve. Henry told me about you and your great adventure. It sounds exciting, but scary. I'm afraid I could never do what you two are doing. I'm too cowardly. Let's go over to the party."

We walked along with her as she continued talking. "Anderson Creek is home to a number of avant-garde authors, musicians, and artists such as yours truly. We residents are pretty much antiestablishment and lovingly referred to as bohemians."

I asked her what a bohemian was. She acknowledged my question with a thin smile, explaining, "Those of us up here tend toward the arts or intellectuality and have no regard for society's rules of behavior. We shun material-ism and try to live a simple life, a life without the stress of extraneous possessions. We attempt to express ourselves through our art. Hopefully, our artistic expressions send positive energy into the world and that energy will flow back to us."

"Because we live without the usual inhibitions, we get a lot of visitors whose only goal is to have a good time without remorse. They tend to visit us in an attempt to attain some level of fulfillment, but unfortunately, they end up leaving without it. Then there are others who just want an orgy."

Henry joined us and continued the conversation. "Bohemians in the old world were gypsies, wandering without roots. We bohemians are like that, and very much like the hobos that you've spent time with. We share many of the same attributes—we wander in search of something…perhaps an understanding of the universe we occupy. We shed modern encumbrances and transcend the normal thoughts of society."

Henry smiled and pointed to a few of the men and women gathered around the bonfire. "We call ourselves the Anderson Creek Gang, and like you hobos, we are searching. We, however, try to describe the hidden meaning of the results of our search in our prose, our art, and our music. Sometimes, our attempts are embraced by modern society, but many, if not most times, our creations aren't understood and are rejected."

He shrugged. "But, enough of that. Let's wander over and help ourselves to the communal meal. While we eat, I'm fascinated by your adventure and want to hear more."

We lined up at a long table and filled our plates with an odd montage of dishes. Most of the fare consisted of one or more vegetables, and very few contained meat. Eve explained, "Most of us don't believe in murdering our fellow creatures for food. We believe that humans are hunter-gatherers by nature. " Her smile returned and she chortled, "But mostly gatherers."

Despite the lack of meat, most of the dishes were quite tasty. I just didn't care for the consistency of many of them—a little mushy. This didn't slow Riley down a bit. She finished off three helpings and then reached over and scarfed up the remaining bites of something called "tow foo" from my plate.

As we ate, Henry peppered us with questions about our travels. He described his travels through Europe and some of the books he had written. We had never heard of any of them, and he told us the reason was because puritanical America found his writings to be blasphemous and too descriptive of things like the natural act of coitus, whatever that was, and were therefore banned in our country. He said he was working on a tome that described his life and friends here in Big Sur. He thought he might include a chapter about us and our adventures.

While we ate and chatted a rugged-looking man named Harry began playing a beautiful melody on a wooden instrument the likes of which I had never seen. Others began accompanying him, and with Henry's encouragement, I tried to follow along with my harmonica. When Harry was finished, he came over and spent an hour helping me to reach new chords. As the sun turned the horizon shades of orange and red, the sweet music in this magical place serenaded all of us—human and nature's creatures.

A short while later, the sun had extinguished itself, and the forest had closed in on the encampment. The flames from the bonfire threw dancing shadows against the wall of trees. Henry said we should get to bed because the debauchery was about to begin. We said our goodnights to our new friends and headed back to our shack in the moonlight.

———•———

I had just awakened the next morning and was lying on my back, staring at the rough boards of the shack and thinking about our next steps, when a rapping on the door of the shack startled me.

Riley was still sound asleep and lightly snoring. I peeked out the window and saw Eve waiting for me to open the door. She rushed in and slammed it behind her. "You and your sister need to stay inside until we come for you. The police are here, and they're looking for two runaway children who were spotted in the area. Henry's talking to them, but some police don't like us and are always trying to find ways to harass us. We'll come get you as soon as they leave."

I snuck a look out of the corner of the window and saw the same highway patrol officer from yesterday standing next to his black-and-white patrol car. Riley rolled over and asked what I was looking at. I backed away from the window and explained what Eve had told me. Just in case we had to make a quick exit, I loosened the rope securing the back door and then collected our belongings into the pack. I crept back to the window so I could keep an eye on the situation.

It wasn't long before the cop got into his car and drove off. Henry stood watching until the car was out of sight and then walked to our door.

"Luke, Riley, it's safe to come out now."

We stepped outside. The air was warm and lightly tinged with smoke from the smoldering campfire. "It seems that you two are infamous. The authorities have put out a bulletin for all law enforcement officers to keep an eye out for you. That cop didn't say anything about your exploits in Cholame. However, he did say that the Pismo police and child protective services were concerned about your well-being. Seems like they're giving your friends the third degree, but they've clammed up and aren't cooperating."

He looked around. "You're welcome to stay here until this blows over, but you would have to stay hidden. There are just too many strangers visiting, and any one of them may report seeing you."

I stood up. "Thank you, sir, but we've caused too much trouble, and now we've put you and your friends at risk for helping us. We need to get on our way, anyway. We need to find our dad."

Henry smiled. "I thought that's what you might say, so Eve and I came up with an alternate plan. Eve's friend Valerie has been staying with us off and on while her husband is stationed at the Naval Postgraduate School. Her husband is graduating, and she's driving home to Monterey this morning. Valerie is a professional photographer of some renown. We explained your situation, and she's intrigued. She wants to hear all about your adventures on the way to Monterey. That will get you out of the immediate area without exposing you along the road."

While we were talking, Eve and a pleasant-looking woman walked up. "Lucas and Riley," Eve said, "I'd like you to meet Valerie."

Valerie had rosy cheeks and long brown hair pulled into a ponytail. Her eyes twinkled, and deep dimples formed with her smile. We made our introductions, and she led us to a tan 1950 Ford convertible with the ragtop pulled down like an accordion behind the back seat. I was immediately enamored with the vehicle. It wasn't as souped-up, but the lines were the same as the moonshine-running hot rod from Thunder Road. Robert Mitchum was my hero—a tough-talking former marine.

After giving hugs to Henry, Eve, and Harry, and getting hugs in return, Riley and I piled into the front seat. Valerie started the car, and the purr of the big eight-cylinder engine gave a thrill. She put the car into gear, and we started down the dirt road toward the highway.

CHAPTER 12

The Long and Winding Road, 1957

This is a lovely place which I am growing to love.
The Pacific licks all other oceans out of hand;
There is no place but the Pacific Coast
to hear the eternal roaring surf.

—Robert Louis Stevenson to W. E. Henley 1879

VALERIE WAS A TERRIBLE DRIVER, scaring the heck out of both of us for the entire trip. She seemed to lose concentration while she chatted with us, and the car would veer over the center line and precariously close to the edge. Other times, she would unconsciously speed up, and the car would slide around corners in the gravel. We learned to act as copilots, keeping a close watch on the situation and reminding her to get control. At least she was warm and friendly, and she delighted in our stories.

She explained that we would be making a series of stops up the coast for her to snap her pictures. We pulled over at the first stop and dashed across the road to a well-worn path leading down to an overlook atop a high cliff. The spot was beautiful, with cobalt blue waves crashing against monoliths of fractured rocks. The nooks and crannies of crags were populated with cormorants drying their widespread wings in the breeze.

The surroundings were awe-inspiring, but then again, so were many spots along this section of coast. I was unsure of the reason for stopping at this particular place until Valerie pointed at the near-vertical cliffs to the south of us. There, in the mist caused by the crashing surf, was a wondrous sight. A stream of water shot from the top of the cliff and formed a perfect parabola as it arced into a vertical descent into the sea. Gulls and terns floated effortlessly around this majestic waterfall.

Valerie set up her tripod and an expensive-looking camera and began taking snapshots. Riley and I sat on rocks and soaked up the beauty of God's creations.

A while later, I helped carry the tripod up the path to the car. As we approached the road, a highway patrol cruiser pulled up and the officer got out. Fortunately, it wasn't the same cop who'd chased us at the rockslide. Valerie frowned and whispered, "Uh-oh, let me handle this. Just follow my lead."

The cop tipped his wide-brimmed hat, and Valerie smiled in return. "Hello Officer, how can we help you?"

He looked at Riley and me. "Good morning, ma'am. We're looking for two runaway children in this area, and these two seem to match their description."

"Goodness me! I should be so blessed if these two were to run away. They're both incorrigible. But I'm afraid that I'm stuck with them. Their father would be downright upset with me if I let them run away." She chuckled. "I do hope you find those kids, though. This is no place for anyone to be alone."

She kept walking to the Ford, and we followed. I tried to look calm, but I was afraid my trembling hands would give us away. "You two wipe off your feet before you get in the car."

Riley and I replied, "Yes, Mother," in unison.

She smiled sweetly at the officer. "Who should we contact if we see these runaways?"

"The alert came from the Pismo Beach police. The kids were last seen south of here near Anderson Creek. Everyone is in a tizzy with them being out here all alone. This is rugged country." He wrote something on a slip of paper and handed it to Valerie. "Here's the number for the Pismo police, and another for highway patrol. Please contact either one if you gain any information about their whereabouts." He gave us another glance, then walked to his car. "Have a good day."

Valerie squealed and began dancing around as soon as the cop was out of sight. "Wasn't that a hoot! I was so nervous, I thought I'd pee my pants. Let's get the heck out of here."

She started up the big V-8 and laid about a foot of rubber as she peeled out. We all started laughing hysterically as the sun shone down on us through the crystal clear air.

We traveled up the winding road, stopping every so often for Valerie to take her pictures. At each stop, Riley and I would explore the cliffs above a roiling ocean that changed from aquamarine to cobalt blue to steely gray and all shades in between. Sea otters played in the surf, and migrating whales breached in the distance. Once, we were able to climb to a beach and discovered hundreds of sand dollars lying there. Some were bleached white, while others were different shades of green, blue, and violet. Their bottom-sides were decorated with an intricate five-pointed radial pattern surrounding a tiny hole. We carefully gathered a few and put them in the pack.

The road turned inland, rising into the lush landscape. Redwood trees as thick as six feet towered over us while gnarled oak and stately pine trees crowded the forest thick with chaparral. Streams and creeks, still feeling the impetus of spring runoff, gurgled and roared down the steep canyons.

Our route eventually left the forest and dropped back down to the coast, where the road straightened from its meandering ways.

We were able to travel at a relatively brisk clip. The highway entered the village of Carmel, and Valerie turned to us. "Dick doesn't graduate for a few hours. How about we stop for lunch up ahead?"

Ever hungry, Riley beamed. "That sounds great. I could eat a horse."

Valerie laughed, and we exited the highway at Ocean Avenue and wound our way to 17 Mile Drive. Suddenly, we were in the midst of well-manicured estates broken up by the fairways and greens of numerous golf courses. Cypress trees, grossly malformed by the winter storms, framed the cliffs above the ocean.

Valerie guided the Ford under a large portico held aloft by timbers. The valet greeted her and gave us a frown. Our clothes must have looked a little shabby for this fancy place. Even our best clothes at home would have been out of place.

Looking at us, Valerie smiled. "I know! Their father makes oodles of money and we buy them all the finest clothes, but they insist on wearing rags because that's what all their friends are wearing. It's the latest thing in

New York and Paris. Come along, children." We giggled as the valet pulled away.

To say the interior of the restaurant was opulent would have been an understatement. Huge twenty-foot timbers held up the open ceiling. Other smaller timbers formed the rafters and held sparkling chandeliers aloft. The walls were adorned with gold lamé wallpaper and swaths of maroon drapes. Floor-to-ceiling windows looked out over a covered porch toward the ocean. The tables were covered in fine linen and discretely placed to provide every diner with an element of privacy. Candles glowed with a warm light on each one.

The maître d' rushed up. "Good afternoon, Mrs. Blaine. Welcome back." He glanced at us. "A table for three, or are you expecting someone else?"

"Thank you, Georges. It will just be the three of us. Would you please seat us near the window?"

Georges nodded and led us to a table near the center of the room, where he pulled a chair out for Valerie and then for Riley. I had to take care of my own.

He left, and a waiter in full livery took our drink orders—white wine for Valerie, Seven Up for Riley and root beer for me.

When we were alone, Valerie said, "This is one of my favorite restaurants in Carmel. The food is adequate, but the ambience can't be beat. And you never know who you might run into. Bing Crosby has that pro-am golf thing here every year, and 'famous' people come from all around to play these courses, though I can't see the attraction to walking around and beating the hell out of a little white ball."

She tittered and nodded toward one corner, then leaned forward with a conspiratorial whisper. "Don't stare, but

I think that's Ronald Reagan and his wife, Nancy, over there. He's not that famous, but you may have seen him in some B-flicks. Now he's on television and hosting the General Electric Theater."

Of course I recognized him. He was the Gipper for gosh sake! Riley even recognized him from her favorite movie, *Bedtime for Bonzo*. We practically squealed with delight.

The selections on the menu may as well have been in a foreign language. In fact, some of them did have foreign-sounding names like "Foie Gras" and "Jerusalem Artichoke."

Valerie watched our confused expressions. "Let me help you. Tell me the types of food you like." After some discussion, she said, "My sister's kids all like spaghetti. How about that?"

We both nodded enthusiastically. She signaled the waiter and ordered two plates of linguine with marinara for Riley and me and a salade Niçoise for herself. She glanced at us. "And give us a large order of garlic bread." The woman knew the way to our hearts.

While we ate, Valerie told us a little about herself and her husband, Richard. "I was born into Southern aristocracy, such as it is. We Morgans can trace our lineage back to the founding of our country. I am a proud member of the Daughters of the American Revolution. Some of my ancestors fought in the American Revolution, and others fought for the Confederacy. My family is long on pedigree, but like many of the old families in Dixie, they are woefully short of cash. At least the amount of cash required to adequately support the lifestyle that they believe they deserve. But, they get by."

She smiled with all of her dimples, but I noted a hint of sadness.

"Dick charged into my life during my junior year at Vassar. He was in his senior year at Annapolis and swept me off my feet. It was love at first sight for both of us. He was away on his first tour while I finished my studies, and we married two days after he returned."

She looked off through the windows, a wistful expression on her face. "Dick is really smart, and everyone says he's on the fast track for admiralship. That's why they assigned him to the school here. They have him studying computers, but because he already speaks fluent Russian from his mother's side, they doubled him up with classes at the language institute. He literally hasn't had a free moment since we got here. That's why I've been spending time with Eve.

"The problem with Dick is that he's very strict and never deviates from the rules. And the navy has a lot of rules. I guess what I'm saying is, he's not going to like finding two 'wanted' runaways in his life. I'll try to convince him to help you, but I think he probably won't want to get involved."

After a delicious scoop of lemon sorbet, Valerie paid the bill and we walked out to the waiting ragtop—love that car!

●————————●

We drove into Monterey and turned into the grounds of a large hotel and circled a well-manicured lawn pulling to a stop under another portico supported by marble columns. A tall, sturdy flagpole stood at the center of the lawn, topped by the American flag fluttering in the wind. Chairs were arranged in neat rows surrounding the flagpole, and a dais stood in the front.

An orderly rushed out and greeted Valerie. "Good afternoon, Missus Blaine. You are just in time. The graduation is set to start in thirty minutes." He took the keys from Valerie and drove away.

I'd grabbed my backpack just in case we had to slip away. Valerie led us into the building. "This grand old place used to be the Del Monte Hotel. The navy used it during the war and decided that they liked it so much they bought it from Del Monte afterward."

We walked up to a huge picture window and looked out over an ocean alive with whitecaps and soaring birds. A huge grin came over her face. "Oooh, there's Dick!"

A tall, broad-shouldered man rushed over and swept Valerie up in his arms, swinging her in a full circle. He had a crew cut of brown hair and was wearing khaki pants with a crease that looked sharp enough to cut. His shirt matched it, adorned with two rows of ribbons above the left pocket and parallel silver bars on each collar.

He pulled Valerie into a full kiss and then held her at arm's length. "Hi, sweetheart! Man have I missed you! You look absolutely gorgeous."

He kissed her again. "Did you have a good time? What kind of trouble have you been getting into with those socialists up in the hills? How are Henry and Eve?" Then he looked over her shoulder at us. "Uh-oh. I don't think I want to know. It looks like you picked up some strays. Who might these two upstanding young folks be?"

Valerie smiled at him. "These are my new friends, Riley and Lucas. We'll explain after your ceremony. Come on, we're late." She turned to us. "You guys can watch from the portico." Then she put her arm in his and they walked out to the lawn.

The ceremony was swift. After a short speech by the commandant, each graduate was called up to receive their diploma. Then, the admiral awarded promotions to the military personnel, including Dick. He was now a lieutenant commander.

We sat in plush leather chairs around a low table in the lobby. A waiter brought drinks while Valerie told Dick our story, emphasizing that we weren't runaways and ending with, "Dick, we need to help these children however we can." She took his hand in hers, and I could sense the love between them.

Dick frowned and thought for a bit. "I understand, sweetheart, and I want to do whatever I can. But we have to be in San Diego in two days. I've been given my orders as the new executive officer on a destroyer that ships out in two weeks. There's no way we can drive them to Seattle and still get there on time. I think the best thing we can do is notify the authorities and let them take care of it."

I had anticipated his answer. Getting up, I grabbed my pack. "Come on Riley. Thank you, Miss Valerie. We appreciate your kindness, and yours too, sir. But we have to find our dad, and the cops won't care about that. They'll just put us into a foster home and we'll be stuck."

We started for the door, but I heard Valerie softly crying. Dick got up and rushed over to us. "Hold on, young man. I can see how you might be wary of the police and the child welfare system. I have an idea. It's not optimal, but how about we take you downtown and get you on a bus to Seattle? That way, we'll be reasonably sure that you're on your way."

Riley started to tell him that the bus company wouldn't let us travel without an adult, but I talked over her. "That would be nice, sir. If you would just drop us off at the station, you don't need to wait around with us. You really need to get on the road, and we don't want to hold you up any longer."

That seemed to satisfy Dick, and he put his arm around Valerie to comfort her.

A half hour later we pulled up in front of the Greyhound station. Valerie had tears in her eyes as she hugged Riley. "I don't know where we'll be living when we get to San Diego. It's the navy way. She pulled a slip of paper out of her purse and handed it to me, "These are the addresses and phone numbers for both my parents and Dick's. I'll let them know what's going on. Please call them and let them know that you made it. They'll put you in contact with us."

She reached over and pulled me into a crushing bear hug. Dick shook my hand and slipped me a twenty, a much-needed addition to the money that our friends in Pismo Beach had given us.

"Are you sure you don't want us to come in with you?"

I assured him that I could handle it, and he wished us well before getting in the car.

We waved as they drove off. Riley and I looked at each other, and I put her hand in mine. "Here we go again." We began walking toward the beach and, hopefully, some shelter for the evening. The sun was dipping into the ocean in front of us, and it was starting to get dark.

A bus pulled into the station, and a group of young sailors got off. They crowded around us in their rush for a night on the town.

CHAPTER 13

Cannery Row, 1957

*Cannery Row in Monterey in California is
a poem, a stink, a grating noise, a quality of
light, a tone, a habit, a nostalgia, a dream.*

—John Steinbeck

W E STARTED DOWN THE STREET and I tried to orient myself so we could find the hobo camp that Clete had described. Riley had just stepped into the street to cross when a loud roar came from around the corner. I pulled her back onto the sidewalk as a caravan of stripped-down and souped-up hot rods cruised past, their engines purring like angry tigers. The lead car was a red Ford coupe, followed by a Hudson with flames painted along the wheel wells. Other street rods followed. The final car in the procession was a jet-black '55 Chevy convertible. The driver had greasy hair slicked into a duck tail, matching the color of the car. A cigarette hung from his lips, and he wore a white T-shirt with a package of cigarettes rolled into his left sleeve. As he rolled by, he spied us and smiled. Then he gave us a thumbs-up and roared away, followed by a police car with its lights flashing.

Crossing the street, I caught sight of railroad tracks and headed for them. We followed the tracks toward a trestle—the landmark that Clete had given me.

I looked up at the graffiti covering the masonry of the bridge and saw three diagonal lines. "Uh-oh! That sign means that this place isn't safe. Come on, let's get out of here." We turned and had just started walking away when we heard some shouting. Quickening our pace, we faded into the bushes and scrambled up a bank and across the street, where we ducked into an alley.

Halfway down, we saw a grizzled hobo sitting on a doorstep, smoking an old stogie. He looked up and gave us a toothless grin. "The bulls razed the camp a night afore last. Burned everything to the ground and beat up a bunch of us. Says they want to make this here town a tourist destination and there ain't no room for us 'bos. Took everything I got except this here cigar." His grin wrinkled into a frown, and he looked away.

I stared at that sad face, then turned to Riley with a shrug. She nodded, and I bent down and untied my tennis shoe, reached in, and handed the old man three dollars. "God bless you, sir. Us 'bos need to look after each other. Hope this helps." Clete taught us right.

His face lit up like the marquee for a Saturday matinee. "Thank you, kind sir. I don't reckon that I've met too many children hobos, but I'm mighty glad I met you. Where you headin'?"

I briefly explained our situation and that we were headed for Seattle. "Wooey, that's a ways. But you sure ain't leaving tonight. Come with me—I've got a safe place to spend the night in one of the old fishermen's shacks on the beach."

As we walked along, he said his name was Seth, and we introduced ourselves. He asked if we were hungry, and Riley gave her usual reply. With a smile, Seth led us to the door of a soup kitchen. "They feed us pretty good here and don't push the religion too hard. Let's see what's cooking tonight."

We entered a steamy room filled with the odor of boiled cabbage and got in line. A heavyset, apron-encased woman ladled soup into our bowls, and we grabbed some bread off a stack and sat at a long, rough-hewn table. It wasn't French cuisine, but that soup sure was tasty. Riley polished off two bowls full, sopping up the liquid with hunks of sourdough bread.

They were handing out chocolate chip cookies at the door as we left, and we each grabbed a handful. Then Seth led us down a hill to the street leading away from the main part of town. We came to a row of dilapidated wooden shacks lining the shore and entered one toward the end. He pointed to a pile of newspapers in the corner.

"That's where I'm sleeping. You two can bed down in that other corner." With that, he lay down, covered himself with papers, and went to sleep.

I did my usual security checks and decided that we were relatively safe. We rolled out the blanket for Riley, and I rolled up a sweatshirt for her pillow. I took the small tarp from my pack and walked over to cover Seth's wiry frame. Then I sank down on the floor beneath my own jacket and propped my head against the pack.

Somewhere in the distance, I heard a ship's horn, and tried to sleep.

•———————•

My mind wouldn't be quiet. Thoughts of our predicament kept popping up. I tossed and turned until early morning before finally creeping out the door to sit on the steps. The ocean was a steel gray in the dim light, the light-colored, foamy waves rolling against the shore. A blanket of fog muted the lights of the town, and in the east I could see a ribbon of red announcing the new day.

My troubled mind kept turning over our situation. We had been gone for nearly two weeks, and I was pretty disappointed with our lack of progress. We were still in California, and I didn't know how much farther we had to go, but I had the sense that it was pretty far. I was leery of asking how far we had to go without raising suspicions. I mulled our options—turn ourselves in or keep going. I suppose the logical choice would be to give up and let the adults take charge. Riley would certainly be safer than out here on our own.

But the thought of putting our destiny in the hands of an uncaring and possibly nefarious bureaucracy was untenable. Then there was the question of Walt. I wondered if anyone in Cholame had found his body and if they were searching for his murderer—me.

I shook my head. There was no way I was giving up until I found our dad and he could take care of Riley. Until then, I just needed to keep us moving north.

I put the bad thoughts away, leaned against the steps, and sat in silence while the world woke up around me. The sound of delivery trucks drifted down from the streets above while the sky lightened and the fog lifted. Terns ran in and out of the surf as they pecked away at the tiny crustaceans in the sand. Out on the breakwater, the cacophony of barking seals split the sound of the surf rolling ashore. I watched a pod of pelicans gliding inches above the water.

As I watched their graceful flight, one large male sailed higher and then dove straight down into the sea, his wings pulled close to his body. I clapped as he came up with a mackerel in his bill. He flipped it in the air, and it disappeared down his large gullet.

The air was beginning to get warm by the time Riley came out and sat beside me. Her hair was askew, and she had lines wrinkling her face from her ersatz pillow. I put my arm around her shoulders. "We're getting there, Riles. It's just taking longer than I thought. We can't afford to stay here too long. We've got to get moving, but I'm not sure how to get back on the road."

"You'll think of something," she murmured. "I know you, and once you start thinking about a problem, you don't let it go until you come up with a solution." She grinned up at me, and I nodded with a confidence that I didn't feel.

We sat there enjoying the antics of the seals as they swam and rolled and leaped thru the water.

A while later, Seth sat down beside me with a grunt. "Some angel covered me up last night. You didn't happen to catch sight of him, did you?"

I just smiled.

"Well now, young 'bos, how about we get something to eat? There's a café a couple of blocks away that's always good for a meal in trade for some chores. Want to join me?"

We got up and started toward the center of town, climbing past the main street and around a corner. A small cottage stood in the center of the block with a neon sign that flashed "oms." When we got closer, I could see that an initial M had burned out and it was meant to say "Moms."

We followed a gravel path to the back door and Seth knocked lightly. After a few minutes. a short man with bushy eyebrows and a stomach shaped like an apple came out. "Hello Seth, how are you? Looking for work?" He glanced at us. "Looks like you brought some help, and they look hungry. Why don't you two come with me and I'll get you started? Seth, you can sweep and empty the trash, and then come see me in the kitchen."

As we followed him into the kitchen, he pointed to a table with a tray of cutlery and a package of paper napkins. "Young lady, why don't you wrap a fork, knife, and spoon into each napkin?"

Then he led me to a large sink. "You look like you know your way around a scullery. Can you handle those pots and pans?"

I nodded. He smiled, and as he walked out into the café, he said, "When you're done, we'll fix you some breakfast."

Riley finished first and helped me with the last kettles. Seth came in and sat at the table. "Mom's a good cook and he takes care of me. I get a meal here just about every day. Everyone calls him Mom because of the sign, but the sign was here when he bought the place. None of us know what his real name is."

Just then, the batwing doors opened and Mom carried steaming plates over to the table. Eggs, hash browns, and bacon covered each. He went to the walk-in refrigerator and brought out a gallon of milk and a pitcher of orange juice. "Looks like you two did a pretty good job. Thank you. We're swamped out front, so I've got to get back. Wash your dishes when you're finished."

The fog had burned off, and the sun was a yellow orb topping the hills by the time we left. Our stomachs were very happy as we walked down the hill. Seth was heading back to his shack, and we wanted to get going.

We were standing on a corner to say our goodbyes when four mean-looking guys wandered up. The biggest one had pock marks covering his face and a scar along his neck. "Well, well, well, what do we have here? I thought I told you to stay away from here, old man. This is our territory, and we don't want any bums around here." He pushed Seth hard enough to make him stumble to his knees. "Now look, you just got your slimy shit all over my street!"

One of the other boys laughed and pushed Seth again.

I stood between the boys and Seth hollered at them, "Just leave him alone! He's not doing anything to you!"

A wall-eyed boy walked up to me and punched me in the stomach, doubling me over. "Shut up, kid, and stay out of this."

I caught my breath and charged him. He wasn't expecting it, and we both went over. The two of us rolled around on the ground. I got in a lucky punch that made his nose burst with a stream of blood, but he was too big for me, and he began pounding my head into the ground. Riley screamed and started to hit him, but another boy pulled her off, laughing.

I was just about done when I saw movement out of the corner of my eye and the guy holding Riley went down hard. Then, the bully holding me grunted and rolled off. I looked up to see the hot rodder from the day before push the leader away from Seth. "How about you assholes take on someone besides an old man and some kids?" He popped the guy in the jaw and then floored him with an uppercut. He turned around to face the others, but they decided that discretion was in order. They gave us one last hard-ass look, picked up their friend, and slithered away.

The hot rodder helped Seth to his feet and brushed him off. He leaned against a wall, crossed one leg over the other and lit a cigarette, "Are you okay old man?"

Seth nodded and mumbled, "Sure, Rick. I'm fine thanks to you and these two. I'm just going to head back to my shack and rest up a bit." He turned to us. "You children take care. It was a pleasure meeting you, and I appreciate all your help." He shook my hand and gave Riley a shy hug before heading down the street.

Rick turned to us and blew out a lungful of smoke. "That was fun. Do you do this every morning?" He grinned. "My name's Rick. Seth is an old friend of mine, but I haven't seen you two around before. What's your story?"

Since Rick had just saved our bacon, I figured we could trust him and took a chance. I sputtered, "I'm Luke, and this is my sister, Riley. We're on our way to find our dad in Seattle, but we're kinda stuck right now and we don't know what to do."

Rick's eyes grew big, and then he let out a breath. "Whoa, hold on there, Ace, that's quite a mouthful. Let's go get a coke and sit on the seawall and you can tell me everything. Then we'll see what we can do." He handed me a handkerchief. "You might want to wipe some of that blood off your face."

•———————•

We stopped at a little grocery store and bought sodas—Coke for Rick, Grape Nehi for Riley, and a Hire's Root Beer for me. Rick said he didn't have any money, so I dug down into my jeans and put a dollar on the counter.

At the last minute, Rick told the clerk, "Throw in a pack of Lucky Strikes and a pack of matches, please." That wiped out my dollar, and I had to dig out another nickel to pay for everything.

We sat on the wall in front of the Monterey Beach Hotel with our legs dangling above the surf. Rick lit a cigarette and took a pull on his soda. "Sounds like you guys are in a bit of a bind. Let's hear the whole story."

We spent the next hour explaining our situation. I told him everything, and Riley chimed in with details that I had omitted or forgotten. I left out the fact that I had killed Walt, but Riley had no reservations about spilling that secret.

Rick was silent while we talked. When we had finished, he shook his head. "That's something else! I never thought I would be hanging out with a couple of runaways." He poked my shoulder. "Much less a murderer."

I almost started to cry. My face got red, and I bawled "We're not runaways! We're going to find my father, and it's my responsibility to take care of Riley. That's why I had to kill Walt. Come on Riley, let's go!" I got up and pulled my sister along.

Concern clouded Rick's face, and then he just looked contrite. "Hey, hold up, Luke. I'm sorry, I was just kidding. Come back and sit down. Maybe we can figure something out."

We went back and sat down.

Rick pulled out a comb and swept his hair back before sitting back with his cigarette hanging from his lips. "My friends and I are heading north for one last trip before we go into the army. Red, Herb, and I all got our draft notices, and we have to report next week. We want to enjoy ourselves before boot camp by traveling up the coast to Santa Cruz and through the peninsula into Frisco.

"We're ready to go, but I'm all tapped out. I need to pick up a few bucks for gas money before we can leave. I can probably earn enough cleaning nets down at the boathouse in a few days. You can ride along with us, and I can get you as far as San Francisco. How's that sound?"

I looked at Riley and smiled. "Thanks, Rick, but we're really anxious to get going. How long do you think it will take you to earn enough money?"

"I usually get around a buck an hour down there. Along with Herb and Zeb's money, I figure I'll need fifteen dollars to get us through and still have a good time. So, we could leave in a couple of days."

I sat on the concrete and unlaced my left shoe, reaching in for the twenty that Dick had given us. I was pretty worried about giving him half of our money, but I was all out of options. And, for some reason, I trusted him.

I handed him the money. "Do you think we can leave today?"

Rick was a little shocked, but he recovered nicely. He grinned, "Hot damn! I'll go round up the guys. But, I have one requirement if you're going with us."

I was worried, but before I could say anything, Riley whimpered softly, "What is it, Rick?"

"I'm not trying to be mean, but you guys are a mess. I can't let you into my car as filthy as you are. Follow me."

I looked at my clothes. They were stained and soiled. Riley giggled and pointed. "Your face is gray, Luke. You look like a raccoon."

I looked at her and almost told her that was the pot calling the kettle black. Instead, I started laughing.

We walked down the street to a beach access area. Rick pointed to a cinder-block building, "That's the beach house. There are men's and women's showers in there. Do you have any clean clothes?"

I opened my pack and pulled out some shorts and a top for Riley. Digging back in, I grabbed a shirt for myself and was rummaging around for some pants when Rick spoke up. "Hold on, Ace. I don't know if you've noticed, but you look like you're expecting a flood. He pointed at my ankles.

I looked down, and it appeared as if my pants had suddenly shrunk. The cuffs were three inches above my shoe tops. "Humph! What the heck?"

Rick chuckled. "You're growing, Luke. It's a natural thing at your age. You've just had a growth spurt. Don't worry, though. My little brother is a couple of years older than you, and I'm pretty sure I can snag some of his used clothes that will fit you. You guys go get cleaned up, and I'll be back in a flash with some duds for you."

Rick walked off with our twenty. I said a little prayer that he would return and handed Riley our one bar of soap and our only towel. "You first, Riles."

While she showered, I sat on a bench and watched the sailboats skittering across the bay in the bright sunshine.

CHAPTER 14

Giant Dipper, 1957

Surf City has nothing to do with Santa Cruz.

—Dean Torrence

I WAS DAYDREAMING IN THE WARM sunlight just enjoying the aquatic panorama playing in front of me when Riley tapped me on my shoulder. "It's your turn, big brother. The water's nice and hot."

Her cheeks were scrubbed pink, and her curly hair was still wet. I handed her my baseball cap. "Here, put this on and tuck your hair under it. I've been thinking that it will be a lot safer if everyone thinks you're a boy. And it will help with our disguise, since they're looking for a boy and girl."

As I picked up the towel and soap and headed for the shower, Rick's Chevy pulled into the parking lot, followed by the Hudson. Rick jumped out and pulled a grocery bag from the back seat. He said something to the Hudson driver, then walked over to us.

"Wow Riley, you look different. I don't think I'd recognize you without the layer of grime." He handed me the bag. "There's a couple pairs of pants and some shirts in there. You can try them on after your shower." He grinned.

"We probably need to burn your old duds. Why don't you go cleanup, and we'll blow this 'burg."

A minute later, the warmth of the shower flowing over me was exquisite. I didn't want to leave its embrace, but after twenty minutes of scrubbing my skin raw, I ran the boiler dry and the water turned tepid. Rick's brother's clothes smelled of laundry detergent and fit almost perfectly. I finished dressing and walked out to the cars. Riley shouted from the front seat of the Chevy, "I've got shotgun!"

Rick and two other young guys were leaning against the Hudson, cigarettes hanging from their lips. One of them was skinny as a stick and had bright red hair that was almost orange. The other was medium height with sandy hair that stuck out in all directions. His teeth were bucked out so much, he had a hard time containing his spittle. They both smiled as they walked up with Rick.

The redhead stuck out his hand and smiled. "I'm Red. My real name's Zebulon, but if you call me that, I'll have to beat you up." He guffawed. "Just kidding. I haven't beat anyone up in my life, but it felt good to say."

Rick snickered and pointed to the other guy. "This here's Herb."

Herb smiled and shook my hand. His voice was quiet. "Nice to meet you. Rick told us a little about you. Quite a story, but I'm not sure why you want to travel with a bunch of misfits like us."

Just then, a police car pulled up next to Rick's car and chirped his siren. Riley scooted down below the dashboard, and I slipped around the corner of the bathhouse. Rick stood up and scowled. "Oh great, it's Officer Dildo. You guys wait here. I'll take care of this."

A portly man pulled himself from the cop car. His belly hung over his belt, and his face was florid with exertion. "You boys need to move along. This parking lot isn't a hangout."

Rick walked up to him. "Oh, yes, sir, officer, sir. We'll get a move on. Just don't write us any more tickets." He cracked up. "Hey, how you doin', Officer Odell?"

"Hi, Rick. I'm okay, and I'll be a lot better as soon as you guys leave town. You know the town fathers don't cotton to you guys racing up and down the street. It's keeping me out of the donut shop just running you down." He offered a laugh in return. "Seriously, I heard you got your draft notices. How long before you have to report?"

Rick shrugged and threw up his hands. "Just one more week of freedom. We're heading up the coast to Santa Cruz and then on into Frisco. Want to join us?"

"Sounds like fun, but I'm getting a little old for that. I'm sure gonna miss you boys. I won't have anything to do besides write parking tickets. You be safe up there." The cop tipped his hat, got back in his car and drove off.

Rick had a funny look on his face as he watched the car drive away. "Who knew Officer Dildo loved us? He's a pretty good ole boy. Let me off with a warning a lot of times when he coulda' busted me." He shrugged and turned back to us. "Well, we better get a move on, it's after nine. I want to make Santa Cruz before one, and we've got a couple of stops along the way. Pile in!"

He hopped into the driver's seat without opening the door.

"Head 'em up, move 'em out," Herb chirped.

As we left the parking lot, Red peeled out, leaving fifty feet of rubber on the asphalt. I looked back at the bay sparkling in the afternoon sunlight.

Rick was chatty as we drove through Seaside and past Fort Ord. He pointed at the base. "Wouldn't it be a hoot if the army stationed me there? I would be near my family and all my friends, but what good is being in the army if you can just go home to Mom after work? I want to see the world before I settle down. Maybe they'll send me to Europe or Japan. Wherever they send me, I'm hoping to work in the motor pool.

"I do want to come home after my service though. This is my home. I'm going to save as much money as I can so I can open my own garage with all the latest tools and equipment. I earned my AA in automotive technology from Monterey Peninsula College." He got a proud look on his face. "I'm the first in my family to go to college. My parents are really proud of me. And then there's Theresa."

He smiled a little dreamily and pushed in the car's cigarette lighter. "It'll be hard being away from her for that long, but we are totally in love and have been since we were your age, Luke. We've made plans and can't wait to start a family, but we want to get the business going first. Our families are all in on us getting hitched, even though they're a little worried. Theresa's Hispanic, and some folks get real heated about people mixing in marriages."

We paralleled the ocean for a while and then crossed a bridge over the Salinas River. An archway over the road announced we were entering Castroville, the "Artichoke Capital of the World." Riley asked what artichokes were, only she pronounced it "artychoke."

Rick pulled onto the dirt and up to a roadside farmer's stand leaving Red and Herb in a dust cloud. "Come along, guys, and I'll show you. I promised my mom that I'd pick up a bunch for her. They'll keep cool in the trunk until I get back. He led us to the bins holding an assortment of fresh vegetables, where he picked up a green plant and handed it to Riley. "This is an artichoke. Be careful, the tips of the leaves have stickers on them."

I picked up one of the plants and examined it. It was shaped like a squat green flower with thick leaves. The stalk at the bottom was about an inch in diameter. I checked out the top and bottom. "It doesn't look like there's anything to eat, and it's too ugly to use for decoration."

Rick and Herb started laughing. "Believe it or not, these are great delicacies. They're typically steamed, and the meat at the base of the leaves and in the heart is very tasty. People garnish them with melted butter or mayonnaise." Rick placed a dozen of the plants in a paper bag and gave the lady tending the stand a dollar. We bought some oranges to snack on for the ride as well, then hopped into the cars and headed down the road. "OK guys, next stop Santa Cruz!"

Our route took us past Moss Landing and a pretty harbor with hundreds of trawlers and other boats bobbing in waves. The sign for a long bridge announced Elkhorn Slough, and looking down, we spied dozens of kayakers paddling along the shore.

"Too bad we're in a hurry," Rick said. "The slough is an amazing place. My parents used to take us there so we would appreciate the beauty of nature—hundreds of different species of birds migrate through here every year. And it's a good place to see sea otters."

We turned inland and passed Watsonville before heading back to the coast. The small towns of Aptos and Capitola went by the windshield in a flash, and then the road intersected with Highway 17, where we turned left onto Ocean Street and dropped down a hill to Santa Cruz. We wound through the narrow streets.

"It's always tough finding a parking space close to the boardwalk," Rick said. "Keep your eyes peeled."

We circled the block twice before we stopped behind an old Buick that was pulling away from the curb. We took the spot and waited for Red and Herb. After a few minutes, Red called from the corner, and we headed toward the boardwalk.

We passed under an arch that read "Santa Cruz Beach Boardwalk" in large letters and on to an elevated lane fronting a mile-long sandy beach. Directly in front of us was a pretty bay penetrated by a long wharf to the right. The wooden walkway was crowded with people. We walked along and took in the sights of arcades, carnival-type rides, and shops. While Rick was buying tickets for the rides, Riley bounded up to a kiosk. "Look, corn dogs! I'm starving. Let's get one." I dug into my pocket and offered to buy dogs for the guys, but they declined. After a little argument, I paid for Riley's and my two.

We slathered them with mustard and ate them as we walked a little farther, then stopped in front of a merry-go-round. Rick pulled us toward it, but I resisted. "Merry-go-rounds are for little kids. Let's go ride something exciting."

He insisted, though. "This isn't a little kid's ride. It's a blast. Just be sure to get a horse on the outside of the ride, and then follow my lead." The ride stopped, and we got onto the wooden horses in a row—Herb, then Red, followed by Rick, Riley, and me in succession.

A bell sounded, and we lurched forward and entered a tunnel into the building. Tinny calliope music was playing from loudspeakers. As we began around the ride's oval,

Rick yelled, "Watch!" and leaned over, reached out, and grabbed a brass ring from a dispenser of sorts. Riley and I both missed the rings as we scooted by. Up ahead, Rick cocked his arm and threw his ring at the large mouth of a clown painted onto the wall. A loud clang sounded when Rick's ring hit home.

The carousel made numerous passes. Riley and I finally got the hang of it and scored clown's mouth bulls-eyes. Before the ride was finished, Rick turned on his horse and winked at us before slipping one of the rings into his pocket. Riley followed suit, but for some reason unknown even to myself I kept two of the rings while the ride slowly came to a halt.

We were all laughing as we got down from the horses. "That was a blast!" Riley giggled. "Can we do it again?"

Rick smiled and waved his arms, "We've just begun the wonders of the Santa Cruz Boardwalk. The best is yet to come. Let's see what else we can find."

We passed numerous old-fashioned carnival games, with hawkers out front trying to lure us in to spend our money. Another building housed rows of pinball machines, and we also passed a glass booth with an animated clown laughing incessantly.

As we approached the eastern end of the boardwalk, Rick said, "And now we have the *pièce de résistance*—the Giant Dipper." He pointed to a large wooden structure dominating the view. As we watched, a train of six cars clattered across the wooden track and entered the station. "Get ready for the time of your life." He ran toward the entrance with a whoop.

We had never seen a roller coaster. Riley looked at me with eyes the size of saucers and then pulled me along.

We boarded the train two abreast, Rick and Herb in the front car followed by Riley and me, and then Red, who seemed to have found a lady friend. As we departed the station, the train immediately entered a tunnel. After some dips and sharp turns, we emerged and began climbing a steep hill. It seemed like the climb took forever, and then we dropped like a rock, screaming in unison. The train rose into a turn to the left and up a couple of hills, and then into a turn that seemed to fly over the park. A few more turns and hills, and then we were gliding into the station.

We were laughing hysterically as we walked back out to the boardwalk. We rode the Giant Dipper four more times until we were dizzy from the twists and turns. Snack booths offering a virtual cornucopia of treats proliferated the park. It seems like we stopped at every other one to feed Riley's insatiable appetite. We had cotton candy, caramel corn, and soft pretzels.

The sun was getting low on the horizon, turning the sky a wild mix of red and orange. We had just finished a cheeseburger when Rick told us it was time to find a place to camp out. "We're going up to Natural Bridges. We can camp in the dunes up there and no one will bother us. As soon as we get you guys settled, Herb, Red, and I are going to go back downtown in Red's car to try to find some action. You two can sleep in my car, and I'll crash on the beach when we get back."

We drove along the coast for a few miles and entered a sand-blown asphalt parking lot abutting the beach, joining about a dozen other cars and trucks. Tents and lean-tos dotted the dunes in both directions. Groups of adults and children sat around campfires stoked with driftwood.

Rick pulled the Chevy up to one corner of the parking lot, pulled the rag top over the car's interior, and secured the latches. He handed me a key. "Here's a spare. You guys should be okay here. The beach is pretty cool, and you can start your own fire if you want. Whenever you're ready to turn in, just lock the doors and crash on the seats. There are enough families camped around the parking lot, so that should keep the creeps away. I figure we'll be back around midnight, and I'll check on you before I hit the hay."

I told him that we'd be alright. He hopped into Red's car, and they peeled out of the parking lot.

It was still light, so we wandered onto the beach and began picking up driftwood for a fire. Walking north, we spied a rock formation straddling the beach. Years of pounding surf had carved a passageway through the granite, giving the formation the appearance of a bridge. Cormorants populated the sides and top, their wings spread wide.

We gathered a nice pile of driftwood, and I snagged some newspaper from a trash can. I didn't remember about the matches I took from Walt and was too worn out from the day's activities to try using my Boy Scout fire-starting skills, so I walked over to a neighboring fire and begged a burning twig.

After a few minutes, we had a warm fire. I pulled the tarp from the backpack, and we lay by the fire, staring up at the stars. "We're getting there, Riles. It's just taking a while."

She patted my hand and dozed off. I lay there day-dreaming about the road ahead. The fog rolled in, and the glow of the stars faded.

I kept the fire stoked for a while until the wind came up and blew the sand in my face and it began to get cold. Shivering, I woke Riley. She crawled into the back seat and was softly snoring again in seconds. I covered her with the blanket and sat in the front seat, watching as the other campfires slowly died.

A soft melody from one of the neighboring campsites eventually lulled me to sleep.

●────────●

I woke to the wind gently rocking the car and sand peppering the windshield. The sky in the east was glowing with the promise of a new day. Riley was out cold in the back seat, arms and legs askew. I needed to use the restroom at the other end of the parking lot, so I quietly opened the passenger door and hopped out.

I stretched my legs under a clear blue sky. Large trees on the other side of the road threw their shadows toward the dunes. The campers were beginning to stir, and I waved to a couple hunkered around their campfire. Then I entered the cinder-block building. The facility was basic but utilitarian, with two urinals, two stalls, and two sinks. Overhead skylights provided the only lighting.

When I had finished my business, I wandered to the beach side of the building and found four shower heads sticking out from the wall. The sand-covered cement apron had a drain in the middle.

I walked out to the beach and wandered down the coast for a while. The wind had subsided, and the water was a calm greenish blue. The waves lapped the sand, and sand pipers scurried around in their search for breakfast.

Back at the car, I found Rick and his buddies sprawled out around the cold campfire. Red's sleeping bag was bunched around his ankles. Herb was blowing bubbles through his wide-set teeth. I peeked into the car and made sure Riley was still okay, then began scrounging up some driftwood.

I was bringing an armful across the dunes when I spotted Rick hunched over the fire. A wisp of smoke drifted up as he huffed and puffed at the coals. The fire caught, and he added more fuel as he stood up. "Mornin', Ace. You're up early. How'd you sleep?"

"I slept pretty well. The steering wheel jabbed me a few times, but I figured out how to curl around it. I didn't even hear you guys come in. Did you have a good time?"

Red sat up and yawned. "Hell no! This town's dead after dark. We crashed a party on the beach, but it was a bunch of old farts playing polka music. I mean, who plays polka music at a beach campfire?"

Herb mumbled through his errant teeth, "Maybe a bunch of Germans?" He and Rick snorted. "Man, that sand is hard. I'm not sure my back will ever be the same. Now, excuse me, I've gotta see a man about a horse." He jogged toward the bathhouse.

The passenger door to the Chevy opened, and Riley popped out. She stretched, and her face brightened. "Hi, everybody. I'm starving."

Rick laughed out loud. "She doesn't mince words, does she? I guess we better find some grub before this little one wastes away to nothing." He rolled up his sleeping bag and tossed it into the trunk.

Everyone started packing up their stuff. I filled my canteen with water and doused the fire, then kicked sand over it until I was sure it was out. We cleaned up the detritus from our stay and piled into the cars. Red was considerate of the still-sleeping families and abstained from leaving a patch of rubber, though I know he really wanted to. And up Highway 1 we went for a few miles until we dropped down into the small town of Davenport.

A neon sign flashed Open in the window of a café perched above a crescent-shaped beach nestled between steep cliffs. We pulled into the gravel parking lot, and the three boys hopped out. I was ready to jump out myself when I noticed a police car among the half-dozen cars there for an early breakfast.

I pulled back ducking behind the dashboard. Rick glanced back and ambled over to the car, his eyebrows raised. "We can't go in there!" I whispered. "The police are looking for us, and whoever's in there might get suspicious when they see us."

Rick squinted at the cop car and nodded. "We'll get something to go and be right out. What do you guys want to eat and drink?"

We said any kind of sandwich would be good, and hot cocoa. Rick smiled and entered the café.

Ten minutes later, a highway patrolman stepped out of the building. He surveyed the parking lot from behind mirrored aviator glasses and then dropped into his cruiser and drove away to the south.

After a while, Rick and Herb came out. Herb was carrying a greasy paper bag and two steaming cardboard cups, and Rick had another pair of cups in his hands. He pointed to a picnic table next to the building. "Let's eat over there. These sandwiches are messy. We don't want to get food crumbs and stains messing up our wheels." Herb pulled four parcels wrapped in waxed paper from the bag and handed one to each of us.

The sandwiches consisted of a fried egg covered with strips of bacon between two pieces of toast. As we bit into them, egg yolk oozed out and dripped down our chins. They were yummy, and we washed them down with the hot cocoa.

I looked around and noticed Red's absence. Herb saw me and chuckled, and Rick said, "Red's in love with the cute waitress in there. He's chatting her up and they seem to be hitting it off. He's going to stick around here for a while, so Herb's going to ride with us. Red knows where we're heading, and he'll catch up later."

He continued, "I did overhear the cop talking to the cashier. He was asking them to keep an eye out for two runaways from Pismo Beach. He said he didn't think you could have made it this far, but all the towns from here south are on the lookout. Good thing you spotted his car. We better head out."

Riley called shotgun, so Herb and I piled into the back seat, and soon we were headed north again.

The highway hugged the coast as we passed sandstone cliffs on one side and groves of redwoods on the other. The ocean had turned the color of slate, and gulls cruised above the pounding surf. After about thirty minutes, the highway split the town of Half Moon Bay in two, with hotels and restaurants competing with tourist shops for our attention.

On the north side of town, we noticed a harbor protected by a jetty and a large promontory jutting into the ocean on the north. Bulldozers and other equipment were busily clearing part of the headland. At the edge of the cliff, a hundred feet above the surf, stood a white building with a large, parabola-shaped dish on the roof. Huge waves were crashing against the north side. I could see surfers riding in the water, and as I watched, a huge wave formed and three surfers began rapidly paddling ahead. The wave began to crest twenty feet above the surfers, and all but one pulled away. The wave picked up the final surfer as he stood, hurtling him toward shore. The surfer traveled along the front of the wave until it seemed to envelope him. I pointed and yelled that we should try to help the poor guy.

Herb just grinned and patted me on my shoulder. "Wait for a few seconds." He pointed at the open end of the wave.

On cue, the surfer shot out and smoothly guided his board up and over the diminishing wave. "That's Maverick's, a world-famous surfing spot. Sometimes, those crazy bastards ride waves that are sixty feet tall. It always amazes me that they can stay on those boards under those conditions."

Our route continued north through Moss Beach, into Pacifica and then Daly City. Finally, we crested a hill and entered San Francisco, where stucco homes were clustered among the hills. Rick exited Highway 1 at Skyline, and we followed the coast for a couple of miles past a lake on the right. We began a long curve to the right, and Rick pointed to his left.

"That's Fleishhacker Zoo over there. My parents used to take us there. It's a really nice place. If you're lucky enough to be there at two in the afternoon, you're in for a treat. That's feeding time for the lions and tigers and all the other big cats. No matter where you are in the park, you can hear them roaring. They're saying, 'It's dinner time! Feed me!' They're so loud you can literally feel the ground shake."

"Kinda like Riley," I quipped. "You don't want to get between her and food." She turned around and stuck her tongue out at me. Herb laughed and tousled her hair, and we headed into Baghdad by the Bay.

San Francisco was a cosmopolitan mecca, teeming with activity. People were scurrying everywhere. I was struck by the multidimensional contrasts. We passed through neighborhoods oozing with wealth right next to some of the worst conditions I'd ever seen. The city was a mishmash of cultures—Hispanic, Chinese, Italian, Japanese, and everything in between. The architecture seemed to vary with the neighborhood and the geographic constraints. Even nature participated in the city's diversity, soaked in a glorious sun one moment followed by chilling fog the next.

Rick got back on Highway 1, and we wound our way to California Street, dropping down Hyde to Fisherman's Wharf. After circling the area for ten minutes, he finally pulled into a parking spot vacated by a delivery van. He hopped out. "C'mon, let's check out the wharf before we head to Chinatown for lunch."

The wharf was full of wonders for Riley and me. Trawlers were parked along a pier, and people scurried about hauling carts of flopping fish destined for dinner tables. Seals barked alongside the boats, waiting for the occasional escapee. One boat held nothing but hundreds of huge crabs with spider-like features.

We wandered under the covered walkway to a jumbled cacophony of shouts, whistles, and laughter. Glass cases held all types of marine life including salmon, tuna, grouper, and cod, all iced down. An octopus reached its tentacle toward the top of its case in a vain attempt at freedom. A large white bucket held squirming eels.

Fishmongers were hawking their wares while customers shouted out their orders. Laborers draped in rubber overalls dashed back and forth, pushing wheeled carts. Shouts were followed by a fish flying through the air to the cashier at the end of a row. The savory scents were making our mouths water, so Rick bought a cup of creamy clam chowder for Riles and a tart shrimp cocktail for me. It was delicious.

We walked the length of the market, then crossed the street and headed back toward the car. We headed back up the hill at Hyde Street and stopped to watch the cable cars as they charged their way down the hill, bells ringing, to the turntable at Hyde and Beach.

Rick and Herb decided they wanted to stop at the Buena Vista Café for an Irish Coffee. Rick pulled out his wallet and slid a driver's license from the interior, winking at me. He called over to Herb, "Got your 'other' license?" Herb grinned and gave Rick a thumbs-up, then handed me two quarters and pointed down the street toward a square of multistory brick buildings. "You guys will enjoy Ghirardelli's much more than this place. We'll catch up with you in a half hour."

The sweet aroma of chocolate enveloped us as we approached the square. Entering from Beach Street, we found a variety of shops and cafes. We opened the door to the main shop and were greeted with row after row of confections. The main theme was chocolate, but lollipops, gums, and other candies dotted the aisles as well.

We wandered about in awe until Riley gravitated toward a display case full of chocolate goodies. I was still pretty full from the shrimp cocktail, so I let her make the selections. And she did pretty well with our four bits, picking out nuts and chews, sea foam, and dark chocolate toffee. I let her sample one before I put the rest in the pack. She frowned, so I said, "Rick said we were going to China Town for lunch. We need to save room."

That did the trick. My sister was easily bribed by the possibility of food.

While we waited for Rick and Herb, we wandered through the many shops and made wish lists of the attractive things we wanted from Santa. A while later, Rick and Herb came bouncing into the square. They were playing around and jostling each other. I thought it was good that they were having a nice time before their induction. Rick walked up, lit a cigarette, and exclaimed, "Are you guys ready to experience China Town? It's one of my favorite parts of Frisco." He charged up the hill toward the car, and we scrambled after.

Rick drove up Columbus Avenue, and we angled across town to Jackson. Parking was even worse in this area and it took twenty minutes to find a spot. We started walking through an area alive with sights, sounds, and aromas. Paper lanterns stretched across the streets from building to building. Murals of dragons and Buddha decorated many of the walls. Pagoda-shaped structures stood out among the more western edifices. It seemed that most of the merchants were shouting at each other in a strange language, creating a discordance with the singsong music that flowed from shop fronts.

And the aroma—I had never experienced anything like the bouquet that assaulted my sniffer that day. The air was tinged with ginseng and cabbage and spices that I could only imagine.

Herb led us into a building and up a narrow staircase to Hung Luk's, a crowded restaurant with white tablecloths. A pretty, young Asian girl seated us near the window.

"Everyone has their favorite restaurant in China Town, and this is mine," Herb said. "The food here is absolutely fabulous."

Rick and Herb ordered Tsingtao beer, and Riley decided on Seven Up. We'd never had Chinese food before, and I wanted to do the whole experience, so I stuck with tea. We perused the menu, written in Mandarin with an English translation alongside while waiting for our drinks.

Rick helped us choose something that wasn't too exotic. Riley and I shared an order of egg rolls for appetizers, while Herb settled on fried wontons and Rick tried the pot stickers. We all sampled each other's choices, and all of them were yummy.

Rick explained that the best way to enjoy a Chinese dinner was for each of us to order one plate, and then we would graze on them together. We decided on sweet and sour pork, moo goo gai pan, steamed dim sum, and General Tso's chicken.

He and Herb were enjoying their second beer when the food arrived. The plates were piled high with so much food that there was no way one person could eat all of it. However, Riley and Herb gave it a good try.

Back on the street, our stomachs were so full we practically waddled. As we left, a voice serenaded us. We walked south a few blocks, and Rick sat on a bench in front of Finocchio's. He rubbed his belly, lit a cigarette, and grinned. "You two are too young to go in here, but I wanted you to check out some of the employees." He pointed at a tall lady in an evening dress heading into the club.

At a distance, she seemed somewhat homely, but as she approached, I noticed a five o'clock shadow and a protruding Adam's apple. "Oh no! Is she a guy? How weird!"

Herb and Rick started laughing. "Yep. Frisco is home to all sorts. This is one of the female impersonator clubs. The, uh, 'people' who work here put on a hell of a show. There's also a lesbian bar near here. Not my thing, but it's pretty entertaining. Let's go up the street and see if we can find a coffee house where a beatnik poet is doing their thing. Some of them are pretty interesting."

He led us to a corner shop with dozens of small round tables and chairs surrounding an elevated stage. Soft jazz was playing from the sound system. Young men in grubby clothes sporting goatees and women in short skirts with black leggings sat around the stage. A woman in all black was just getting on the stage, sitting on a high stool in front of a microphone. We slipped in and quietly sat in the back.

The woman in black introduced herself and began reciting a poem that spoke of the "pure and beautiful but downtrodden masses" and "personal release and illumination." She went on about something called "Zen." I really didn't understand much of it, and I found her poem to be pretty depressing. When she finished, there was reserved applause. She took a slight bow and then tittered, "Now I would close with a short piece by Friedrich Nietzsche that reflects my current mood:

"'God is dead. God remains dead. And we have killed him. Yet his shadow still looms. How shall we comfort ourselves, the murderers of all murderers? What was holiest and mightiest of all that the world has yet owned has bled to death under our knives; who will wipe this blood off us? What water is there for us to clean ourselves?'"

This sad recitation brought a standing ovation by the folks around us. I found the words struck something within me, but part of me felt that they rejected hope and were too melancholy. I wondered if all of these people were always despondent and why they didn't do something about it.

The lady stepped from the stage. Some people left, while others formed into groups and began animated discussions while smoking and sipping the strong coffee. Rick got into a discussion with a couple at the next table.

Riley and I were pretty bored, so we whispered to Herb that we'd be outside and waved to Rick as we left.

The air seemed particularly fresh without the cloud of cigarette smoke that had accumulated inside. We wandered into the City Lights Bookstore and perused the stacks crowded with books and periodicals. One table held a dozen books titled *Howl and other Poems* by someone named Alan Ginsberg. I wondered if the whole book was as depressing as what we had just heard, so I picked up a copy and flipped through it.

Not only was it depressing, it contained some pretty explicit descriptions of sex acts. Not my type of literature.

While we were waiting, I found a map of the West Coast and opened it. It showed the route we would need to take, and I started to feel a weight pressing down on me when I realized how far we still needed to travel. I folded it, paid thirty-five cents to the clerk, and stuck it in my pack.

A while later, Rick and Herb wandered in and took us to a reading corner with overstuffed chairs. Rick looked sad as he stammered, "Here's the deal, guys. I've enjoyed our time together, and I love you like you were my own brother and sister. I really wish that I could take you all the way to Seattle, but you know that Herb and I have to head home tomorrow. And we're going to be bar hopping tonight—not something that kids your age can participate in. That said, I'm not leaving you here in Frisco, it's too dangerous.

"Anyway, I was talking to that couple in the coffee shop and explained the situation to them. They said that there's a community in the hills above Sausalito across the bay. They said the place is safe and that other families with children stay there as they pass through. You should be able to connect with someone heading north from there. It breaks my heart, but it's the best I can do."

He looked like he was ready to cry. Riley walked up to him and hugged him hard. "Rick, don't be sad. We understand. Thank you for helping us. We wouldn't have made it this far if it wasn't for you and Herb."

Rick must have gotten something in his eyes because he looked away and rubbed at them. I got up to shake Herb's hand, and Rick pulled me to him for a bear hug. His voice was raspy. "Okay then, let's get across that bridge and check this place out. Make sure they'll take care of my brother and sister!"

We left the bookstore and stepped out into the street. The diverse population of San Francisco passed us by and Dave Brubeck's *Take Five* emitted from the doors of a nightclub as we headed to the car.

———•———

The fog was rolling in as the Chevy rumbled across town. The orange towers and just the top section of the parabolic suspension cables of the Golden Gate Bridge glowed brightly in the afternoon sun. As we drove over the bridge, we could see Mount Tamalpais in the distance. Rick exited to the left after crossing the bridge and followed Highway 1 for a few miles until we turned on a dirt road heading uphill. The muddy clay track wound around and through the coastal redwoods before terminating at a cleared space. Towering eucalyptus trees dominated one side of the clearing. Rustic farm structures dotted the landscape.

We pulled up to the largest building, and a man with a receding hairline and wispy goatee walked out with a slender woman, both of them smiling. Rick and I got out and walked up to them. We introduced ourselves, and the man volunteered, "Hi, I'm Roger, and this is my wife, Mary. How can we help you?"

While Rick explained the situation to them, Riley got out and joined us. As our story unfolded, Mary reached out and put her arm around Riley. "You poor, sweet thing. Come on in here and we'll get you set up with some sweet tea and cookies. Roger, we need to do what we can for these angels." It didn't sound like there was much room for discussion.

She and Riley went into the building while we continued talking.

After we finished, Roger grimaced. "That's some story. I think we can help in the short term. We try to protect our privacy up here, but we do invite guests. Some of those will be visiting in the next couple of days, and maybe one of those will be heading north." He pulled at his goatee, looked at me, and chuckled. "I suppose I could use a gopher."

The two men shook hands, and I walked Rick back to the car. Rick hugged me and jumped into the driver's seat. "Damn, Ace this is hard," he murmured. "Are you going to be okay?"

I reached in and softly punched him in his arm. "We'll be fine, Rick. You've done enough." I looked at Herb, then back to him. "I'll never forget how kind the three of you have been. Good luck in the army. Tell Red thanks, and please be safe. I hope the army works out for you."

Rick put the car in gear, and it slid away.

I walked back to the building with a heavy heart, as a jay's scolding broke the silence of the surrounding woods.

CHAPTER 15

Monterey, 1969

Lean on me.

—Bill Withers

I SPENT THE NIGHT IN MORRO Bay. Early the next morning, I ate a breakfast of eggs, hash browns, and bacon at a small café before heading up the Pacific Coast Highway. I passed the turnoff for Hearst Castle and tooted my horn for old time's sake. A while later, I turned up the dusty road to the remnants of the buildings where the Anderson Creek Gang had taken us in. I got out of the car and stretched my legs. The buildings were in bad shape, and there wasn't anyone around. Eve had passed away, and Henry was living in Pacific Palisades and protesting the war. I wondered if he had added that chapter to his book about two vagabond children. There wasn't much to see, so I drove back down the hill and continued up along the Big Sur coast, surrounded by some of the prettiest scenery in the world.

After passing Carmel, I reached Monterey. The town was shrouded in fog as I drove into its center. Crowds of tourists jammed the sidewalks. Many of the old buildings had been either replaced or gentrified. An ice cream store stood where Seth's shack had been. Up the hill, Mom's was no longer, replaced by a McDonald's. The old bathhouse still stood, and young men and women cleaned their surfboards and stripped off their wetsuits in the showers.

The Drifters were singing "Under the Boardwalk" as I turned up the hill and into an industrial area crowded with light-industry and service shops. Turning into a cul-de-sac, I spied a sign announcing Rick's Automotive at the end. Mechanics were busy in all four bays, two with cars balanced on the lifts. The shop was immaculate, and a young man pushed a broom across a spotless floor. The fifty-five was parked beside the building, still shiny and black.

I pulled into the parking space in front of the office. As I was stretching my legs, Rick walked out in a pair of clean overalls and a cigarette sticking out of his mouth. He gave the Mustang a once-over. "Nice wheels. Sounds like she's running a little rich, though."

He didn't recognize me, so I decided to have a little fun. "Yeah, I just bought her and haven't had a chance to make her right. But, even as outta tune she is, she can still leave that junk pile over there in the dust." I pointed at the Chevy and smiled.

He stood up tall and started to reply. Then he squinted at me and roared, "Oh my God! Is that you, Ace?" He pulled me to him and tried to crush my ribs. I let him—it felt good. He pulled a lollipop that I had assumed was a cigarette from his mouth. "Look at you! I think you've had a few more of those growth spurts. Get your ass in here."

He practically dragged me into the office and sat me down on one of the plastic chairs. Then he grabbed two RC Colas from a small refrigerator, handed one to me, and sat across from me. "I can't believe it. I was so worried about you guys after I left you in Frisco. I even thought about skipping my induction physical and going to find you. But by then, it was too late. I was so relieved when I got to call home from boot camp and Mom told me you had called from Seattle and were alright. Oh my goodness, look at you. Fill me in on the last ten years." He flipped the used lollipop stick into a nearby trash can.

He peppered me with questions while I described the rest of our adventure traveling through California and Oregon after we had parted. My description of some of our encounters made him smile, while others made him wince. He asked about Riley, and I told him about her school and how proud I was of her and her upcoming valedictorian speech.

I tried to skim over my navy service, but he wasn't having any of it. His face grew grim while I filled him in on some of my experiences as a medic assigned to a marine battalion. He shook his head. "Fucking war! Theresa would have my ass if she heard me cuss like that, but Kennedy and Johnson really outdid themselves with that fuck-up. I hope Nixon really has a secret plan to get us out of there."

It didn't take much prompting on my part to get him talking about his life since we had parted ways.

"Well, I got half of my wish and was assigned to the motor pool after boot camp. But I wasn't assigned to an exotic paradise. I ended up at Fort Sill, Oklahoma. Nice place—if you don't mind lotsa bugs and humidity in the nineties. No ocean either, but I learned a lot working on those big diesels. They wanted me to re-up and offered me a big promotion, but I was homesick and anxious to return home. The good thing about Fort Sill was the complete lack of any nightlife beyond the bars. I was able to save a pretty good nest egg, which I used to start this business.

"The business was pretty touch and go for a couple of years, but after my reputation for quality at a good price got around, things turned around. Now, I've got six employees and a good backlog. I'm even teaching a couple of classes at the college, and I do a volunteer class at the high school for underprivileged kids.

"As soon as I got on my feet, Theresa and I married. She's the best thing that ever happened to me." He pulled a lollipop from his shirt pocket, unwrapped it, and stuck it in his mouth. "She even got me to quit smoking. Said she didn't want to end up being a thirty-year-old widow."

He pulled out his wallet and handed me a picture of a beautiful woman and four young children, one infant on her lap, two boys who looked to be around five, and a pretty girl of around three. He sat straight and puffed up. "These are our bambinos. The dark-haired boy is our first born. His name is Anthony Lucas. We named him after his grandpa and some waif that we knew. The other boy is Benjamin Alexander. We adopted him and his sister, that sweet young three-year-old, Grace Anne. Ever since our little soiree up the coast, I seem to have a thing for kids in need. The baby is our first girl, Mia Riley. Theresa's mom and your sister get the honors for that.

"After our induction, Red was sent to Germany as an MP. He fell in love with a fraulein. They married, and he decided to stay over there after his discharge. He's in security for some multinational corporation over there, and they have two little ones.

He got up and walked me through the shops. Each bay held an assortment of tools and was spotless. The pride glowed from his face as he pointed out different areas of specialty.

We wandered back to the office, and he continued talking about the gang, "Herb is a real success story. After the army gave us a battery of tests, it turns out his IQ is off the charts. They convinced him to extend his service in exchange for training in electronics. After his training, he was assigned to a Nike Radar site. The army fixed his teeth, too. But after his commitment, he went to work at Vandenberg Air Force Base down by Lompoc. He works at a radar site up on a mountain peak and tracks those big missiles they're launching down there. He snuck me onto the site for one of those launches, and it was pretty exciting, especially after the missile self-destructed."

We talked for a couple of hours, and then I got up to leave. Rick hugged me and shook my hand. "It may sound silly, but I cherish those memories. You and your sister brought a change in me—you made me stop thinking about myself."

I started the Mustang, and the Beatles' "All You Need Is Love" was playing on the radio. I fingered the brass ring in my pocket and drove away. My next stop was going to be tough.

CHAPTER 16

Love and Ferries, 1957

Such was life in the Golden Gate:
Gold dusted all we drank and ate,
And I was one of the children told,
"We all must eat our peck of gold."

—Robert Frost

RILEY AND MARY WERE SITTING at a table, gig-gling and munching on cookies. Roger was seated at a drafting table on the other side of the large room. Mary handed me a glass of sweet tea and three cookies. "Here you go, sweetheart. I made up the spare room for you and your sister. It's got a twin bed and a cot. I'm afraid your sister has already claimed the bed."

A wicked smile crossed Riley's face, and she giggled.

I was getting pretty tired, so I grunted, "Thank you, ma'am. We really appreciate your help. Is there anything we can do to earn our keep? We don't want to be a burden."

Roger spoke up from across the room, "I'm sure Riley can help Mary and Elsa in the 'Love Garden,' and I've already made a list of chores that you can help me with tomorrow. Elsa's and my dreams for this place result in a lot of work. But it's getting late, and I can see your eyes are getting heavy. How about we eat some dinner and then call it an evening? Mary, what's on the menu for tonight?"

Mary was already at the stove, stirring the ingredients in a large pot. The aroma of seafood filled the air. "Tonight, we're going to enjoy soup made from some of Elsa's garden vegetables. It's got potatoes, carrots, leeks, tomatoes, spinach, and celery. For an entree, I'm baking those brook trout that you caught in the creek. I breaded them and added some garlic and spices. Everything should be ready in about ten minutes. Riley, would you mind setting the table while Luke washes up?"

Mary's cooking was exceptional, and Riley and I both put away two helpings. The conversation was light, and thankfully, we all skirted the topic of our predicament. After dinner, Riley cleared the table while I washed the dishes.

While we sat around the fireplace and ate Mary's apple pie, Roger lit his meerschaum pipe and talked about their community. "This used to be a chicken ranch. Elsa and Isabel, along with Mary and I, bought this place in 1954. Some call us bohemians, while that journalist in San Francisco has coined the term 'beatnik.' It's strange how people try to categorize and pin a name on things they fear or don't understand."

Riley had fallen asleep with her head in Mary's lap, and I was fighting to stay awake. Roger's eye's twinkled. "I think we should call it a day. We've got lots to do tomorrow."

•———————•

The weak morning light woke me around six. Riley was snoring in the other bed, and I could hear activity coming from the front of the building. I got dressed and quietly headed out to find Mary softly humming and stirring a pot at the stove. I looked around, but Roger wasn't there.

Mary smiled and told me to have a seat, then brought me a glass of juice. "Good morning, Luke. How did you sleep? Would you care for some oatmeal and toast?"

I nodded. "Yes, please, but I don't want to be a bother. Is there anything I can do to help?"

Mary had a kind face, and when she chuckled, her laugh lines deepened and her face glowed. "My, aren't you just the perfect gentleman. Thank you for the offer, but everything is ready. All you need is a good appetite. I'm sure Roger will find some chores to keep you busy when he returns from town." She placed a bowl of steaming-hot porridge and a plate stacked with toasted bread in front of me, then sat down with a cup of coffee. Reaching over, she pushed a jar of homemade blackberry jam in front of me. "Roger filled me in on some of the details of your exodus. You two have had quite a time of it. It must be very hard to keep going—and pretty frightening. I'm not sure how you can continue. It worries me that you're on your own without anyone to look after you. Maybe you should just stay here until someone can find your father. I'm sure the authorities would help."

Roger walked in and listened to Mary as he filled his coffee cup and sat down. He looked at me expectantly, waiting for my answer.

I was scared, my mind immediately rushing to how we were going to get away from this remote area. "Thank you, ma'am, that's a very nice offer, but we can't do that. I'm pretty sure if you notify the authorities, they won't let us stay here. They have rules and checklists that they think are in our best interests but are really just processes meant to methodically take care of a problem without caring about Riley or me. They would place us into foster care and probably separate us. I knew some kids from school who were in foster care. Most of them said the caregivers were only in it for the money and didn't care about them. Plus, I don't think they would really try to find our dad. Once we're out of sight, the problem is solved in their minds."

Roger smiled and clapped his hands. "That's great, Luke. I'm happy to see you have a healthy distrust of authorities at your young age. It gives me hope for the future of humanity. Mary, I think the best way to help these young people is to aid them on their journey. I'm hoping that we'll find a kind soul who might get them all, or part, of the way to Seattle. In the meantime, I could use a little help with our many projects. Sometimes I need an extra hand."

Riley wandered in then with her hair poking everywhere and sleep still resident in the corners of her eyes. She smiled and murmured, "I'm kinda hungry. Is there anything to eat?"

I silently thanked my little sister for the great diversion away from a difficult subject.

Roger laughed, and Mary rushed her over to the table. She was soon spooning hot oatmeal into her mouth and chatting amiably with the woman. Roger got up and headed outside. I followed him into the morning sunlight.

As we walked up the hillside, Roger pointed at a small cottage. "That's Elsa's house. We wanted it to be a quiet living and working environment. We didn't set out to create a formal commune, so we just ended up being an 'unintentional community.' Because of our proximity to San Francisco, yet relative isolation, we're free to function as a breeding ground for countercultural exploration. We provide a peaceful setting for a myriad of artists, philosophers, and musicians. Living so close to nature inspires their social and artistic energy."

We passed a large redwood water tank and began following a line of pipes headed up the hill. "I built that tank to provide a community water source. It's fed by a creek farther up. We need to reinforce the diversion dam and clean up some of the spillway."

Roger and I worked in the creek and spillway for a few hours. When he was satisfied that we had repaired the integrity of the water system he sat on a rock and lit a pipe. "You're a good worker, Luke. You don't mind getting your hands dirty." He pointed at the compound below us, "Many of those structures existed when we bought this place. My vision is to reuse salvaged materials to create a living environment that's a part of nature rather than competing with it. I studied Frank Lloyd Wright and Japanese architecture, and I hope my creations complement the twists and turns of all the living things around here."

He pointed with his pipe to a considerable craggy rock sticking out of the hillside among gnarled cypress trees. "That piece of granite is a perfect example of the unobtrusive impact that I hope my designs bring to this place. Alan Watts has dubbed it Cloud Hidden. Seems appropriate. Let's head down and see what Mary's prepared for lunch."

Mary, along with Riley, had put together a pot of chili that emitted a spicy aroma. Fresh lettuce, tomatoes, and other veggies made for a bright garden salad on the side. Under Mary's supervision, Riley had baked a score of cornbread muffins.

Maybe it was because of our physical activity, but lunch was a true delight. I wolfed down two bowls of the chili and ate six muffins slathered with butter and honey. I was ready for a nap, but Roger said we had more chores, so off we went.

We worked side by side all afternoon, altering a structure that Roger lovingly called the "Meditation Shack." It was somewhat ugly, with windows that looked like eyes popping out. We had just finished and were washing up at an outdoor sink when some guests arrived in an old Buick. Three men and a woman exited the car.

Roger told me we were finished for the day and went over to speak with them. The men were all dressed in dark clothing and sported scroungy beards. The woman had long stringy hair and was wearing leotards and a black sweater. After some discussion, he led them to one of the buildings, and they unloaded their luggage.

I wandered around the compound and finally found Elsa's "Love Garden." It was a remarkable creation, and its name truly reflected its character. Roses of all colors and shades provided the border. Rows of colorful vegetables were alive with their bounty. Fruit trees hugging the hillside created the backdrop.

I found Mary and Riles bent over a row of radishes, pulling weeds, giggling and gaily chatting without a care in the world. Mary's kindness and motherly instincts were just what Riley needed. I wondered if she and I would ever find that serenity in the future. I missed our mother and father. I couldn't do anything about our mother, but we needed to find our only family.

I helped with the weeds until the sunlight began to weaken behind the trees and cold fog rolled in. The three of us washed up and headed back to the barn.

Dinner consisted of a slowly baked ham and a navy bean soup. After we finished, Riley and I washed the dishes and sat around the fireplace while Roger softly played on his bongo drums. He noticed the harmonica sticking from my pocket and asked me to play something.

Embarrassed, I stuttered that I was just learning and not very good. He smiled and said it didn't matter, and that all music was good as long as it came from the heart. I struggled through "Amazing Grace." He sat back and picked up a saxophone and started to play along. He was really good, and his talent helped cover up my flubs. We played for a spell while Roger offered me pointers and helped me reach some of the more difficult notes.

The fire was burning down, and Riley's eyes were drooping when the two of us headed for bed.

That night, I had what I initially thought was a weird dream. There was loud shouting and singing coming from outside. When I looked out the window, I spied one of the men who had arrived the day before, jumping up and down on the hood of their car and chanting in some strange language. The woman, who had arrived with him, was dancing around the car and she was buck naked. She had her arms in the air, and her small breasts were kinda bouncing around—and not in an attractive manner. I rubbed my eyes, shrugged, and went back to sleep.

The chiding from that scrub jay woke me at first light. I dressed and wandered outside, where the jay screamed at me and flew off. No one else was around, so I walked over to the newcomers' car, and sure enough, the hood was full of concave dents. Strange people.

I wandered around the compound for a while and then went back to Roger's place. Mary was puttering around the kitchen and greeted me with a huge smile. Roger was drying his hands as he came out of the bathroom. He grabbed a cup of coffee and sat at the table, indicating to me that he wanted to talk. "I don't know if that ruckus woke you two last night, but it was quite a scene. Seems our new visitors use drugs to expand their minds and help them with their creativity. Last night, they dropped some acid to help them along on their journey to full awareness. By acid, I mean LSD, which is a hallucinogen. Mary and I aren't into that scene, but many of our visitors are. The beauty of Druid Heights is that one can express oneself as one sees fit. There is no judgment."

Mary sat down next to me, ruffled my hair and continued, "That said, when people are under the influence of these drugs, they can get crazy and do dangerous things, not to mention excessive or unnatural sexual indulgence. Anyway, Roger and I have had second thoughts, and this isn't the best environment for you and your sister."

I slowly got up. "I understand. I saw a little of that weirdness last night. I'll get Riley and we'll be on our way. We really appreciate your help and don't want to be a concern for you."

I had started for Riley's bedroom when Roger spoke up. "Hold on, Luke. We're not abandoning you just yet, we're just going to relocate you to a safer spot while we're arranging your transportation. We'll take you there and get you set up after breakfast."

Half an hour later, Riley drifted into the room, and we sat down to another scrumptious breakfast of eggs, bacon, and thick waffles containing morsels of blueberries. Riley outdid herself with three waffles, but my mind was churning. I ate enough to not hurt Mary's feeling without really tasting it.

We washed the dishes and cleaned up the kitchen, then packed our clothes. Mary handed us a paper bag filled with sandwiches and fruit. She hugged both of us, then Roger led us to an old GMC pickup, and off we went down the clay two-track. Backtracking to the highway, we turned left, and after a couple of miles we dropped down into the town of Sausalito.

The bay was sparkling with thousands of tiny diamonds in the morning sun, and sailboats scooted along ahead of the slight breeze. Boutiques and coffee shops lined the opposite side of the street below large houses clinging to the hillside above. A large chandlery dominated one corner, and three long piers thrust themselves into the bay. Hundreds of colorful houseboats of all sizes crowded along these wharfs, interrupted only by an occasional yacht.

Roger pointed at them. "The navy built those as shipyards for the fleet during the war. When the war ended, the navy abandoned them. Artists and free spirits moved in, and now there are three houseboat communities along and adjacent to Sausalito's shore."

He scowled and pointed up the hill. "The rich people living in their big houses up there don't like looking down on the riffraff crowding the waterfront, and they're always trying to rid the city of what they feel is a detriment to the ascetics. However, most of the houseboat residents were here before those homes were built."

We pulled up to the curb in a cul-de-sac and parked. Roger told us to grab our stuff, and we headed down a wharf crowded with multicolored houseboats. Some appeared to be made from barges, while others looked like Chinese junks. Still others seemed to be resting on logs lashed together. Flowerpots and other containers full of blooming flowers decorated the walkway.

We stopped in front of a dilapidated ferry. "Vallejo" was visible in faded paint on its stern. It was surrounded by a nice wooden fence, and a ramp led up to its deck. Roger opened the gate and led us onto the derelict. "Our friend Jean owns this. I'm helping with the renovation and design. He's touring in Europe, but he lets visitors use the boat in his absence. You two should be okay here."

He led us inside, up one deck and into a oversized bedroom adorned with statuary and artwork. After we put our pack away, we followed him on a tour of the old boat. Some rooms had been remodeled and looked quite nice, while others were under construction and some were in complete disrepair.

We walked outside and down the ramp, heading back down the wharf. Roger wanted to familiarize us with the neighborhood, so we followed him through the surrounding streets. Light-industry and shops associated with marine activities crowded the buildings. We came to another pier, only this one seemed to be dedicated to charter boats and trawlers. At the end of the pier was a fish-cleaning station.

Roger pointed it out and commented, "If you want to earn some money, you can pick up some easy cash cleaning the fish that the charter boat clients bring in. It's kinda funny that people want to 'catch their dinner' but don't want to be bothered with or dirtied by preparing it."

We were walking back to our new shelter when I first saw her. She looked to be about my age and was holding hands with a man who was probably her father, and she was staring directly at me. Something bounced inside my chest, and I smiled shyly.

When she returned the smile, my chest got a little tighter. She had dark brown hair cut into a pixie, and brown eyes that crinkled at the edges when she smiled. She stood about my height and was wearing white capris and a summery light blue blouse. I couldn't take my eyes off of her, but her father said something to her, and they turned and walked away. Halfway up the block, she turned and gave me a small wave.

Riley pulled at my arm and laughed. "She's pretty. I think you just fell in love."

I stared at where she had stood and grumbled, "She sure is! I'll never see her again though, so what difference does it make?"

We walked Roger back to the truck, and he handed me a dollar. "This is for helping me yesterday. It's not much, but we don't have a lot of cash. Mary and I will drop in to check on you, and we'll be working on finding you some transportation."

He started the truck and drove away. Riley and I started back to the old ferry. People on the boats smiled and greeted us as we walked on those rough boards out into the bay. My mind was swirling. I wondered about the girl.

When we got back, we continued our exploration of the ferry. We went to the top deck and looked out at the bay and Angel Island in the distance. At the end of our wharf, a float plane bobbed gently in the waves. Many of the rooms on the next deck were unfinished or partially so, but when we opened one door, we happened upon an extensive library. Shelves lined the interior walls, while sunlight illuminated large leather chairs gathered around an oak table.

Riley examined the books and beamed. "I think I'll like it here. There's lots of interesting reading." She pulled one out from the bookcase and curled up in one of the big chairs. "I'm starting with *Peter Pan*. "Then it's *Swiss Family Robinson*! Maybe I can get some ideas for our survival."

I left her there, happy and cozy, fully engrossed in the story in front of her. Out on the end of the dock, I found a place to hang my feet over the side. As I looked back toward the town, the hillside seemed alive, cars scooting between homes on narrow, winding streets. The bay was a deep blue. I turned and watched sailboats with full sails gliding across its bright surface.

I was deep in thought about our predicament when she plopped down beside me. "Hi, you look lonely. Mind if I sit here?"

All my worries vanished, and my heart jumped to my throat. I had a hard time catching my breath, but I managed to blurt out, "Be my guest." Damn, if she wasn't the prettiest thing I had ever seen.

"I saw you up on the street. Is that girl your sister? Do you guys live here? She sighed and took a breath. "I'm sorry, I was rambling. I'll slow down. My name is Margaret, but my mother is the only one who calls me that. Most people call me Maggie. What's yours?"

I let out the breath I'd been holding and laughed. "It's okay. My name is Lucas, and most people call me Luke. My sister's name is Riley or Riles. We don't live here— we're just staying on that old ferry for a while until we can get to Seattle."

"Seattle!" she gasped. "How exciting! That's a long way. Is your family moving there, or are you going for a visit? I hope you don't leave too soon—I just met you."

I looked into her big, welcoming eyes and began to tell our story. I felt relieved to be sharing my troubles with someone my age and who seemed to honestly care.

I started with my dad losing his job, then continued our sordid tale, from Helen's duplicity and Walt's meanness to riding the rails. I smiled when I told her about all the kind people who had helped us along the way. I thought about skipping the fact that I was a murderer, but there was no way I could ever deceive her, even if it meant she thought I was a monster and ran for her life.

She didn't run away, though. Instead, she picked up my hand and held it in hers, sending little chills through my body. "Oh, Luke, how horrible. You must be so scared, yet you don't show it. You're taking care of Riley and acting so brave."

I'm not ashamed to admit, I melted. Feeling her hand squeeze mine filled me with a strange emotion. Beyond the physical stirrings that she evoked, it felt good to have someone my age to talk to without the inhibitions that seemed to hold back most adults.

We talked for over two hours, still holding hands. She had none of those adult restraints, and she unabashedly shared her story with me. Her father was a lobbyist for a giant corporation that had business all over the world. He commuted to Sacramento and worked with the governor and assembly. She said that they might move to Washington, D.C., for a while because he had been selected for one of the president's councils.

Her mother and father came from old money. "Mother is a devout member of the Westport Historical Society, tracing her ancestors all the way back to the Mayflower. She was the chairperson of a committee that reviewed school textbooks for any slant toward socialism. Daddy is a true blueblood—grew up on Beacon Hill in Boston, attended Yale and Harvard Law. He avoided service during the war, yet he's a hawk in regard to national defense and protecting America from the perils of communism."

Apparently, both were dedicated "Hill People" and looked with disdain down at the houseboats that sullied "their" community with bohemian ways. They had forbidden Maggie to hang around the houseboats, but she would sneak away whenever she could. She found the environment vibrant and exciting.

She was an only child and attended a private school. Her dream was to get her teacher's credentials and to help underprivileged children find a way out of poverty.

When I described my family and how much I missed my dad, Maggie squeezed my hand and held it to her cheek. I told her about Riley and how smart she was and how I wanted to attend college and enter a field where I could help people.

We walked back to the ferry and found Riley still curled up in the chair, sound asleep. *Peter Pan* lay open on her lap, and it looked like she was halfway through already. While we quietly talked, Riley woke and rubbed hers eyes with the heels of her hands. I introduced Maggie while she yawned and stretched. She and Maggie hit it off right away and began communicating in that girl-talk that men will never understand. Watching them, I was filled with tranquility—it seemed like Maggie was filling a mother/big-sister role for Riley that neither my dad nor I could ever approximate.

Maggie looked at her watch and shrieked, "Uh-oh, look at the time. I was supposed to be home fifteen minutes ago. Luke, would you mind walking me out to the street?"

Mind? I would have dragged myself across broken glass just for the privilege of spending another minute with her. I hid my exuberance though and quipped, "It'll be my pleasure."

Maggie and Riley hugged and air-kissed before we walked down the ramp and out toward the street. Maggie took my hand as we walked, and nothing ever felt more natural. When we got to the street, she turned and hugged me before dashing up the hill. She called over her shoulder, "I'll see you tomorrow, as soon as piano practice is over."

As she slipped out of sight, I turned and walked down the wharf, but I don't think my feet ever touched the ground.

●───────●

The three of us were inseparable over the next few days. We bought bread and bologna and peanut butter for our meals, augmented by Hostess Twinkies and chocolate chip cookies. A little café on the beach provided somewhat healthier sustenance. I used Walt's old fillet knife to earn some money at the fish-cleaning station. Maggie and Riley would keep me company until they got bored and headed back to the ferry to read and play chess on the board they'd found in the parlor.

When I finished, I would join them. Riley was savvy enough to give us some time alone, and Maggie and I would wander along the docks and through town. We never tired of just being together. Sometimes we would sit on the end of the pier and talk about the future. Other times we were happy to just look out at the bay and daydream. Like the song said, we were "happy just bein' around together."

But there was an undercurrent of sadness. I was torn between the need to continue our journey and never wanting to leave Maggie. I could tell she felt it too by the sad look that came into her eyes when she thought I wasn't looking.

The last day I saw her started off the same as the others. Mary had come to check on us in the morning and to bring us some fried chicken and potato salad. Maggie showed up shortly after, and the three of us played around the docks for a while. I left the two of them at the ferry and went to clean fish from the party boat that had just pulled in. When I returned, Riley had fallen asleep in one of the big chairs, so the two of us went to the upper deck and soaked up the afternoon sun.

I must have fallen asleep and woken to Maggie gently shaking me. "Hey, buddy, I've got to get back. Wanna walk me home?"

We headed up the hill for a while, and she stopped at the corner and pointed toward the middle of the block. "I live right down there. Since I'm late, I don't want Mother to see you and think you're the cause. She already gets upset because I hang out at the docks as it is. She's such a snob."

I was a little hurt, and I think it showed. "Okay," was all I said. My voice came across as chilly, and it betrayed my resentment. I felt like she was embarrassed to be seen with me, some poor kid living on a houseboat. I got my back up and turned to walk away.

Maggie squealed and grabbed my arm. "Please don't be upset. It has nothing to do with you and me. I want to spend more time with you, but I can't control my mother. If she gets into a tizzy, she'll cut me off and ground me. Please!"

Her brown eyes were filling with tears, and I just melted. I turned toward her and grabbed her hand. "Don't be sad. It's alright. Your world is so much different than Riley's and mine. I just feel like an outcast and maybe I don't belong."

She pulled at my hand. "Oh, you silly boy. Can't you feel it, Lucas O'Connor?"

I knew exactly what I was feeling. I was feeling that this lovely creature had entered my life and I never wanted her to leave. My feelings were as strong as they'd ever been, yet I was afraid to express them for fear that she was talking about something else entirely and would laugh at me. Instead, I mumbled, "What is it you feel?"

I shouldn't have been surprised that Maggie had no such inhibitions. She put both hands on my shoulders and turned me toward her. "Luke, this may sound crazy, but ever since the first time I saw you, I knew we were meant to be together. I get such a warm feeling inside of me whenever I even think about you. Please don't laugh at me, but I think that I love you." She was smiling, but her eyes were moist and showed fear.

I was dumbstruck—for a while, I couldn't find my voice. She must have taken this for rejection, because the tears began to flow down her cheeks and she hung her head. "It's okay," she mumbled. "I know that things like this don't happen, and it's silly of me to think that you would feel the same way."

Seeing her cry broke my heart, and my words came rushing out. "Oh jeez, Maggie, please don't cry! I just didn't think that you felt the same, so I was afraid to say it. I have such strong feelings for you, and I'm absolutely sure that I love you, too. I never want to be without you and the joy you bring me."

Now she was crying full out. She pulled me to her and kissed me—my first kiss, and I never wanted to kiss anyone else.

"You and I are meant to be together. It doesn't matter what people like my mother and dad think. They're stodgy old dinosaurs, but they can't keep us apart forever. You're going to be leaving soon to find your dad. And my dad's relocation to Washington is going to happen at any time. Promise me that no matter what happens, we'll find each other and live our lives together."

I was never more sure of anything in my life, but the kiss sealed it. This girl brought a whole new dimension to my existence, and I said so. "Maggie, I will find you no matter where you are."

I reached into my pocket and pulled the brass rings from Santa Cruz and handed one to her, "This isn't much, but I want you to keep this. Whenever you get discouraged, just know that I have this other one and I won't rest until our rings are together."

Maggie pulled me into a hug and kissed me again. "This is now my most cherished possession. I'll keep it with me, always." She turned and ran toward her house, yelling over her shoulder, "I'll see you tomorrow."

I felt like I was literally floating as I headed back to the ferry. My mind was swirling with thoughts of Maggie and her kisses. I couldn't wait for tomorrow and spending time with her.

Life has a way of interfering with your plans.

———•———•———

The next morning, I headed down to the fish-cleaning station to earn a little more money. Business was good, and I kept busy for over two hours. I kept looking over my shoulder, expecting to find Maggie, but she never showed. I didn't think much of it. She had a whole life in that big house that I didn't know anything about. I just thought she had forgotten about piano practice or some such. After gutting and cleaning my last fish, I headed back to the ferry, four dollars richer.

I was walking up the ramp when a woman's voice called out, "Are you Mister Luke?" only it came out as "Meester Yuke."

A young Hispanic women walked up to me and held out an envelope. "I am the housekeeper at Maggie's home. She asked me to give this to you." She turned to leave, then paused and turned back. "She's very sad."

She left before I could think of anything to say in response.

I looked at the envelope in my hand and held it as if it carried the plague. My name was scrawled across the front in shaky handwriting. I tore it open—the writing inside was just as shaky and smeared in places from teardrops. My eyes were blurry, and I had a hard time focusing on the words.

My Dear Luke,

The absolute worst has happened. One of Mother's friends saw us downtown and reported it to her. She was livid, grounded me, and forbade me to see you again. She is such a horrible person.

I would have snuck out this morning, but we got word from Daddy that his assignment to Washington had been approved. We're leaving today for Sacramento and flying from there.

Oh, Luke! I'm devastated. If I could, I would run away with you and Riley, but Mother has this place locked down like a prison.

Please don't forget me. I will always love you and will be waiting for you to find me just like you promised. You'll always be in my heart. You and I are meant to be together!

Love Forever,

Maggie

P. S. Give my love to my little sister, Riley. Please write when you find your dad.

Before I'd even finished reading it, I was letting out a long, incoherent shout. I dropped the letter and sprinted down the pier and up the hill. As I approached her house, a black limousine was pulling away from the curb. I could see Maggie peering out the back window, waving the brass ring.

I pulled up and collapsed to the curb, where I began sobbing. I had no idea how long I sat there, but the tears kept flowing. I just couldn't stop them. Pedestrians crossed to the other side of the street to avoid me. One kind old man stopped and asked if he could help. I managed to thank him and just shook my head.

Riley appeared and sat beside me, the letter clasped in her hand. "My poor, poor Luke."

She put her arm around me and slowly rocked me back and forth. "My poor brother." It was time for a role-reversal—little sister was taking care of big brother for a while.

CHAPTER 17

Sausalito, 1969

The fountains mingle with the river
And the rivers with the ocean,
The winds of heaven mix forever
With a sweet emotion;
Nothing in the world is single;
All things by a law divine
In one spirit meet and mingle.
Why not I with thine?—

—Percy Bysshe Shelley

THE "ARTICHOKE CAPITAL OF THE World" appeared in my windshield, and a roadside stand hawking a multitude of vegetables including "Five Large Artichokes for a Dollar" lured me to the side of the road. I bought ten of the big thistles and a sack of apricots before heading back north.

Huge instrumentation parabolas forty and eighty feet across dominated the bluff at Pillar Point in Half Moon Bay. I slowed down and watched surfers catch massive waves at Maverick's. At one time, I had thought they were extremely brave, but since then I'd learned what true bravery consisted of. Thoughts of Johnny and Huey and the others filtered in.

The Mustang purred as I passed through Pacifica and up and over the hill into Daly City and then the city of San Francisco loomed in front of me. The fog was slowly burning off as I drove in circles and finally found parking space in Chinatown. The food at Hung Luk's was just as spicy and delicious as years before. Still wanting to enjoy the whole experience, I washed down the Dim Sum with Tsingtao beer this time instead of tea.

My belly was pretty full, so I decided to walk it off by leaving the car and trekking over to City Lights. I browsed through the shelves and finally decided on *Stanyan Street and Other Sorrows* by Rod McKuen as Riley's graduation present.

Back in the car, I cruised over to Fisherman's Wharf. Luck was with me, and I found a parking spot right away and headed to Ghirardelli's. I knew I was dragging my feet, but I just couldn't face the answer yet, so I browsed the aromatic aisles and picked out sweets for everyone at home.

I was contemplating a visit to the zoo to see if they still fed the big cats at two o'clock, but finally decided that enough was enough. I needed to face the future. I had one more stop to make first, though, so I headed across the Golden Gate. After the bridge, I turned west and found the clay two-track heading into the woods.

Mary was walking back to the barn when I pulled into the compound. She shaded her eyes and squinted at me when I got out of the car. I said hello, but she didn't recognize me until I walked a little closer. Then a light went on, and she smiled that infectious smile of hers and let out a little laugh. "My, my, just look at you. You've grown into a man. Roger will be thrilled to see you. Come sit on the porch, and I'll fix you some tea. I want to hear everything about you and Riley."

I described our adventures after we had left them and settled down in Seattle. She delighted in my stories about Riley and her academic achievements. I avoided talking about myself much, but she wasn't falling for it. She reached over and ran her hand through my crew cut. "Not exactly a stylish hairdo. I guess you were in the military. Did you have to go to that awful place?"

I described my service with a broad brush. Telling her I had been a corpsman, I talked about the more innocuous tasks that I had to perform, like taking temperatures and giving shots.

She smiled, shook her head, and squeezed my hand. "Oh, Luke, you never were one to talk about yourself. Methinks there's a lot more to that story, but we'll just let it be. You're strong, and many people love you. You'll heal eventually."

Mary had just convinced me to try a slice of her freshly made apple pie when Roger wandered up. He smiled at her and then gave me the once-over. He was about to ask who I was when recognition came to him and he let out a cheery laugh. "Well, if it isn't our wayward child. Goodness, Luke, I barely recognize you now that I have to look up to see your eyes. And that haircut—I guess you've had some experiences since you left here." He grabbed my hand in both of his and gripped it like a vise. His hair was dusted with gray and had completely abandoned the front of his head.

We chatted while I ate the pie, going over the same questions as Mary. After the pie and some more talk about Riley and my dad, we wandered around the property.

Roger proudly showed off some of his handiwork. He pointed to a circular building near the rock that they had christened "Cloud Hidden" years before.

"That's Mandala House. We built it for Elsa's sister, but she's moved on." He walked a little farther and pointed to a large redwood barrel with pipes running into it. "That contraption is the darndest thing. Ed Stiles built it as a big soaking tub where people can immerse themselves. He's rigged up a gas heater and a pump to heat and circulate the water. I'm not sure why anyone would want to take a bath in front of God and everyone, but people are raving about it. It's quite a sight when the young flower children strip down and jump in.

He became quiet and looked at me with concern. "How was it over there?

I assured him that it wasn't as bad as the news made out, but he shook his head. "I can understand that you don't want to talk about it. We've had many visitors lately who were just as reticent. I can't claim to have experienced what they or you went through, but if you ever just want to talk about it, I'll be here."

As we walked around the property, Roger commented on the changes over the last few years. "This younger crowd are very different than the beatniks of yesterday. The beatniks were contemplative, where these hippies seem to be all about themselves. They're arrogant and rude, but that may be because they see the situation in a different light than their predecessors. The war is certainly an existential threat to them. That said, my observation is that most of them are in it for the good times."

Our route brought us back to the Mustang. Mary stepped out of the barn, handed me a sack full of cookies, and hugged me. Roger shook my hand with both of his.

"Good luck to you, Luke. I'm not a religious person, but if there is a God, may he watch over and bless you and your sister."

I drove through the cypress trees and looked in my rearview mirror to see those two kindly people, arm-in-arm and waving.

The clay road was leading me to a moment of truth, and wouldn't you know it—Van Morrison was singing "Brown Eyed Girl."

———————

I parked along the curb in the cul-de-sac and wandered out onto the wharf. The ferry was still there, and it looked like more improvements had been made to her. People were all about, watering their plants, washing down their boats, and otherwise just socializing. The Righteous Brothers' "Unchained Melody" floated over the water, and some of the crowd were joining the chorus, asking the same questions as me, it seemed.

I knew I was putting it off, but I was afraid of hearing the answers. I had written as soon as Riley and I had reached Seattle and then again once a month through my school years, and even for the first few months in Vietnam, but never received a reply. I gave up after that. Maybe, I was on a fool's mission. I knew it was more than curiosity that was driving me. The wounds that I had sustained in service had healed. Unfortunately, the ache I felt deep inside had never left. I needed closure.

And so, I began a long walk up the hill. I turned left and sat on the curb opposite her house, just staring. I wondered if the stains on the street below my knees still contained remnants of my tears from so long ago.

I never considered myself a coward, but my knees were shaking when I walked up to the front door. I could hear the stereo within playing Patsy Cline's "Crazy." Maybe that was what I was. I sucked in my breath and rang the bell.

Voices grew louder on the other side, and I was ready to bolt when that same Hispanic lady, a little older but just as pretty, answered the door. "May I help you?" she asked in that wonderful accent.

When I asked for Maggie, she shook her head. "I'm sorry, *senor*, but she is busy. Maybe you call next time." She started to close the door.

Well, I knew that there wouldn't be a next time. I had summoned up all the courage left in me. I reached into my pocket and blurted, "Wait! Perhaps you could give her this." I handed her my brass ring.

She looked at the ring, and a glimmer of recognition crossed her eyes. Her face lit up with a huge smile, and she tittered, "Oh, *si*! *Bien*! You wait here." She threw up her hands and ran down the hall. "Meese Maggie! Meese Maggie!"

An answer came from a room in the back. "What is it, Maria?

I heard them talking, and then a loud shriek. "Oh my God! Yes! Yes! Yes!" She came running up the hallway, arms spread, and literally threw herself into my arms, throwing me back against the door.

She kissed me hard on the lips and then held me at arm's length, "Oh, Luke, I knew you'd find me! I never stopped believing." Tears streamed down her face. "Where have you been? Why didn't you write? Oh, never mind, you're here now." Panic crossed her face. "Oh dear, I'm babbling and being presumptuous. Please say you're here because you want to be with me and not just here out of curiosity." Now the tears really started flowing.

I took in the sight of her. She was a woman now, even more beautiful than when she left. Her hair was pulled into a ponytail, and she wore jeans and a sweater that showed off her figure. The brass ring hung around her neck on a leather cord. Her big brown eyes were shiny with tears.

I brushed them away from her cheek. "Maggie, I never stopped wanting to be with you. I loved you the first day I saw you, and I'll never stop. I've been miserable since you left." This time, when she came into my arms, we melted together. The kiss was long, deep, and passionate. Tears of joy ran down my face, and a weight lifted from my soul.

Maria had stayed discretely in the background, but now she cleared her throat. "Meese Maggie, I go home now. I think you'll be okay." She hugged Maggie and squeezed my arm, "You take good care of her. She happy now."

———•———

Maggie pulled me down the hallway, and we sat on a couch facing a huge picture window that framed the bay in all its beauty. However, I didn't appreciate the view. My eyes were locked on to Maggie as we cuddled, and she told me everything that had happened to her since we parted.

She fingered the ring on the leather strap. "Mother was such a bitch. She sequestered me in this house and wouldn't let me leave to tell you goodbye. Then, we rushed off to Washington, and I kept waiting to hear from you. I know the mail was being forwarded because I received letters from here. Why didn't you write, Luke? I was so hurt."

I held her hand and looked directly into her eyes. "I wrote as soon as we reached Seattle. In fact, I wrote for years, but I never received an answer. After that, I just tried to bury my feelings and forget about you, but I carried my pain all this time."

Maggie pulled me to her. "Mother must have intercepted your letters. At least, that's what I've hoped happened. I knew deep in my heart that you loved me and we were meant to be together. I never believed otherwise, so I waited where I knew you would look."

She had spent the last twelve years back east and attended all the right prep schools in Georgetown, then Wellesley College in Massachusetts, where she'd earned her degree and teaching credentials. As soon as she graduated, she moved back to the Sausalito house and worked as a substitute teacher in Corte Madera.

Her mother and father were firmly entrenched in Washington life and would probably never leave the East Coast again. Mother reveled in the social life, and Daddy was a power broker on K Street. He served on some of the president's panels and threw his weight around whenever he could.

The conversation shifted to me, and I described our life in Seattle. My dad had continued to work at Boeing, becoming one of their master machinists. He was their go-to guy whenever they had a problem. Both Riley and I had attended parochial schools all the way through high school. After graduation, I'd taken a few night classes while I worked at a grocery store and saved money for Riley's college tuition. We knew she was exceptionally bright and wanted to make sure she could attend a college of her choice, even if it was an expensive private school. Scholarships helped, but the costs of tuition, books, and boarding would have been prohibitive on our income. We were delighted when she chose Gonzaga, where she'd excelled and would soon graduate *cum laude* from their engineering department.

After I received my draft notice, I enlisted in the navy and was fortunate enough to be accepted to corpsman training. Eventually, I ended up in Southeast Asia, assigned to a marine unit. I continued to send money home to help with Riley's expenses. Now that she was graduating, it was my turn to pursue a degree. I told Maggie my aspirations in the medical field, and she pulled me to her as I described my desire to help people.

Our snuggling was turning into heavy petting, and our hands explored as much of each other as our clothes would allow. Maggie smiled demurely and whispered, "I have a confession to make. I've never been with a man. I wanted to save myself for you."

I laughed. "That makes two of us. I attended an all-boys high school, so none of my friends knew that I was celibate. The ribbing would have been merciless. I just knew that saving myself for you was the right thing to do."

She stood up and took my hand. "Come with me. I may not know what I'm doing, but I know I want you right now." Then she pulled me toward the bedroom.

Our first attempt may have been clumsy and amateurish, but it was absolutely wonderful. We started off shyly, averting our eyes while we began to undress, but the heat of our desire took over, and some articles of clothing would never be the same.

We laughed and touched and kissed and pulled at each other. Finally, we could enjoy the whole of each other, and when we finally climaxed, all of our past pains melted and slipped away.

The second go-around was just as good, only different. We took our time, exploring and testing and looking for ways to delight each other while we slowly approached the summit.

I woke entangled in Maggie's arms and legs and watched her slow breaths. I was filled with wonder at how blessed I was to be loved by this beautiful woman. I knew that I wanted to spend the rest of my life with her.

She stirred and opened one eye, a huge smile dominating her face. "Mmmmm! That was yummy, even better than I imagined." A frown began to darken her face. "Oh dear, was I okay for you? Why do you look so serious?"

I pulled her to me and kissed her, then whispered, "It was amazing. My dreams of this day didn't even come close to how wonderful it is. And you were perfect." I got down on the floor and held her hand. "I want you to be my wife so we can have a perfect life together. Maggie, would you consider marrying me? I don't just want a girlfriend—I want a partner."

Pulling my face to hers, she purred, "Great minds think alike. Before I fell asleep, I said a little prayer that you would ask me." She giggled. "I don't want to wait! I want to ensnare you before you get bored with me. And I think the sooner, the better. You go make coffee, and I'm going to make some phone calls." She reached for the phone as I shook my head, put on my boxers, and left to find my way around her kitchen.

The Mr. Coffee had just finished percolating when she walked into the kitchen. "I always thought my parent's snobbery was appalling, and I still do, but there are advantages to having friends in high places. You need to get dressed. We've got an appointment at the courthouse. I'll explain on the way."

Twenty minutes later, we were in the Mustang and crossing the Golden Gate Bridge. Maggie sat next to me, squeezing my arm. "I only have two close friends in the area. Suzie and I attended Wellesley together—she was prelaw, and now she clerks for a superior court judge here in the city. The judge is single and has a crush on her, so after I explained the situation to her, she used her womanly wiles to get us a marriage license, predated and everything. Pull over here and I'll be right back."

She started up the steps to the courthouse, then paused and ran back to the driver's side, "By the way, I love this car. What are you going to drive?" She kissed me and disappeared into the building. Ten minutes later, she was back, clutching a sheaf of papers in her hand. "Okay, big boy, now to North Beach.

In between giving me directions, she explained, "My other friend is Timothy Byrne. He's a priest at Saints Peter and Paul Cathedral. I met him back east when he was attending the seminary. He helped me through a rough spot when I was really missing you, and we've been friends ever since. You'll really like him."

•━━━━━•

Father Byrne had bright red hair and stood six feet, six inches tall in his stocking feet, and he was one of the gentlest men I've ever met. Maggie was right—I did like him. We entered the church through a side door, and after hugging Maggie, he enveloped my hand in a huge paw. "So this is the man who holds Maggie's undying attention. I have heard nothing but stories about you and your sister's exploits since we became friends. It looks like you made it through your odyssey alright. Welcome, young man."

He pulled me into a hug and chuckled. "We're going to be cutting a few corners here, but if there's anything I know, it's that you two belong together." He ushered us into a side chapel adorned with statues of Jesus and Mary. "The choir is practicing, so we'll have a little background music." Then he sighed. "It seems we forgot something in our haste—witnesses. Wait here."

Five minutes later, he returned with two nuns. They smiled and stood behind us while Father Tim performed one of the shortest marriage ceremonies ever. When he got to the ring part, I started to pull my high school ring off my finger to use as a temporary solution, but Maggie stopped me, pulling the brass merry-go-round ring from around her neck. "Luke, this ring is all I'll ever need. I've been married to you in my heart since you gave it to me."

The rings were an inch and half in diameter and too big for our fingers, but they meant much more than the finest Tiffany's creations.

I removed the other ring from my pocket. Father Tim blessed them, and just like that, I was kissing the bride. The nuns tittered and laughed, giving us both hugs before signing the certificate and leaving.

Father Tim walked us to the car. I handed him two fifties for the poor, and we hopped in the car.

As we pulled away from the curb, Maggie purred, "Let's hurry home so I can pack. I can't wait to see my little sister. While we're on the road, you can tell me about the rest of your trip to Seattle. I especially want to hear about that scar on your forehead."

The choir was belting out, "Alleluia, alleluia!"

CHAPTER 18

On a Wing and a Prayer, 1957

*When once you have tasted flight, you will forever walk
the earth with your eyes turned skyward, for there you
have been and there you will always long to return.*

—Leonardo Da Vinci

R ILEY WALKED ME BACK TO the ferry. She sat me
in the library and heated some hot cocoa. After she
put the cup in my hand, she enveloped me in her arms and
let me cry. Soon, the tears were replaced by anger, and I
released a string of expletives that would have shocked
even the saltiest marine. I used words whose meaning I
didn't even know.

I moped around the docks all day. Riley tried to cheer
me up, but I was too far gone, and she finally decided to
let me work it out for myself.

That was one of the longest nights of my life, tossing
and turning for hours. Every time I would start to doze
off, thoughts of Maggie would shake me awake. I finally
left my bed and went out to the end of the dock, where
Maggie and I had held our first conversation. I sat down
and let the soft lapping of the waves calm me.

Dawn was breaking over the hills to the southeast, and darkness turned to lighter shades of gray when I finally worked it all out. I knew how I felt about Maggie, and I was pretty sure I knew how she felt about me. I made a promise to myself that we would one day meet again and rekindle our relationship. Until then, I had to take care of Riley and find our dad.

The sun had breached the hills and was warming the chill in my bones when Roger walked up and sat down beside me. Rather than pry, he put his arm around my shoulders and silently sat there. After a while, he sighed, "You probably don't think anyone my age can remember that far back, but I remember being your age, and I'm really glad that I'm not anymore. It seems like you have no control of your own destiny. Despite that, I promise you things will get better. It may take a while, but you'll grow out of this situation even stronger."

He stood up and smiled. "How about I treat you and your sister to breakfast at that café on the corner? I have some news for the two of you."

The café was busy, but we found an open table, and after the waitress took our order, Roger began, "It's been impossible to find anyone who's going all the way to Seattle. That said, I have found someone who's willing to take you as far as Fort Bragg in Northern California. That will get you another couple hundred miles toward your goal. It's the best that I can come up with, so far. I'll keep trying, but…"

I smiled at Roger and put my hand on his arm. "Sounds good to us. We want to keep moving or we'll lose our momentum. The longer we stay in one place, the higher the risk that someone will get suspicious about two kids running around without an adult. When do we leave?"

Roger let out a laugh. "You're a tough kid, Luke. When I found you this morning, I thought sure you were going to jump into the bay and drown yourself. Now, you're focused on your goal." He pointed to the end of the dock. "See that seaplane? Sam provides charter flights to sportsmen and tourists. He's leaving in the morning to pick up a couple of fly fishermen at Fort Bragg. He'll let you hitch a ride, no questions asked.

Riley started bouncing up and down in her seat. "Oh goody, I've never flown in a plane before. I call shotgun!" She reached for my plate. "Are you through, Luke? You didn't eat much, but if you're finished I'll eat it. I'm starving."

I smiled as she chattered on about flying and the book she was reading and how much she'd miss Roger and Mary and ten other subjects without seeming to catch a breath. She was unperturbed by our situation, but not blissfully so. She had comforted me during my crisis, and I wasn't going to let her down.

•———————•

The next morning, Roger walked us out to a Cessna 180 at the end of the wharf, where Sam was waiting. He was quite the colorful character. He stood about five feet, three inches tall, with bushy red hair and a mustache to match. His bomber jacket was festooned with a half-dozen patches. His diminutive size was put to rest by his booming voice. "Top of the morning, Roger. Are these my cargo? Doesn't look like they'll put a strain on my weight limit!" He let out a hearty laugh and threw my pack into a storage area behind the seats.

"Looks like Frisco's security blanket is burning off and we'll have great weather for flying. Climb on in and make yourselves comfortable. We're going to have a slight headwind so I'm figuring about an hour and a half flying time. Might even do some sightseeing along the way."

I got into the back seat while Riley buckled up in the right front seat. Roger stuck his head in and handed me another dollar bill. When I protested, he pushed my hand away. "You earned a lot more than this. You two stay safe and let us know when you're home with your dad." He ruffled my hair and gave Riley a sideways hug.

Neither of us had flown before, and my stomach lurched with anticipation. Riley didn't seem concerned at all—she just peppered Sam with questions. Sam went through his preflight checks, turned and shook Roger's hand, then jumped into the pilot seat. The engine roared, and he shouted, "Here we go, kiddies! Off into the wild blue yonder. Cross your fingers."

The guy really filled me with confidence, so I said a quick prayer.

The Cessna seemed like it was stuck for a few seconds. Then it lurched forward. We bounced across the small waves of the bay, and in an instant, the bouncing stopped. We were airborne, skimming a few feet above the water. As we lifted off and headed toward Angel Island, Sam adjusted a few controls and smiled. "If you promise not to tell, we'll take the scenic Golden Gate route. The weather's perfect for it. The authorities don't like it, but it always puts a smile on my passenger's faces."

The right wing dipped, and we banked to where we were heading in the direction of the Golden Gate Bridge. It was glowing orange in the morning light as we approached. Sam laughed and yelled, "Hold on to your seats, kids. If it's low tide, we'll have just enough room." The guy was a laugh a minute.

Sam pushed the nose down, and we were soon skimming a few feet off the water. The bridge seemed to be only a few feet above the wings as we sailed under it. Sam let out a whoop, and Riley giggled. I tried to unclench my fingers from the seat where I had embedded them. It was certainly exciting, and once it was over, I even thought I enjoyed it.

After clearing the coast, Sam brought the plane around and pointed to a mountain dominating the hills of the peninsula. "That's Mount Tamalpais, highest peak in the area."

We flew in a northwesterly direction, and after a few minutes, Sam brought the plane lower, toward a large bay complemented by a crescent-shaped sand beach. "This is Drake's Bay. They believe Sir Francis Drake landed here on his circumnavigation of the world in the 1500s. Off to the left is Point Reyes. And it looks like we're in luck." He banked the plane and pointed at a large pod of gray whales swimming below. As we passed over, one of the large animals breached and crashed into the water on its side.

We continued on while Sam pointed out some of the highlights of the coast, including the Russian River, Timber Cove, and Salt Point. The weather was clear and the ocean a deep blue. Every once in a while, we'd pass over schools of sea lions and families of sea otters. Sea birds floated lazily on the currents below. We circled the Point Arena Lighthouse, and Sam dipped his wings to waving tourists on the ground.

He began our descent as we passed by Jug Handle Cove, swinging out to sea and then banking toward Fort Bragg. We bounced a few times as the plane made contact with the waves, and then we were motoring through the water into the Noyo River, and up to a wharf populated with small boats. Sam secured the plane and helped us onto the pier, where he handed me the pack. "Here you go, young fella. Roger wasn't real clear on why you needed to get here, but I suspect there's a story there. Hope you and your sister are okay." He shook my hand and turned toward his waiting customers.

Riley and I walked down the pier and into the town. It seemed like there were soldiers everywhere I looked. We had walked a while when I spied a hobo in an alley behind a café and asked him if there was a camp in the area. He nodded. "It's a couple blocks up that way. Take a left on Laurel Street, and the camp is in a thicket near the train station. Not many of us there, though, since there's only one train."

We found the camp under a trestle, and I went up to a hobo standing at his tent and asked if we could share the fire. He nodded and walked away. We found a spot and set up camp near an old fence, where we made a lean-to with the tarp. I scrounged around and gathered enough dry leaves to make a soft bed, then spread the blanket on top. When we had finished, I walked over to the fire and introduced myself to an old woman hunched over a pot. I probed her. "We're passing through on our way north. When do the northbound trains come by?"

She looked at me and shook her head. "Ain't no trains going north. There's just one train, and it heads east from here. Your best bet is to hang around at the front gate of the fort. There's an area there where the soldiers catch rides up the highway. Charitable folks pull over, and the soldiers pile in. Lotta pickup trucks where you could probably sneak aboard."

She told me the best time to hitch a ride was first thing in the morning. It was midafternoon, so we would have to wait another day. We went back into town and found a grocery store, where we bought a pack of hotdogs, plus chips and soda. After we roasted the hotdogs and shared them with the 'bos around the fire, Riley and I set about making ourselves useful by gathering firewood.

Sitting around the fire that evening, we shared stories with the others. When we mentioned Clete, one of the men spoke up. "My name's Hal. I know Clete. He's a good man. He sent word up the ole hobo telegraph and told us to be on the lookout for you. He says to take care of you. If you're headed north, I can take you to the hitchhiker pickup point and get you on your way."

The next morning, Hal led us past the front gate of the base to an empty lot where about a dozen soldiers were waiting. He wandered among them, making small talk. He wound his way back to us, pointed at two soldiers, and whispered, "Those two are headed north to Leggett. Stay close to them and try to catch the same ride as them. The road splits at Leggett, so when you get there, you're going to have to find another ride in the direction of Eureka." He pointed to a highway sign. "Just be sure to stay on the 101, north." He shook my hand and murmured, "I'll send word to Clete that you made it this far. Good luck to you." Then he walked away.

Cars and trucks came and went, picking up soldiers as they drove off. We sidled over close to the soldiers who were heading our way, and I heard them talking.

"I'm telling you, Joe," said one, "the steelhead are as long as your arm up there in the Eel River. They practically jump into your net. I promise, we'll have a blast." He held up a hand-drawn sign that read Leggett as a car and a pickup truck pulled over to the shoulder of the road. An old farmer waved to them from the cab of the truck. They took off running and jumped into the bed.

Riley and I followed, and I boosted her up just as the truck started to pull away. I ran hard after the truck and almost didn't think I'd catch it, but one of the soldiers grabbed my arm and swung me up and over the tailgate. He grinned. "There you go, partner."

He sat against the cab of the truck and soon fell asleep alongside his buddies.

Highway 1 followed the coast through the town of Westport, past sand dunes and steep cliffs falling into the ocean. It was cold and foggy, making the water a steely gray. After a while, we left the coast and began climbing into the coastal mountains.

The winding road made it difficult to remain in one spot, and eventually the soldiers woke up and began to banter. After trading friendly insults for a while, they turned their attention to us. We told them our story, and a slender black soldier got a sad look on his face. "I can understand how you feel," he drawled. "I joined the army to see some of the world, but I sure do miss my momma and daddy." He grinned at Riley. "Even my little sisters. I wish you luck and I'll say a prayer for you." He went on to tell us that there was another hitchhike spot north of town, where we should be able to catch a ride farther north.

After winding along through twists and turns and switchbacks, the truck passed over a wide river and entered the town of Leggett. We all jumped out when the truck slowed, then headed south on Highway 101. Waving goodbye, the soldiers headed into town, while Riley and I headed toward the hitchhike area.

An old Hispanic woman was sitting along the road at a makeshift table that was covered with baskets of fruits and vegetables. She watched us while we waited for a ride. Unfortunately, the traffic was almost nonexistent, and there wasn't anyone else waiting for a ride. I was reluctant to stick out my thumb for fear of attracting attention. As long as we were part of a group, we didn't stick out, but two kids on their own was taking a risk. I checked the map and was grateful to see that we'd made good progress, but we still had a long way to go.

After watching us for a while, the lady waved us over and in broken English asked us why we were there. She nodded and smiled as we explained our reasons for being there. Then she nodded some more, and I soon realized she'd fallen asleep. We started to walk away, but her head popped up and she exclaimed, "Not good today! Very little cars, and they no stop. You come back manana. Mateo, he come early morning and drop us here to sell las verduras and then he go to Eureka. He give you ride. Be here early, *si*?"

We thanked her, gave her a dime for two apples, and headed back to the river. We followed a path and went upstream to a secluded spot. Up on a narrow ledge, the river and erosion had carved a cave like depression into the hillside. The cave was hidden from view by a large creosote plant. We arranged the tarp and blanket and set about exploring along the bank of the river. The water was placid in spots where it could spread out, but it ran fast through narrow gorges.

We collected firewood along the way, piling it on the beach below our hidden cave. After poking around for a while, Riley was tired, so we climbed up and she lay down. I did a check of our supplies and found them sorely lacking. All we had left were the two apples, a jar of canned green beans, a few pieces of jerky, and a half-melted Hersey Bar. Riley's eyes were drooping, and she didn't want to join me on a trip to the store, so I cautioned her about leaving, then headed out.

I crossed through the trees on a path and headed along a two-lane into town. I spotted a sign for the mercantile and headed toward it. Just then, two police cars pulled up in front with their lights flashing red and blue. I ducked behind a large redwood tree and watched as the cops piled out and headed into the store. I heard shouting and a loud pop that could only have been a gunshot. A while later, an ambulance pulled up, and the EMTs ran into the building.

Two uniformed cops led a bearded man out. He had a bandage on his arm, and his hands were cuffed behind his back. He was fighting against them as they pushed him into one of the patrol cars. Then the EMTs exited, carrying a stretcher with a body strapped to it. A tarp covered the head, and I figured whoever it was had passed away. It reminded me of Walt. and I shivered.

The ambulance left without its lights flashing, confirming my suspicions. Two of the cops departed with the man in handcuffs, while the other two began stringing yellow tape around the front of the store. A crowd had gathered, and I wandered up and stood among them. One of the cops told us that the store would be closed until detectives could finish their investigation. Some of the crowd started grumbling, and the cop told us to go into South Leggett if we needed any supplies.

That pretty much cinched it for me. I'd already been gone longer than I should have been, and there was no way I could get to some other town. It looked like Riley was going to be hungry tonight, and she got pretty grumpy when she was hungry. Two apples and some jerky weren't enough keep her spirits up. I turned and walked toward the river.

•————————•

Riley was relatively upbeat about our lack of food. "That's okay, Luke. That winding ride made my stomach a little woozy. Let's go down to the river and clean up while it's still light."

We found a sandy beach where the water was slowly flowing and stripped to our underwear. The water was ice-cold, so we hurried our bath, then sat on the beach in the warm sun. I could see fish slowly wiggling by the shoreline, but every time I tried to catch one it would quickly skitter away. I finally gave up and watched the Flycatchers swooping down and skimming across the water to snatch the hovering butterflies and gnats. A lizard sat on a rock not far from us slowly doing pushups as it waited for its prey. Across the beach, an egret took slow steps through a marshy area, head down in search of frogs.

Bald Eagles drifted above us, constantly scanning the water for an unsuspecting fish. I watched as one eagle dove into the water in a clumsy manner. I thought it was hurt the way it was slowly moving its wings, trying to get airborne. It finally took off with a silvery mass between its talons. As soon as it got into the air, six crows began harassing it, yelling out their obnoxious "caws." The eagle defended itself valiantly, but the constant assaults by the crows got the best of it, and it finally dropped the fish about twenty yards from where we were sitting.

I jumped up and ran to where it had fallen. It was still flopping in its attempt to reach the river. The crows were cawing at me as I approached, and a few even swooped down, trying to scare me away. I waved them away and picked up a rock to quickly put the fish out of its misery with a smack to the head. It looked like a salmon, or maybe a steelhead trout, and seemed to be about two pounds. The crows were really unhappy with me and told me so in no uncertain terms, but we now had dinner. God was looking out for us.

Riley started the fire while I cleaned and gutted the fish. I pushed a stick lengthwise through the meat and placed it on two forked branches above the coals. Riley slowly rotated the fish while I heated the green beans. The grilling aroma filled the air. We sat on driftwood near the fire and satisfied our hunger with another fine meal.

Our tummies were happy, and I broke the Hershey bar in two and gave half to Riley. "Here's dessert. We're down to apples and jerky though after that, unless we can find somewhere to get food."

We sat around, basking in the warm afternoon sun as the fire burned down. The fish carcass was lying on the other side, and I had just gotten up when we heard a snuffling sound from the brush a few yards away.

Riley let out a small yelp when a bear came ambling out. It stood on its hind legs, sniffing at the air. I grabbed her hand, and we scrambled over to the ledge and up into the cave.

We watched while the bear devoured the remains of the fish in three bites, grunted, and walked to the river. It walked into the stream and swam over to the other bank, where it disappeared onto the brush.

"That was scary," Riley squeaked. "Do you think we'll be okay up here?"

I wasn't sure, but we had nowhere else to go.

———•———

I didn't get much sleep that night. I had tied the pots and utensils from the mess kit to some string and stretched it across both sides of the ledge leading to the cave. Nothing would be able to get past without setting off a clatter of metal on metal. I'd also scoped out a couple of escape routes and a tree that we could climb if necessary. I was pretty sure most bears weren't interested in humans, but "most" was the word that worried me.

I tried to stay awake, but my eyes would droop, and my head would slowly fall against my chest. As soon as that happened, an owl would hoot, a coyote would yip, or a small animal would rustle the brush. My head would snap back, and I'd be fully awake again. I'd stay vigilant for a while, and then the cycle would repeat itself.

Dawn slowly crept up on me. The stars began to give way to the morning light, and I began to discern shapes that had been hidden in the dark. As soon as it was light enough to see, I woke Riley, and we packed up and headed to the highway. Riley was being brave, but I could tell that she was hungry. I reached into the pack and gave her one of the last pieces of jerky.

The sun was shining brightly through the foliage of the evergreen trees around us when we reached the road. No one was around, and we sat on the ground and leaned against the old wooden table. I would doze a little until the sound of a car or logging truck racing down the highway startled me awake.

The sun was creeping higher, and I was beginning to worry that we hadn't understood correctly when a flatbed truck pulled up to the table.

Four people crowded the cab, three women plus a middle-aged man in the driver's seat. The old lady that had counseled us the day before and the man got out and began transferring boxes of produce to the table. Then they walked over to us.

She smiled and volunteered, "This Mateo. He no speak English, but he take you to Eureka." She pointed to the two women in the truck. "He drop my sisters off on the way. You have money? Mateo go get gas and come back"

I pulled out a crumpled dollar bill from my pocket and handed it to him. He smiled, jumped into the truck, and headed into Leggett. While we waited, the woman reached into her pocket and handed us two toasted rolls stuffed with beans, sausage, and cheese. "Tortas." She smiled and pointed at the rolls. They were still warm and smelled enticing. I tried to give her some change from my pocket, but she pushed my hand away and began setting up her table. Five minutes later, Mateo drove up, and we hopped into the cab with Riley on my lap. The woman waved, and we started up the road.

Her sisters ignored us and chatted in Spanish, and we ate our tortas while we drove up hills and around hairpin turns. Mateo stopped at a roadside stand in Garberville, and I helped him and one of the ladies set up.

A while later, we rounded a bend and were suddenly in the midst of the biggest trees I had ever seen. The trunks of some were the size of a small house, and I couldn't see their tops when I looked. We dropped the final lady at Weott and continued on after setting up her table.

We descended through a dozen small towns carved out of the thick forest and finally approached the coast. Traversing one last hill, the sight of a large bay greeted us, and we dropped into the town of Eureka. Mateo drove to a large warehouse in the center of town, then stopped and got out. He opened the passenger door and mumbled, "Aqui! Adios," and walked into the warehouse. A man of few words.

CHAPTER 19

Follow the Yellow Brick Road, 1957

*We're expecting a lot of rain in the state of Oregon,
so let's just get rid of Oregon.*

—Ryan Stiles

W E WALKED UP THE STREET, looking for any hobo signs that might lead us to a camp. There were people all about moving briskly to and from their destinations, but not one 'bo.

We'd wandered a few blocks when Riley spotted a grocery store, so we went in to replenish our supplies. It was a large store, and I lost track of her as I grabbed essentials: bread, two cans of chili, Hostess Twinkies, and a package of bologna. Turning a corner into the produce section, I wasn't paying attention and almost ran into Riley. She was chatting with a very pretty lady and smiled when she saw me. "That's my brother, Luke. He and I almost got eaten by a bear, but it only ate the fish head and guts. It was yucky." She giggled and held up a bag of potato chips, "Luke, this is Miss Amelia. She helped get these off the top shelf. She lives here."

We greeted each other, and I thanked her for helping Riley. Her hair was pulled into a bun, and her figure was curvaceous without being heavy. I grabbed some bananas while they continued their banter, then called to Riley that we needed to leave. She seemed like a nice person, but I was worried that she might get suspicious about two kids on their own.

After checking out, we walked across the street to a park and sat on a bench, sharing a package of Twinkies, which we washed down with cans of coke.

I was throwing our trash into a can when a commotion broke out across the street. A woman was sitting on the ground, screaming and pointing at a teen boy sprinting across the street. "Stop! That's my purse. Help!"

I didn't really think about it—I just reacted and ran toward the boy. He was taller than me and running full speed ahead. He was looking back and laughing, so he didn't notice me as I just kind of plowed into him from the side and we both went down in a heap. Somehow, I grabbed the purse strap and tried to wrench it free. The boy got up and pulled the purse toward himself, swinging me around. I slammed into a brick retaining wall, fell to the ground, and almost lost my grip. He screamed, "You little bastard, I'll kick your ass," and proceeded to kick me. I tried to curl into a ball with the purse under me and heard people shouting just as one of his kicks caught me in the head and things went black.

●———————●

I woke to an angel patting my head with a moist cloth and the sounds of Riley sobbing. I was lying across the seat of a car. The angel was yelling at the crowd that had formed. "It's okay. He's coming around. I'll take care of him and get him to a doctor."

I tried to sit up, but a pain shot through my head behind my eyes and I had to lie back. I panicked that we might get caught after all this time. I thought I might throw up, but I mumbled, "I'm okay. I don't need a doctor. Please, we have to go." I tried one more time to sit up, then proceeded to pass out again.

The next time I woke, I was lying between two cotton sheets under a thick blanket. Silky shears muted the sunlight that angled in through a lushly curtained window. I ached all over and felt nauseated. My ribs hurt, and when I reached to my head, I felt a bandage covering it. I was a mess. I heard a voice coming from somewhere below and tried to sit up.

Big mistake. The curtain came down once again and I drifted off, to dreams of Maggie.

•————————•

My eyes popped open to a dark room. I was still sore, but my head felt better, and the nausea was gone. I eased myself up and looked around in the dim light. Soft gurgling sounds were coming from an overstuffed chair in the corner, and I could just make out Riley's curls peeking out of the blanket covering her.

She must have heard the covers rustling because she popped up and jumped onto the bed beside me. "Oh good! You're awake." Her eyes glistened as she grabbed my hand and said, "I thought you were dead. I was so scared."

My mouth felt like it was full of cotton, and I could hardly squeak, "Are you alright? What happened? Where are we?" A million questions filled my mind. Especially if we were finally captured after everything we'd been through. Was our odyssey over?

Riley laughed. "We're at Amelia's house, and we're safe." She jumped off the bed and opened the bedroom door. "Amelia, he's awake." She turned and smiled. "You're everyone's hero, big brother."

The angel walked in holding a tray and a pitcher. "Well, young man, you're back among the living. You sure know how to put a scare to everyone. Your sister's right—you're my hero, and I was hoping you'd wake up so I could thank you." She put the tray down and sat on the bed beside me, while Riley jumped up on the other side. The angel brushed the hair from my eyes and kissed me on the cheek.

Amelia's voice was soft, and she smelled of soap and a floral perfume. She poured me a glass of water, and after I'd drained it, she murmured, "Let's see how your head is doing. It may sting a little when I remove the dressing, but I'll try to be gentle."

She was more than gentle. I didn't feel a thing except the warmth and caring of this lady. After the dressing was changed, she and Riley explained what had transpired. During the tussle with the purse snatcher, a passerby had heard the screams and pulled the boy off of me. He had run off without his prize—the purse. Amelia had wanted to call an ambulance, but something in Riley's pleading had convinced her otherwise. A couple of gentlemen loaded me into her car, and Amelia whisked us home and called her physician, who came over promptly. Seemed like they still did house calls in Eureka.

The damage to me wasn't life-threatening or permanent—bruised ribs, contusions, and a mild concussion. The jagged cut on my head required twelve stitches and would probably leave a scar. The doctor left strict orders for me to rest for at least forty-eight hours.

I started to protest and say that we had to get going, but she stroked my cheeks and whispered, "It's okay, Luke. Riley told me all about your situation. What you did for me was the bravest thing I've ever seen, and I'm not going to let anyone hurt you." She wrapped me in her arms, and it felt wonderful. It had been so long since I'd felt safe, but she did that for me.

I fell asleep again, and this time I dreamed of our mother.

The next time I woke, it was to the unmistakable smell of frying bacon. The dawn light filtered into the bedroom as I eased out of bed and out to the top of the stairs. The old wood floor creaked, and Riley poked her head out of a doorway below. "Good morning, sleepyhead. How are you feeling? Do you need help coming downstairs?" Flour dusted her cheeks and she tittered, "Amelia's showing me how to make biscuits. It's a blast!

The kitchen was bright and cheery, all white tile and stainless-steel appliances. I sat at the table, and Amelia brought over a glass of orange juice. She knelt down and examined my eyes and then my bandage. Tousling my hair, she smiled. "Looks like you're mending well. Another day and you'll be good as new. Are you hungry?" Just then, my stomach growled, and she and Riley laughed. "I guess that answers that. How about scrambled eggs, bacon, and biscuits?"

My stomach gurgled again, and I turned bright red. "I'm starved. Can I help?"

I tried to stand, but Amelia put her hand on my shoulder and kept me seated. "You just sit there. Your sister and I have things under control."

I sipped my juice and watched as the two women chatted amiably, moving effortlessly around the kitchen. My thoughts went, again, to Riley's need for a woman to help her into maturity. Dad and I could love her and protect her, but there were some things only a woman could do. This woman, and Mary and Maggie before her, made a connection with Riley that we could never hope to duplicate no matter how we tried.

Breakfast was wonderful. Riley beamed when I told her how light and delicious her biscuits were. In between bites, she went on and on about our adventure and how happy she would be to find Dad.

Even though Amelia was smiling, I could sense a sadness below the surface. It seemed similar to the sadness I detected in Dad when he let his guard down.

She allowed me to help with the dishes after breakfast. I washed while Riley dried, and I asked Amelia to tell us about herself. She told us she had moved to Eureka with her new husband right after the war. He was a commercial fisherman and had been lost to the sea just before she discovered she was pregnant. Her face turned dark with sadness when she told us she lost the child a short time later.

Riley let out a sob and rushed to her, wrapping her short arms around the woman.

Amelia choked out the words, "I've been on my own ever since. I have a little savings from my husband's life insurance, and I make ends meet working as an aide at the school and taking in laundry. It's enough to pay the mortgage, and my needs aren't great. My sister keeps after me to move back to our hometown in Iowa." She let out a little laugh. "Claims there are lots of eligible bachelors there and that I need to stop wallowing in pity and get on with my life. I know she's right, but I just can't seem to get going."

She was quiet for a while, then lifted her head with a huge smile on her face. She hugged Riley and exclaimed, "I think you two are just the catalyst I need! It's about time I got off the pity pot and started to live." She pulled me to her, and the three of us enjoyed a group hug. "You two are my little saviors. I think God sent you into my life."

It seemed like a weight had been lifted from her soul. She was practically giddy. "You've rescued me from a blue funk and now I want to reciprocate and help rescue you. I think that old car of mine can make it all the way to Seattle—how about I join you on your trek?"

It took three days to get underway. Amelia insisted that the doctor check me over before we left. He removed the stitches, applied a butterfly bandage, and instructed Amelia on how to care for my wound. She arranged to have someone look after the house and put together a bunch of traveling food, including sandwiches, fried chicken, and sodas. I scrutinized my map and traced the best route for the trip up the coast.

While we were making our preparations, she had her car tuned up. And what a car it was—a 1941 Cadillac Series 62 convertible. It had four doors and was so wide it didn't have room for running boards. It was, quite possibly, the prettiest car I had ever seen. "My parents gave us this car as a wedding present. My husband loved it and took immaculate care of it."

Of course, Riley called shotgun when we finally took off. I didn't care. The back seat was huge and luxurious. The big car floated over the highway. We traveled along at a good clip through huge redwoods. It was foggy when we left, and by the time we reached Crescent City, two hours later, the weather had turned to drizzling rain and we had to put the top up. The rain turned into a downpour at the Oregon border, limiting our visibility of the ocean or the forest.

Small towns flew by in the mist. After an hour, we stopped at a pretty overlook in Gold Beach to enjoy sandwiches and stretch our legs. We didn't stretch them too much, however. The rain forced us back into the car after a short time. Then it was back on the road again through more tiny beach towns. After driving for another couple hours, we made it to Coos Bay, where we filled up with gas.

The sun was approaching the horizon, and Amelia was pretty wrung out by the time we pulled into a Motel 6 in Tillamook. It was still raining as we dashed to our room and relaxed on the two beds. Amelia decided to take a nap, but Riley's and my energy levels were overflowing after sitting for so long, so we wandered around town. We wandered up the street to the Tillamook Cheese Factory and into a showroom, where a hostess was handing out samples of cheese. Some were quite delicious, but others were too stinky for me. Riley didn't have a problem, though, and cleaned one of the platters.

Amelia was refreshed by the time we returned, so we spread out a towel on one of the beds and had a fried chicken picnic while we watched cartoons on the old black-and-white television. The rain had become a torrent, so Amelia dug a deck of cards from her purse and we played "Go Fish" until we started to fade. She and Riley shared a bed, and I smiled as their giggling conversations lulled me to sleep.

The next morning, we walked to a small diner, in the rain of course, for breakfast before taking off. Riley and

Amelia continued their chatter while we ate, and I could sense a bond building between them. It was heartwarming, and I let Riley call shotgun without any protest.

Off we went through the sheets of rain. I began to appreciate the sign in the café that read "Oregonians don't tan, they rust." The big Cadillac sneered at a little rain, and we sailed along stopping for gas and a potty-break once until we reached Astoria, where we had to wait for a ferry across the Columbia River.

While the ferry churned through the river water, I stood along the rail, just watching the seagulls swooping and diving. We were getting close to our quest, and I could hardly wait to finally find Dad.

The crossing took half an hour through the rough current. A rainbow appeared as we passed into Washington, and the rain stopped. We landed outside McGowan and headed through Long Beach. Our route turned inland, and eventually we passed by Olympia, its pretty capitol dome visible from the highway. A short while later we left our old friend Highway 101 at Tacoma and headed toward the Emerald City on Highway 99.

CHAPTER 20

Seven Hills, 1957

*Let us be grateful to the people who make
us happy; they are the charming gardeners
who make our souls blossom.*

—Marcel Proust

THE CADILLAC PURRED AS WE drove up the four-lane highway, past Federal Way and Des Moines. A taxiway sided by a row of hangars came into view. Long, sleek aircraft were parked alongside. The propellers of these silver behemoths were missing, and in their place I could see conical-shaped cowlings hanging under the wings. "Boeing" was stenciled in blue on the sides of the hangars, and I yelled over the sound of the highway noise, "Dad said he hoped to get a job at an aircraft company—we should stop and see if he's there."

Amelia turned at a stop light and pulled up to a guard shack. The guard put the magazine he was reading down and ambled over, admiring the car and then Amelia. After a short discussion, he directed us to a building marked Administration. We parked and entered through a single door that led into a musty-smelling hallway with more doors on either side. We traipsed down the corridor past Finance and found a door marked Human Resources.

Amelia explained our situation to the clerk, who smiled. "Let me see what I can find out for you." She disappeared behind rows of filing cabinets, then came back five minutes later with an apologetic look on her face. "I'm sorry, but my supervisor says we can't give out personal information. Although, I can tell you that a Mr. Sean O'Connor is employed here, and you can leave a message for him. It's Friday afternoon, and the first shift has already left, so he probably won't get it until Monday, but that's the best I can do."

We left with conflicting emotions. We were elated that we knew where to find him but depressed because we had to wait for at least two days. Riley and I were so worked up, there was no way we could wait that long. We would just have to find him wherever he was living.

We got back on the highway and headed into town.

The highway ran parallel to the waterfront, and while Amelia drove, she assured us, "Don't worry, we'll find him. However, we're not going to find him driving up and down these streets. We need to develop a plan that helps us search in the most logical places, so start thinking the way your father thinks." She followed the road around a curve and pulled into a Best Western overlooking a lake on our right. "We'll use this as our base and fan out from here."

I jumped out of the car and said, "Let's go check in and see if they have a map of the area."

The clerk was cheerfully helpful, and after she gave us a map, she annotated a few areas where she thought we should concentrate our search. "Seattle was originally built on seven hills just like Rome, and most people refer to them to help get their bearings. We're on the border between Denny Hill, which is mostly made up of businesses, and Queen Anne Hill, which is residential. The downtown area lies south of us with hotels, apartments, restaurants, and shopping.

"First Hill and Capitol Hill are to the east. First Hill is also called Pill Hill because of all the hospitals and clinics. There are some nice apartment complexes there, but they're expensive. Capitol Hill has night clubs and is home to all the millionaires. Cherry Hill is just south but just the opposite—lots of low-cost housing and some rough areas. I would steer clear of there, especially after dark.

"Since you say your dad is working at Boeing, I would look hard around Beacon Hill. That's where a lot of Boeing workers live because of its proximity to the plant. The other areas of Seattle are residential suburb types, and there's not many places for single people. Anyway, since it's not very busy, I'll call around to other hotels and see if he's staying at any of them. I'll let you know. Good luck with your search."

Riley carried the map to our room, and I unloaded the pack and Amelia's luggage. Once we were settled, Amelia grabbed the complimentary pad off the bedside table. "Okay, let's put our heads together and figure out a strategy. I think we need to list where he might stay. I'll start. Based on what you've told me about your dad, I think he would probably want to save money and might stay at something like the YMCA. I'll get on the phone and call any in the area. How about it—do you guys have any ideas?"

Riley sat next to Amelia, frowned, and shook her head. "Dad was with us whenever he wasn't working. I don't know where he would go."

I was so worked up I could hardly think straight. I thought about our father and tried to categorize him beyond being "our dad." I mean, he had friends, and he went to church regularly. "Maybe we can call the Catholic Churches in the area. They may know something." And then a thought popped into my head. "Dad is a veteran. There's a whole bunch of veteran support organizations. We should contact those."

Amelia was writing everything on the pad of paper. "That's a good start." She reached under the bedside table and handed me the phone book. "Luke, if you look up the numbers, I'll start calling around."

Riley fell asleep on Amelia's lap while she made calls and I paced. Thirty minutes later, I heard a light rap on the door. I opened it a crack, and the hotel clerk was outside with a grin on her face.

"I haven't found him, but a clerk at a Motel 6 south of town remembers him. Says all he talked about was you two kids. Anyway, he checked out last week, and she's pretty sure your dad found a house to rent on Queen Anne Hill. She says he was really excited about getting back together with you." I thanked her, and she ruffled my hair as she left. "I'll keep calling around. By the way, my name's Patsy. Be sure to let me know what you find out. This is a lot more fun than checking on maids or balancing the cash in the register."

It was getting late when Amelia decided to call it quits for the day, but I convinced her to drive around the Queen Anne Hill neighborhood on the off chance that we might spot Dad. Using the hotel's map, we headed east on

Mercer and turned right on Queen Anne Avenue, where a steep hill topped with three orange and white TV towers piercing the sky confronted us. The hill looked almost vertical, with three tiers giving it the appearance of a wedding cake. I almost expected to see the bride and groom when we crested the summit. Electric buses with their tentacles reaching the wires above sparked at each splice. The Cadillac had no problem reaching the top, even though it felt like we might slip backward at any time.

As we crisscrossed the streets, a beautiful vista opened up before us on the west side. Ferry boats passed back and forth in the sparkling waters of Elliott Bay below us. A navy cruiser was slowly approaching a large pier at the base of the hill, and freighters steamed across the horizon in the distance. A deep ravine lay to the west, separating Queen Anne from another hill.

Turning back to the east, we encountered another smaller body of water below the hill. Smaller craft plied their way through the calm waters, and I could see a relatively narrow canal entering this lake to the north. Small shipyards and chandleries populated the shoreline.

Back and forth we went through a well-maintained, middle-class neighborhood. Scouring the streets, we spied an IGA grocery store and St. Anne's Catholic Church. A pretty cemetery shrouded in maple and birch trees bordered one street coexisting with a small tennis court.

No Dad, though.

Dusk was settling in, and we decided to head back. Amelia was nervous about taking the big car back down steep Queen Anne Avenue, so we wound our way down to the ravine on the west side, passing another church. Railroad tracks traversed the ravine, and I spotted a hobo encampment under a bridge as we turned left onto

Fifteenth Avenue. I wondered if any of our friends had made it there. As we headed back to the hotel, the overwhelming odor of raw garbage from the landfill to our right permeated the car until the avenue bent left and we passed the cruiser, which was finally docking at the pier.

Arriving back at the hotel, we were exhausted and hungry, but mostly depressed. We cleaned up and walked to a restaurant overlooking Lake Union advertising a Friday Special, "All the Fish You Can Eat for $1." The meal included hush puppies and coleslaw. It was good but not nearly as tasty as Merle and Al's Fish and Chips. Amelia was a light eater, but Riley and I put enough away to put the restaurant into the red. We walked back to the hotel and watched television late into the evening. I looked over to the other bed, and Amelia and Riley were curled up together under the blankets, gently snoring. I turned the TV off and lay awake staring at the popcorn ceiling for a while until the sandman finally overtook my spurious thoughts and I slipped into a deep sleep.

Sometime during the night, I woke with a start. The sheet was tangled around my legs, and I was sweating. It took me a while to figure out where I was. I had been having a nightmare where Riley and I were running up and down the big hill on Queen Anne Avenue. I could see Dad ahead of us, but we couldn't catch up to him. Running down the hill, I stumbled and fell, calling out, but he just kept going.

———•———

I tossed and turned for the rest of the night but must have finally fallen asleep. The sound of water running in the bathroom woke me. Riley was sitting at the end of her bed, watching cartoons with the volume turned down. She turned and murmured, "Hi, sleepyhead. I thought you'd never wake up. Amelia's in the shower. Don't you just love her? She's the nicest adult I've ever met." She thought for a minute, then laughed. "Except Dad, of course." A pout came onto her face. "I wish she could stay with us."

After Amelia was done, we showered and put on clean clothes. I was ready to go, but Amelia made us walk to a nearby Denny's restaurant for breakfast. Amelia and Riley dug into their food, but I just picked at my scrambled eggs. I wanted to get going. Amelia paid the check and we headed over to the car.

Amelia had just put the car in gear and was pulling out of the hotel parking spot when Patsy ran up, jumping up and down with excitement, "I've got news! My friend from the Motel 6 remembered something and called me back. He remembered that your dad told him he was join-ing a VFW in Ballard because they serve hot meals every morning and evening and he doesn't have to eat alone." She handed another hotel map with the VFW circled in red pen. "Good luck!"

Amelia gave her a hug and we zipped away, back-tracking down Elliott to Fifteenth and past the smelly land fill. Smoke was rising from a fire at the hobo camp as we raced by and over a bridge crossing the canal. The Cadillac pulled into the club's parking lot, and we all jumped out and ran to the door where a burly man sporting a handle-bar mustache stopped us. His gaze wandered over Amelia, and he stated, "Hold on, little lady. This is a private club and not open to the public."

Amelia explained our plight, while Riley and I craned our necks around the man to possibly catch sight of Dad. I could see a dozen or so men sitting at tables, but I couldn't make him out in the dim light. We couldn't see around the corner, either.

The man smiled. "Sure, I know Sean. He's a good guy. Let me go see if he's here."

Five minutes later, the burly guy came out accompanied by a bald man missing an arm. The bald man grinned. "So, you two are Sean's kids. I'll be damned." He looked sheepishly at Amelia. "Sorry about the language, ma'am. Sean was here on the phone all morning trying to find you two. He was really upset and said he couldn't get hold of your aunt. Said the number was disconnected. He called a neighbor of yours, and they told him that you guys had left a few weeks ago. Anyway, he left about twenty minutes ago and said he was going to talk to the police. Ballard only has a substation, so I'm pretty sure he headed downtown."

After they pointed out the location on our map, we scrambled into the car and headed downtown. We made pretty good time until we reached the center of town and traffic ground to a halt. After taking five minutes to barely travel a block, Amelia veered off to the side streets, and we finally reached the city hall a few minutes later. The area was heavily congested with weekend shoppers, and we had to park two blocks away.

Pushing through the crowded sidewalks, we had to wait for a traffic light at the corner.

Then we spotted Dad talking to an officer in front of the station. He was waving his arms and shouting something. Riley let out a little yelp and started to dart across the street in front of traffic. Brakes squealed, and Amelia's hand shot out and grabbed her collar, pulling her back a split second before a delivery truck blazed past. The driver laid on his horn and fired a few expletives at us. By then, the light had changed, and we ran toward our father.

Dad and the cop turned to see what the commotion was about. When he spotted us, Dad's eyes lit up and he sprinted over, tears streaming from his eyes. We literally jumped into his arms, and we all crumpled to the sidewalk.

"Oh my babies, you're here," he stammered. "You're okay. Oh, thank you Lord."

We sat there, hugging and kissing, and Dad blubbered, "Luke, Riley! How?" He couldn't finish a sentence, and he looked up as Amelia walked toward us. A tiny spark lit behind his eyes for just a second.

Riley jumped up and grabbed Amelia's hand, pulling her toward us. "This is Amelia. She's our friend. She drove us here from California."

Dad stood up and took Amelia's hand in both of his. "Thank you so much. How can I ever repay you?"

She smiled. "That's not necessary. Your wonderful children gave me so much more than I could ever give them. You should be very proud of them." She turned to us. "Please stay in touch. Thank you for the adventure and for helping me to find myself. I'll miss you terribly."

Riley jumped up and grabbed her arm. "You can't leave! You have to come with us."

Dad looked at the two of them and chuckled. "Well, you can't leave yet. Come to the house I just rented. I want to hear all about your trip, and the least I can do is fix lunch for you."

"I'll ride with Amelia," the words tripped out of Riley's mouth. "We'll follow you."

After thanking the cop, Dad and I walked to the old Chevy and circled the block so Amelia could pull behind us. Once we were on the way, I began talking. "Dad, we can't let Amelia go. She helped us, and if it weren't for her, we wouldn't be here and may never have made it."

Dad smiled. "Don't you think Amelia might have a say in that? I'm sure she has her own life to live. Besides, how would that work with a strange woman living in our house?"

I'd thought about it a lot, though, and I countered, "But she doesn't. She was lonely, and we helped her out of her loneliness. I don't think it's right to let her go back to that kind of existence. I know that she would stay if we asked her."

"But, Luke…" he started to respond.

I interrupted him, something I'd never done before. "She's not a strange woman! She's kind and caring, and Riley loves and needs her. Look, Dad, I've watched the two of them, and they're right together. Riley needs a woman to help her with women's things. You and I can love her to death, but we'll be hopeless about girl things. I mean, do you know anything about bras?"

I looked over to his wide eyes. "Well neither do I, and Riley will need some help with bras pretty soon. Besides, there's probably a lot of other woman things that I don't even know about where she'll need help in the future."

He started laughing, reached over, and tousled my hair, "You're a good man, Lucas O'Connor. You win. We'll talk to her and see if she's interested in becoming a nanny. We can make the master wing of the house into private quarters for her." He let out another laugh. "How did you even know about bras?"

Our route took us back up to the crest of Queen Anne Hill. Dad chuckled when I told him it reminded me of a wedding cake, "This big hill is called the Counterbalance for the small, weighted vehicles that offset gravity so streetcars could make it to the top."

We turned west and stopped in front of a charming two-story house that overlooked the bay, framed by two huge maple trees. Amelia pulled behind the Chevy and followed Dad into a sparsely furnished but bright, sunlit living room. Dad apologized for the lack of furniture while he hustled about the kitchen and brought us glasses of tea. "I found this place and thought it would be perfect for us. It has five bedrooms, and that's a lot, but the rent is really reasonable, and the landlord has given me an option to buy as soon as I can save up the down payment. Now, everyone sit. I want to hear the story of how you got here."

So, we told him our saga. He was visibly upset when we talked about Helen's duplicity, and he had to get up and walk outside for a while when I described Cholame and what had transpired with Walt. After he'd cooled down, he went to the phone and made a number of calls. I sat next to him and listened to his half of the conversation.

He was upset and tried to be patient while he tried to sort out the situation in California. Waiting for someone on the other end, he put his arm around me and whispered, "My little man. I sure am proud of you." He looked at me and smiled. "Wait, you're not so little anymore. I think you've grown a foot."

He continued making calls before returning for the rest of the story.

Amelia had her arm around Riley while we finished our saga, and I saw Dad glancing their way. It was obvious that he could see how close they had become—and I thought I detected an appreciation of Amelia's beauty in those furtive looks.

Riley had fallen asleep on her lap by the time we'd finished our tale and Dad started telling us a little about what he'd been up to. He'd spent two weeks on the road, stopping and searching for work at every opportunity. He picked up odd jobs along the way, but nothing permanent until he got to Seattle.

Boeing was always looking to hire veterans for their commercial airplane business, and they'd picked up dad within weeks of his application. It didn't take long for them to realize he had a lot of potential, so they entered him into a machinist apprenticeship program. I could see him fill with pride when he told us he was working on the Boeing 707, the first commercial jet airliner.

As soon as he was sure his job was secure, he tried to get hold of Helen so she could get them up here, but Helen's number had been disconnected. He didn't think too much of it at first—he just figured she hadn't paid the bill—but after a week, he began to get concerned. When he found out from neighbors that Helen had moved, he really became frantic, and that was why he had gone to the police just before we'd shown up.

While we were talking, the phone rang, and he left to answer it. His face was bright red when he returned. "That was the Redfield Police Department. They tracked Helen down to a rehab facility in Los Angeles. She's hooked on heroin and isn't doing very well. They've got a call into the San Luis Obispo County sheriff to find out about Walt, and they'll let us know."

The discussion turned to Amelia, and my dad described what we'd talked about.

"Your son is very astute," she softly said. "And very sensitive. He's correct that I've formed an attachment to Riley, but I love both of your children. Lucas is my hero."

She described the tussle with the purse snatcher, and Dad pulled my hair back to inspect my new scar under the butterfly bandage.

Amelia put her head back and closed her eyes. "What you two are proposing is very intriguing, and very scary for me. I had wrapped myself in a very comfortable and safe cocoon that Luke and Riley started to unravel." She was silent for a few seconds, then looked at me. "And you know what, I don't want to return to that life! I'll do it, Mr. O'Connor. I'll take care of your children and give them all the love I have."

I reached out to her, and she opened her arms to me. It felt warm in her embrace.

The next morning, I was exploring our new house and all of its secrets when the phone rang. Dad answered it and spoke to the caller for a long time.

Riley, Amelia, and I were eating breakfast in the kitchen when he finished the call and walked in. "That was the police down in California. The sheriff went to check on Walt and found him still alive—seems you gave him a nice scar on his head, though."

Tears formed in my eyes, and I started to shiver. I hadn't realized how much killing Walt had weighed on my conscience. Amelia came and pulled me to her while Dad continued, "The cops used their visit to snoop around and discovered a few nasty things. It seems that one of the garden plots was a shallow grave with human bones." My stomach turned at the thought of eating vegetables that had grown amongst bones in that garden. "Neighbors said Walt's wife disappeared a few years ago, and the cops think the grave may be her remains. They also found jars of moonshine whiskey in that root cellar. After checking around, they rounded up some of Walt's buddies, and they're singing like birds about the illicit whiskey business he was running at an abandoned building. He'll be spending a long time in prison."

We spent the rest of the day contacting all those guardian angels from our trip. We reached some by phone, and to the others we wrote long letters of gratitude. Then I went to my room to write one special letter.

The four of us began a life full of joy and love. Summer was pretty much used up, and Dad enrolled us in the neighborhood Catholic school that was down the hill, just a block away from the hobo camp I'd noticed the day before. Riley and I cherished each day with Dad and Amelia. She sold her house, and as soon as dad could take a week off, the four of us traveled down and packed up her belongings and brought them to Seattle.

Amelia and Dad danced around each other and stole glances whenever they thought no one was looking. Then one night, about six months after school started, I wandered down for a glass of milk and found the two of them asleep on the couch, entwined in each other's arms.

The two of them snuck around for a few more months until one day, they called us together for a "discussion."

Dad was bright red and stammered, "Well, kids, you see, Amelia and I, uh… Well, uh…"

Riley jumped on his lap, laughing. "We know, Dad, and it really makes us happy." She giggled. "I'm gonna have the best mom ever."

I sat on the couch next to Amelia and held her hand. "I've been hoping this would happen. You two have been lonely so long."

•——————•

They married in a small ceremony. Riley carried the rings, and I proudly walked Amelia down the aisle to my dad's arms. Patsy from the Best Western served as one of the witnesses. I'm not saying it was a shotgun wedding or anything, but it was close.

Nine months later, Amelia presented us with a miracle: twins. Michael Sean O'Connor became the best little brother anyone could have, and Caitlyn Amelia O'Connor stole my heart as soon as I looked into her pretty blue eyes. I was going to have my hands full looking after two sisters. The day we brought the twins home, I went to my room and wrote another letter.

The new arrivals didn't diminish the love that either Dad or Amelia showered on Riley and me. In fact, they seemed to amplify it. He and Amelia seemed to have unending love and patience for all of us, and we wallowed in it happily.

CHAPTER 21

Seattle, 1969

Tell me not, in mournful numbers,
"Life is but an empty dream!"
For the soul is dead that slumbers,
And things are not what they seem...
Let us, then, be up and doing,
With a heart for any fate;
Still achieving, still pursuing,
Learn to labor and to wait.

—Henry Wadsworth Longfellow

I FINISHED THE STORY OF OUR exodus while we drove through the pounding rain of Oregon. As I navigated the wet road, it made me wonder if the sun ever came out in this part of the world. Maggie and I spent the night in Tillamook. While I was showering, she called her parents with the news of our wedding. It didn't go well, and Maggie was softly crying when I came out of the bathroom. I tried to comfort her as her body quivered under my arms and she summarized their conversation.

Her parents were livid and threatening to get the marriage annulled. Her voice shook, "I love my parents, but you and I are meant to be together, and I told them so. I hope they'll come to their senses some day and grow to love you as I do, but it will be a while before that happens."

I kissed her forehead and held her tight until she fell asleep.

The next morning, we headed into Washington across the newly completed bridge across the turbulent waters of the Columbia River.

The sky opened up as we crossed the bridge, and a beautiful rainbow led us up the highway, past the big Boeing plant and into Seattle. Maggie was driving and stared up at the Counterbalance. "I'll bet that's fun in the winter," she muttered. She downshifted, and the Mustang squirted up the hill easily.

Amelia's Cadillac was sitting regally in the driveway when we pulled up. "I've changed my mind!" Maggie exclaimed. "You can drive this old Mustang, *that's* the car for me."

Mike and Caitlyn streamed out of the house and practically bowled me over jumping into my arms. Caitlyn squealed, "Oh, Luke, we thought you'd never get here. Welcome home, big brother."

Mike was eyeing Maggie, shyly giving her the once-over as only a boy would look at a beautiful woman. I think he might have been smitten. Just then, a shriek emanated from the porch, and Riley practically flew into my arms.

"Luke, where have you been? We've been waiting—" She stopped short and let out another shriek as she ran to Maggie. "Oh my God, is that you? Look at you. But, how…" She looked back at me. "Luke, this makes me so happy. I've been praying that you two would find each other. Now you can be completely happy."

She turned to Caitlyn and pointed. "Cay, this is the woman I told you about. She's the one that can make Luke truly happy. She became my sister long ago, and now she's yours, too." She grabbed Maggie's and Caitlyn's hands in hers and pulled them toward the house, then stopped abruptly, turning toward me. "Luke, Maggie, are you—I mean, did you?" When she saw the smiles on our faces, she began to cry. "Oh my, we truly have another sister, kids." She did a little dance and ran to the house with her sisters.

Mike took my hand. He had grown a foot while I'd been gone "Hi, big brother. I'm really glad you're home. I missed you. She's really pretty."

I ruffled his hair. "Yes, she is. I think you'll like her." We walked to the house, and Dad's big arms enveloped me. "Welcome home, son. My prayers are answered." His cheeks were wet. "I understand you have some news for us. Let's go find your mother so we can properly meet your bride."

Amelia and Dad fell in love with Maggie that day and accepted her with open arms and hearts. Mike shyly stood off to the side until Maggie walked up to him. "Hello, Michael. Luke told me all about you, she smiled tenderly, but he didn't tell me how handsome you are. I think he was afraid I'd fall for you." She pulled him into a full hug, and I could see his grin as he let himself go.

———•———

Clete and Marilou came in that night, and we all sat around telling stories, Mike on my one side and Maggie on the other. Caitlyn and Riley snuggled close to Maggie, and I could see the youngsters' eyes grow wide with some of the stories of our adventure. I could hardly believe some of them myself.

The next day, we piled into the Mustang and Cadillac and drove to Spokane for Riley's graduation. We cheered until we were hoarse when they announced our sister as *magna cum laude* and again for her valedictory speech.

After the ceremony, we gathered together for a group picture, and I noticed a handsome young man standing to the side. He was tall and lean, and I recognized him as one of the graduates. He was gazing at Riley, and I had a feeling, so I walked over to him and introduced myself.

He smiled shyly and stuck out his hand. "Hi, my name's Peter. I know who you are. Riley talks about you all the time."

I could tell from the way he said Riley's name that they were more than just friends. Riley was blushing a little when she and Maggie walked over, and that confirmed it. "Hi, I see you met Peter. Luke, Peter, and I are going together. We're in love just like you and Maggie." She smiled at Peter and gushed, "He makes me feel really good. I hope you two will become friends, because I think he's about to become part of the family."

I took Peter's shoulders in my hands and stared into his eyes. "Riley, if you love him, then I'm sure that I will too. Come on, let's all go home and celebrate my little sister's day. You too, Peter."

We piled into the cars and headed out.

That evening, Maggie and I were sitting on the porch with Dad when he asked, "Son, I'll never question your decisions, but I am curious—why did you extend your tour in Vietnam? We were worried to death about you. We expected you home, and then you stayed."

I fidgeted a little and sat up. "I'm sorry that I put you through that. When I got to Nam, they assigned me a to a hospital in Da Nang for four months until a new marine unit rotated in and I was assigned to them. That would have meant that I would leave four months before they would, but by then they were my brothers, and I couldn't bail out on them. I had to take care of them. I hope you can understand."

Maggie squeezed my arm, and my dad smiled. "That sounds just like you," he said. "And that's when you got wounded."

"Yes, sir, me and a bunch more."

Dad got up, took my face into his hands, and kissed me on my forehead. "I'm just grateful that you're home. I'm going to get some tea. Anyone else want any?"

Amelia scooted into his chair as he walked away, and she and Maggie chatted for a while as I turned thoughts over in my mind.

"Something's bothering me," I said, and they turned toward me. "I sense that you guys aren't telling me something. Will you please tell me?"

Amelia looked a little uncomfortable and fiddled with her hands, but then she said, "You're right, there is something. Your dad and Riley didn't want to tell you because they knew what you'd do, but I know you, Luke, and I know that you'd really be hurt if you found out after the fact."

She cleared her throat and went on, "Riley has been accepted as a Rhode's Scholar. They want her to spend two years at the University of Oxford in England. They provide a stipend, but it's not nearly enough to cover expenses, and with Mike and Caitlyn getting older we just can't afford it. So she's going to turn it down."

I was dumbfounded. What a great honor for my sister. There was no way she should miss this opportunity. Maggie squeezed my arm and reassured Amelia, "You and I both know my new husband, and I'm pretty sure he's going to ensure Riley gets her opportunity even if it means delaying his plans. That's what we love about him." She reached up and kissed me on my cheek."

In bed that night, Maggie and I discussed the situation. "This is quite a quandary," I murmured. "It wouldn't be fair to you if I delay college for another two years, but I just can't let Riley pass up this chance."

Maggie punched me in the arm. "Silly boy. The only thing I care about is you. And if I'm with you, then everything else is fine. You forget that Riley is my sister, too. We formed that bond a long time ago. Besides, you can work part-time and attend a community college for two years, and I'm sure I can get a job teaching. With your GI Bill, we can surely help Riley make ends meet."

I nodded and held her tight as she faded off to sleep.

———•———

I was up early the next morning and went for a run. It felt good to stretch my legs, and I pushed through the pain from the wound. The cool Seattle air helped clear my head, and I resolved to talk with Riley as soon as I could before she turned down the scholarship.

But by the time I'd returned, Riley and Peter had gone into town to do some shopping, and I had to settle for a discussion with Dad and Amelia.

Dad was uncomfortable with Maggie's and my decision, but he said he knew that I wouldn't let my little sister down. We all talked for a while until Riley and Peter returned.

When they came in, I asked them to sit down so I could tell them something, but then the phone rang. Mike hollered from the kitchen, "Luke, it's for you! Some guy named Admiral something or other."

I wondered who it might be as I headed for the kitchen with Maggie in tow. She sat next to me, and I picked up the receiver. "This is Lucas O'Connor. How may I help you?"

Richard Blaine's big voice boomed over the phone's speaker, and I had to hold it away from my ear. Maggie would have no problem listening to both sides of this conversation. "Petty Officer O'Connor, it's a pleasure to talk to you. You may not remember me, but we met in Monterey a few years back. Valerie, my wife, still corresponds with your sister, and she sends her regards. She said to give Riley a big hug and tell her congratulations."

I told him I remembered him vividly and how much I appreciated the help he gave us back then.

"Well, I didn't do enough, and Valerie gently reminds me of that now and again." He chuckled and went on, "I called for a couple of reasons. First, I just received official notice from congress, and I wanted to be the first one to congratulate you on receiving the Congressional Medal of Honor."

Maggie's body stiffened and her brown eyes grew to the size of saucers. "But, sir," I sputtered, "I don't deserve that. Please give it to someone else."

He harrumphed. "Luke, I read the citation, and there's no one who deserves this medal more than you. You saved those men and that orphanage. You're getting that medal if I have to hog-tie you so the president can drape it around your neck. The navy needs some good press right about now, and your story will resonate even with the most cyni-cal. So just accept it, please."

Maggie pulled me to her and kissed my cheek.

"The other item is this," he continued. "I want you to come back into the navy, and I have an offer that you shouldn't refuse. The navy has a program for enlisted men to attend college, all expenses paid. The program goes even further for special cases such as yours. Your test scores qualify you for entry into the medical educa-tion program. We want to send you to Seattle University's premed program, and then on to medical school at a col-lege of your choice."

This was better than a dream come true. I looked at Maggie and asked her if she wanted to be a navy wife. She just nodded. "Lucas O'Connor, I told you I'd be happy just as long as I'm with you. And it sounds like I get to be a doctor's wife, too. Sounds like a heck of a deal."

I turned my attention back to the admiral. "Well, sir, it sounds really good, but my status changed a few weeks ago and I'm now married. Will that impact the program?"

He laughed. "I heard about that when an arrogant lobbyist came into my office and pounded on my desk, demanding that I withdraw your citation. Says you kid-napped his daughter. I made him read the citation before I threw him out on his ear. Damn lobbyists! Sorry, I hope I didn't offend your wife."

Maggie giggled.

"Now, here's the deal. You'll be commissioned, and based on your years of service, you'll start out as a Lieutenant JG. I'll arrange for the navy office in Seattle to get in touch with all the particulars. Congratulations, son. And thanks again for your service."

Maggie and I walked into the living room, where I announced, "I think our problem is solved."

———•———

The Seattle night had turned chilly, and we all sat around the big fireplace chatting and enjoying the company of family and good friends. Riley had her head on Peter's shoulder, and she said with a sigh, "I heard about a big rock concert being organized back east at a place in New York called Woodstock. Maybe the four of us should drive there before heading off to school. It would be fun."

Maggie clapped. "That sounds like a blast. I heard that some really big names will be playing there, like CCR and the Grateful Dead."

"Speaking of music," Dad said, "why don't you and Mike play us a little song on your harmonicas."

I had given my old Horner to Mike when I left for Vietnam, and he had gotten pretty good. We were warming up when Dad pointed at Riley and Maggie and declared, "If you go to that concert, Luke, I want you to take care of these two daughters of mine."

I thought to myself, *Here we go again, another adventure. Hopefully a less stimulating one!*

Mike and I blew on our harmonicas to get into tune with each other. Then we looked each other in the eye, counted down with a few nods, and began to play.

THE END

I hope you enjoyed reading *Mensch* as much as I enjoyed writing it. If you can, I would appreciate a review. It will help me in my future writing efforts as well as giving potential buyers a feel for the book. Thank you in advance!

THE MAKING OF MENSCH

Mensch is a product of my experiences and my imagination with some actual history thrown into the mix.

Having spent time in the Marine Corps in addition to being an avid student of military history, I was very familiar with the Vietnam conflict, but more importantly, the dedication and bravery of the enlisted medical personnel, including the Navy corpsmen and the Army medics. These brave individuals shared the front lines with their combat friends while selflessly putting their lives in danger for their safety and well-being. While I was not directly in combat, these brave men were and many were wounded or killed in action.

The Jack Ranch Café in Cholame was real and existed in Cholame until its demise at the hands of Covid in 2022. Cholame is also real, and I don't believe my description of this "town" is far off the mark.

As I mentioned in one of my blogs, I have always been intrigued by hobos. Based on my research, I don't believe that I stretched the truth in my description of hobo life.

While their hometown of Redfield is fictitious, it pretty much depicts the many towns that dotted southern California in the mid twentieth century. The towns that Luke and Riley visited on their odyssey, though, are all real, with no embellishments except the establishments located in each. I don't know if Oxnard had a Spudnuts. I drew upon my experiences with a Spudnuts in the Ballard section of Seattle for that one. The same is true of Merle and Al's Fish Bowl that I conveniently located in Pismo Beach. The Fish Bowl was owned and operated by Merle and Al in north Seattle on Aurora Avenue. They were friends of my father, and I spent many Sunday afternoons enjoying their fish and chips and trying to improve the vocabulary of their Myna bird.

The Anderson Creek Gang existed in the hills above the California coast, but I doubt Henry Miller or anyone in that community helped two vagabond children on their adventure. The same can be said about the Bohemian community near Sausalito. Roger and Mary existed along with many other famous people as well as the creations by Roger and his friends in that camp, but my story about their encounter with Riley and Luke are fiction. The ferry, *Vallejo*, also existed in the Sausalito harbor, but I'm not aware of any children living alone in its rooms.

Unfortunately, Riley would not have been a candidate for a Rhodes scholarship in 1969. Women were not admitted until 1976. I don't feel guilty about this fabrication since it never should have been an issue.

My description of Seattle is pretty much through my eyes as an adolescent where the Counterbalance was a blast to sled down in the winter!

ABOUT J MILO

J Milo spent his formative years in California and Washington. After trying his hand at upper education, he moved on to an all-expense vacation in southeast Asia courtesy of the Marine Corps. His training there led him to the aerospace industry where he honed his writing skills by trying to convince customers that his products were better than his competitors'. Sometime truth but mostly fiction. After tiring of the hustle-bustle of corporate life, he escaped to the Pacific Northwest. After moping around for a while, his wife kicked him out to the studio and urged him to write what he felt rather than what might sell. The result was his first book, *Mensch*. More to come.

Receive updates from the author by signing
up for his mailing list at jmiloauthor.com
Connect with the author on Twitter at @jmiloauthor

ACKNOWLEDGEMENTS

First and foremost, I must give thanks to God for blessing me with the ability to put these words to paper. Without Him, I am nothing.

I cannot begin to thank my wife, Vickie, for the support she has provided in the writing of this book. She is the one who believed I had the ability to create. She was my first editor and most helpful critic. Her assistance while I struggled through the maze of publishing and marketing *Mensch* has been invaluable.

Many thanks to my grandchildren, Kaela and Brendan, in helping me through the mysteries of social media.

Finally, I must thank Debra L Hartmann and the professionals at IAPS with their editing and design expertise. *Mensch* would be a much lesser product without their help.